"Wait a minute. At least tell me your name."

Travis loved pretty women, and this lady was in a class all her own with her long, willowy body and the most incredible head of curly golden-red hair he'd ever seen. And she wasn't wearing a wedding ring. He couldn't let her walk out of his life.

Serena drew a breath. "I'm Serena Fanon," she said coolly.

Travis cocked an eyebrow. "And you live… where?"

"Right here in Rocky Ford. Goodbye, Mr. Holden." Turning, she began walking toward her car.

Travis chuckled, then took off at a jog to catch up with her. She heard him coming and turned around to glare at him.

"Why are you following me?" She didn't speak kindly.

"Why do you think, beautiful lady?"

Dear Reader,

Whether or not it's back to school—for you *or* the kids—Special Edition this month is the place to return to for romance!

Our THAT SPECIAL WOMAN!, Serena Fanon, is heading straight for a Montana wedding in Jackie Merritt's *Montana Passion,* the second title in Jackie's MADE IN MONTANA miniseries. But that's not the only wedding this month—in Christine Flynn's *The Black Sheep's Bride,* another blushing bride joins the family in the latest installment of THE WHITAKER BRIDES. And three little matchmakers scheme to bring their unsuspecting parents back together again in *Daddy of the House,* book one of Diana Whitney's new miniseries, PARENTHOOD.

This month, the special cross-line miniseries DADDY KNOWS LAST comes to Special Edition. In *Married... With Twins!,* Jennifer Mikels tells the tale of a couple on the brink of a breakup—that is, until they become instant parents to two adorable girls. September brings two Silhouette authors to the Special Edition family for the first time. Shirley Larson's *A Cowboy Is Forever* is a reunion ranch story not to be missed, and in Ingrid Weaver's latest, *The Wolf and the Woman's Touch,* a sexy loner agrees to help a woman find her missing niece—but only if she'll give him one night of passion.

I hope you enjoy each and every story to come!

Sincerely,

Tara Gavin,
Senior Editor

Please address questions and book requests to:
Silhouette Reader Service
U.S.: 3010 Walden Ave., P.O. Box 1325, Buffalo, NY 14269
Canadian: P.O. Box 609, Fort Erie, Ont. L2A 5X3

JACKIE MERRITT

MONTANA PASSION

Silhouette ®

SPECIAL EDITION ®

Published by Silhouette Books

America's Publisher of Contemporary Romance

SILHOUETTE BOOKS

ISBN 0-373-24051-1

MONTANA PASSION

JACKIE MERRITT

and her husband live just outside of Las Vegas, Nevada. An accountant for many years, Jackie has happily traded numbers for words. Next to family, books are her greatest joy. She started writing in 1987 and her efforts paid off in 1988 with the publication of her first novel. When she's not writing or enjoying a good book, Jackie dabbles in watercolor painting and likes playing the piano in her spare time.

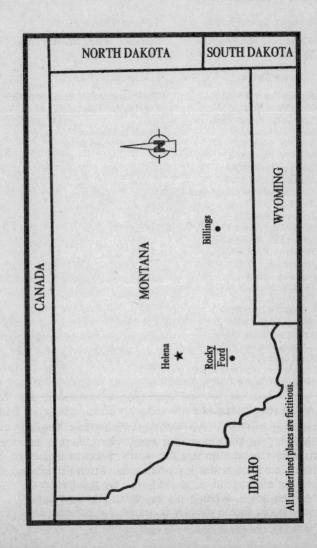

CANADA

NORTH DAKOTA | SOUTH DAKOTA

WYOMING

MONTANA

Billings •

Helena ★

Rocky
Ford •

IDAHO

All underlined places are fictitious.

Chapter One

*Y*es, *this is the one,* Serena Fanon thought as she once again walked through the two rooms available for lease on the second floor of the Ridgeport Building. Serena had ferreted out every commercial rental in Rocky Ford, Montana, her hometown, checked each one several times—pondering location, interior space and parking—and was finally approaching a final decision. The Ridgeport Building was almost new and in excellent condition. It had an ample parking lot and appealing landscaping. The two connecting rooms she was seriously considering each had a large window with a pleasant view of trees, shrubbery and grass, and a slanted peek at a portion of the parking area.

Her gaze went to the bare walls of the room she was in, and immediately she began thinking of that list of items she would need to buy before opening her law practice. Office furniture, a computer, law books and shelves on which to put them were not inexpensive, and her bank account wouldn't begin to cover the cost.

But she didn't need the money for those things today. At present, she was waiting for the result of her bar exam from the Montana Bar Association. Instinct told her she had done well. In fact she was quite confident that she had passed each segment of the lengthy exam. She could be receiving notification from the bar any day now, but it wouldn't surprise her if she heard nothing for several more weeks. In the meantime, she had been looking for the very best site in which to open her practice, and if she wanted this particular space, she had to make a decision today. The rental agent had explained Serena was first in line but she had other clients who were very interested in that space, a building contractor, especially. She was pressing Serena for an answer.

Serena didn't doubt the space was in demand. The Ridgeport Building already housed a medical doctor, a dentist, a real-estate office and an insurance agent. In truth much of the space had been snapped up almost before the building had been completed. She might procrastinate on purchasing a desk and a computer, but if she wanted these two rooms, she had to lock them in with a sizable deposit.

Okay, she thought with a surge of courage. *This is it.* It was the best the small town had to offer, and she didn't want to hide her practice in some out-of-the way place that offered no prestige whatsoever.

Locking the door as she left with the key the rental agent, Myra Farthing, had permitted her to use for one more look, Serena descended the carpeted staircase to the first floor. Myra had a small office within the real-estate company's area of the building, and Serena went directly to her door.

"I'll take it, Myra."

The agent smiled. "Glad to hear it, Serena. Come in and we'll go through the paperwork."

A half hour later, Serena left the building and walked to her car. Her bank account was a thousand dollars lighter, bringing her balance down to a worrisomely small amount, but she had her office. Now all she needed was the legal right to practice law in Montana.

And the money to get started, she added wryly while settling herself behind the wheel and turning the ignition key.

With the decision on where she would put her education to use behind her, Serena felt both excited and deflated. She wasn't good at twiddling her thumbs, and that was about all there was to do until she heard from the Montana Bar Association.

She could worry, of course. Think about broaching her father, Charlie Fanon, for the money to furnish her office. But she hated asking Charlie for one more cent. He had funded most of her extensive education from his retirement account, and when she came home after graduation from law school, he had bought her a car from a friend of his. "It's not new, but Jake took real good care of it, honey," Charlie had said.

Serena had a private vow: someday she would repay her father with interest. She knew if she went to him with her present financial plight, he would give her whatever she needed. But she hated even the thought of bringing up the subject with Charlie. He was the most generous, loving father anyone ever had, yet she felt as though she had taken enough from him. More than enough.

Backing out of her parking space, Serena stopped to look at the building's impressive sign. It was situated on tall wood pillars, and there was one empty space among the lineup of names of the other lessees. That was where her own name would be placed: Serena Fanon, Attorney.

For a moment, she frowned and bit her lip. Having her own law practice was what she had planned for many years, then had changed her mind when she met and fell in love with Edward Redding. Her law degree was from Georgetown University, and she had also worked part-time in a senator's office. She had loved Washington, D.C., with its bustle of political activity, its feeling of being the very center of what was important in the country. Meeting Edward had brought to a head an idea that had been gradually gaining momentum all on its own: to stay and work in Washington rather than return to Rocky Ford.

But Edward hadn't been the man she'd believed him to be.

Serena tossed her head, making her red-gold curls bounce, and got the car moving. She was not going to think about Edward's lies and deceit today. It was a beautiful day in early August, but unless the area should be fortunate enough to see one of those pleasant autumns that were so rare in Montana, winter weather was just around the corner. Wasting a day like this one with disturbing memories was practically a sin. Instead she would ... she would ...

A sigh lifted Serena's shoulders. Beautiful day or not, her options on how to spend it were limited. Everyone she knew was busy. Her father ran his business, Charlie's Place, during the week. It was a low-key sort of business that he conducted from his own home, which he had remodeled to accommodate customers years ago, after his retirement from the local telephone company. He sold coffee and sweet rolls, magazines and newspapers, and had some tables for card-players. Serena was positive that he didn't make very much money with his business, but it kept him active and involved, and he seemed to love it.

Her sister-in-law, Candace, had mentioned at breakfast that she was taking Ronnie, her toddler son, to the park for a picnic lunch today. Candace and Ronnie had come to live with Charlie when her husband, Ron, was killed in Germany. Ron had been in the military, and losing her only sibling had been a terrible blow for Serena. It had been a terrible blow for the whole family, as far as that went, so she wasn't the only one who missed Ron with an ache in her heart. At any rate, Candace wouldn't be home until after lunch, so if Serena went home now, she would be eating alone. Unless Charlie had no customers to tend to, which wasn't very likely.

Lola, Serena's cousin, came to mind next. Charlie had taken her in at the age of nine to raise as his own when her parents were killed in an auto accident. As the owner and on-site operator of the Men's Western Wear store in downtown Rocky Ford, Lola was usually very busy.

As for friends, Serena had discovered upon her return that her dearest friends from high school had moved away. There were some she knew well enough to drop in on, but these people held jobs and were rarely at home during the week.

Realizing that she was driving aimlessly, Serena decided to take a chance on Lola. Maybe she could get away for lunch, but even if she couldn't, Serena wanted to tell her about signing the lease for that space in the Ridgeport Building.

She was on the east side of town, and Lola's business was downtown. The shortest route was to cut through a residential district, which Serena did. Driving through this area brought back some pleasant memories. She'd had girlhood friends who had lived in these twenty- to thirty-year-old homes. It was a nice neighborhood, with mature trees and well-tended yards. A small smile played on her lips as she recalled sleep-overs and backyard barbecues at some of these homes.

Then, quite suddenly, her smile vanished, and her brow furrowed. There was smoke up ahead in the next block, billowing above the treetops—too much smoke to be an innocent, deliberate fire to burn trash, for instance. Besides, the town had a strictly enforced ordinance against trash fires. Years ago people had burned their leaves in the fall, but not anymore. It wasn't yet fall, and the leaves hadn't started dropping to the ground, anyway.

With a faster heartbeat, Serena stepped on the gas and sped down the street. The source of the smoke came into view almost at once: a house!

"Oh, no," Serena whispered with a catch in her throat. Quickly she stopped at the curb, then realized she was too close to the house and her car would be in the way when Rocky Ford's volunteer fire department arrived. Surely someone had called them. People were appearing, running out of their own houses. Backing her car up, Serena parked some distance from the developing chaos, then hurriedly got out and ran toward the gathering crowd.

"Has anyone called the fire department?" she called out as she ran up to the group.

Several voices said yes. It occurred to Serena that the onlookers consisted mostly of women and children. There were a couple of older men, one of them leaning on a cane, but this was a workday and the younger, family men weren't at home.

A roaring came from the house, and flames suddenly shot through a portion of the roof.

"Oh, it's bad," a woman next to Serena said worriedly. "I hope Lorraine went somewhere this morning. You can't tell with her garage doors closed. She always leaves her car in the garage."

"You mean someone might be in there?" Serena gasped.

"Lorraine Brack. She has a little girl, too," the woman replied. "Her husband works for the forest service. Does a lot of traveling. Leaves on Monday and usually doesn't get home until Friday. Oh, dear, I pray that Lorraine took little Katie and went somewhere this morning."

Serena's heart was in her throat. Without thinking, she started for the burning house. Someone had to do something, and the volunteers might not arrive in time.

She was suddenly shoved hard and yelled at.

"Get back!" a man shouted as he ran past her.

Startled, Serena froze in her tracks and watched him drive his shoulder against the front door until its lock gave. Then he disappeared into the smoke and flames.

Frantically Serena looked back at the small crowd, who all seemed too stunned to do more than stare. It seemed an eternity, but it was only minutes before the man brought out a woman. She was coughing and crying. "Katie... Katie..."

Several women rushed forward to help. "Lorraine, thank God," one said. Lorraine collapsed on the lawn.

"Oh, she's hurt," a woman cried. "I'm going to call the fire department again and make sure they send an ambulance." She took off running.

The man had vanished again. Serena stared wide-eyed at the burning house. The fire was spreading voraciously, popping and cracking as it consumed the wood house and its contents. He must be a man of enormous courage, she thought. To enter that conflagration not once but twice made him someone very special.

Lorraine was sobbing on the grass. Someone had produced a light blanket to cover her. Serena had seen the burned tatters of her clothing, and the woman had to be in pain. But she obviously was thinking of only one thing: her daughter.

The crowd fell silent when the man ran out again, this time carrying a blanket-wrapped bundle. His face was sooty and his clothing scorched. He had to have received some burns, but he had brought out both mother and daughter. The question on everyone's face was the same: was Katie all right?

He carried his bundle to Lorraine and laid it down. On his knees, he pulled back the blanket. "She's all right, ma'am," he said gently. "A few burns and she's scared to death, but she's all right."

A wail from Katie proved his words. Lorraine burst into fresh tears. "Thank you, oh, thank you."

Just then the scream of sirens pierced the air. In seconds the fire truck and an ambulance had arrived, along with a good half-dozen cars. The volunteers went to work on the fire. The paramedics from the ambulance bent over Lorraine and little Katie. Everyone moved back.

Feeling totally drained, Serena leaned against a tree. She couldn't take her eyes off the man who had risked his life in the most inspiring show of courage Serena had ever seen. He was tall and lean, with thick black hair and expressive dark eyes—a handsome man. A stranger to her, and a stranger to the others standing around watching the firemen. A stranger with endless courage, who had come along at a very crucial moment in Lorraine and Katie Brack's lives.

A woman dashed up to the man. Serena recognized her as Kathleen Osterman, the owner of the local newspaper. She could hear Kathleen's strident voice. "I understand you're the man who rescued Lorraine and Katie Brack," she said. "May I ask you a few questions?"

To Serena's surprise, the man grinned. "Ask away."

Serena left the tree and moved closer so she wouldn't miss any of this interview. Kathleen had to be in her fifties, an extremely attractive gal who knew how to dress, one of those ageless women that people referred to as a tough but classy woman. Serena remembered admiring Kathleen while she was still in high school, and she found herself admiring her again today. Her makeup, hairstyle and clothes were perfect for her. She had class, no question about it.

And she knew how to use her megawatt smiles in an interview. "First your name," she said, flashing one of those smiles.

"Travis Holden. Trav, to my friends."

Kathleen was writing in a notebook. "Then I'll call you Trav. I'm Kathleen Osterman. You're not from Rocky Ford, Trav. I know everyone in town. Where *are* you from?"

"The entire state of Montana is my home, Kathleen. Holden's my name, used cars are my game."

Kathleen's eyes widened. "You're *that* Holden? Well now, isn't this interesting? I believe you advertise in my paper, Trav."

"All the time, Kathleen."

Serena frowned, trying to make sense of this peculiar conversation. Holden...Holden. Should she know that name? And how could the entire state of Montana be anyone's home? Travis Holden had to have an address. What was he, some kind of wandering weirdo?

He didn't look like a weirdo. In fact, up close—as Serena was now—he was the best-looking man she'd ever seen. Until now, Edward had carried that title in her mind, and it felt good to drop him to second place, petty vengeance that it was.

"So," Kathleen said, "how did you happen to be in Rocky Ford today? And how did you happen to be in this part of town at this particular time?"

"I'm often in Rocky Ford, Kathleen. I keep a pretty close eye on all of my car lots. As for being in this particular location, I was on my way to Herb's Diner for some lunch. Just passing through this neighborhood, as it were."

"Pure coincidence," Kathleen said. "Lucky for Mrs. Brack and her daughter that you chose this route, Trav." She smiled. "How does it feel to be a hero?"

Trav laughed. "Feels pretty damned good, Kathleen. Pretty damned good."

"May I quote you on that?"

"Only if you mention Holden's Used Car Lot at least twice in your article." Trav was grinning.

Serena finally knew who he was. Holden's Used Car Lot had not been a part of Rocky Ford's business community before she went away to college, but she had noticed it in passing several times while searching the town for the best location in which to start her law practice.

But it was a bit shocking that Trav Holden would use this unhappy event to obtain some free advertising. He was a crass opportunist, Serena thought with a startlingly discomfiting disappointment. A hero with feet of clay.

Still, she felt compelled to wait until Kathleen had finished her interview so she could say a few words to the man who had braved an inferno to save a woman and child he didn't even know.

But Serena wasn't listening so hard now. Her gaze wandered to the burning house and the all-business activities of the firemen. She noticed a young man with a camera snapping pictures, moving here and there to get different angles. It didn't surprise her when Kathleen called out, "Jason, come over here and take some shots of Mr. Holden."

Jason trotted over. Trav Holden smiled for the camera as Serena watched, and then, quite suddenly, it was over. Kathleen thanked him for the interview, and she and Jason walked off.

The ambulance pulled away about the same time, heading for the hospital. The crowd began dispersing. The fire was all but out, reeking of water-soaked, charred wood.

Pulling a handkerchief from his back pocket to wipe his face, Trav headed for his car. Serena watched him for a second, then hurried to catch up with him.

"Mr. Holden?"

He stopped and turned. "Yes?"

Immediately Serena felt his gaze boldly go up and down her white slacks and yellow tank top, and a pink flush crept into her cheeks. It was a predatory look if ever she'd seen one. Her spine stiffened, but she couldn't just walk away now without saying something.

"I just wanted to, uh, express my gratitude for your quick action," she mumbled lamely, wishing with all her heart that she had let him leave without speaking to him. There was no good reason for them to meet, even if she did applaud his courage.

"Nice of you," Trav murmured, studying the beautiful woman standing before him with such a distant expression in her gorgeous blue eyes. "Did you see it all?"

"Yes. I stopped before you arrived."

"Then you don't live in this neighborhood."

"No, I don't. Well, that was all I wanted to say, so goodbye."

"Wait a minute. At least tell me your name." Trav loved pretty women, and this lady was in a class all her own with her long, willowy body and the most incredible head of curly golden red hair he'd ever seen. And she wasn't wearing a wedding ring. He couldn't just let her walk out of his life.

Serena drew a breath. Trav Holden's interest was strictly personal and much too obvious, but she had no one to blame but herself for this unnecessary conversation. He hadn't even noticed her until she'd called his name. The last thing she wanted or needed was a man. It might be unfair to blame all men for Edward's treachery, but she couldn't help how she felt. She was an intelligent person and knew that time diminished pain. At the moment, however, her man-made wounds were too new and raw to ignore.

Still, how rude could she be? After all, she had approached him.

"I'm Serena Fanon," she said coolly.

Trav cocked an eyebrow. "And you live ... where?"

"Right here in Rocky Ford. Goodbye, Mr. Holden." Turning, she began walking toward her car.

"Are you any relation to Charlie Fanon?" Trav called.

Damn, she thought irritably. Saying goodbye to Trav Holden was not going to be the end of this mistake in judgment. But she'd told him enough about herself. Pretending not to have heard his question, she kept on walking.

Trav chuckled, then took off at a jog to catch up with her. She heard him coming and turned around to glare at him.

"Why are you following me?" She didn't speak kindly.

He grinned. "Why do you think, beautiful lady?"

She tensed at his outrageous flattery. "You wouldn't want to hear what I'm really thinking, Mr. Holden. Let me put it in simple language. The only reason I spoke to you at all was because of what you did for the Bracks. As far as I'm concerned, our relationship began and ended in the space of five minutes." Again she turned away.

Trav fell into step with her. "You've really got a chip on your shoulder. Did I cause it?" After a second, he answered his own question. "Nope, wasn't me. So it had to be another man."

His perception startled Serena so much she stopped walking and looked at him. "You're much too cocky for my taste, Mr. Holden. I'm sorry I spoke to you at all, and you want to know something else? I'd bet anything that I'm going to be even sorrier in the future. You plan to intrude on my life, don't you?''

He couldn't help grinning. ''She's not only beautiful, she's bright. Dynamite combination, Serena. What are you to Charlie Fanon?''

''He's my father, if it's any of your business, which it isn't. Now, if you'll excuse me, I have things to do.''

''What things?''

Her jaw dropped. ''You have more gall than any person I've ever met.''

He rubbed his jaw. ''That's probably true. I've never lacked gall. Probably why I'm so successful in the used-car business.''

''And to what do you attribute your remarkable modesty?'' she asked sarcastically.

He laughed. ''Do you know that you're an absolute doll?''

''Good Lord,'' she muttered. ''Listen, I'm going to get in my car and drive away, and I hope I never have the misfortune of running into you again.''

''But what about our date tonight?''

''Our what?''

''I want to take you to dinner. I want you to look at me across a candlelit table with those fabulous blue eyes and tell me how wonderful I was today.''

''Oh, get a grip.'' Fuming, Serena whirled and marched off.

''Honey, you're breaking my heart.''

She glanced back to see the tragic expression on his face, the big phony. Obviously he thought he was the cutest thing in long pants.

''I'm sure you'll live,'' she called over her shoulder, feeling pretty good about her parting shot. She had finally reached her car, thank goodness. Climbing in, she immediately started the engine. Her last look at Trav Holden was when she drove past him. He was standing on the sidewalk with his hands on his hips and a brash, cock-of-the-walk expression on his face. An I'll-get-you-yet expression.

"Like hell you will," Serena mumbled. Deciding to skip that drop-in visit with Lola, she drove directly home.

Chapter Two

Serena was at the breakfast table with Candace and little Ron, eating at a leisurely pace, sipping coffee and chatting about this and that. There were moments when she wondered if she hadn't made the decision to leave Washington too hastily, permitting her pain over Edward to chase her away. Even so, she truly enjoyed being with her family and living in this big old house again with its innumerable memories and comfortable homeyness.

Charlie came in and laid a folded newspaper next to Serena's coffee cup. There was a teasing twinkle in his eyes. "Looks like we have a celebrity in the family," he said. "Front-page news, yet."

"Pardon?" Puzzled, Serena reached for the paper, unfolded it and found herself looking at a photo of Trav Holden and herself. "Good Lord," she muttered. Trav was looking every bit the hero with his broad smile and tousled hair, even with grime from the fire discoloring his skin. And she was gazing at him as though he were some sort of god.

This was not a photo to cherish, and it was on the front page of the newspaper.

"For crying out loud," she said in disgust, tossing the paper to the table. "One would think that fool Jason would have made sure Holden was the only person in the pictures he took." She had told her family about the fire yesterday, including Trav Holden's bravery in rescuing the Bracks.

Candace reached across the table for the paper and looked at the photo. "It's a very good shot of you, Serena. And listen to what's written beneath the picture. 'Travis Holden, owner of the chain of Holden's Used Car Lots spread across Montana, displayed admirable courage in rescuing Lorraine and Katie Brack from their burning home. The lady in the background, one of the many onlookers at the fire, is Serena Fanon.'"

"My name, too?" Serena was aghast. Kathleen hadn't had to identify her, dammit. But that was Kathleen, never leaving any stone unturned to write a story that would catch her readers' interest. The woman was a natural-born gossip, Serena thought peevishly. No wonder her little newspaper had remained successful for so many years.

"There's a lengthy article about the fire," Candace said. Her gaze lifted from the paper to Serena. "Would you like to read it?"

"No, thanks," Serena replied with blatant distaste. "Jason took half a dozen pictures of Travis Holden. I'm sure I wasn't in all of them. Why did Kathleen pick this one for the front page?"

Charlie chuckled. "Probably because a pretty girl adds gusto to any picture. Kathleen's a sharp cookie."

"She's also rude and inconsiderate," Serena retorted, holding out her hand. "Let me see that photo again, Candace."

Candace handed over the paper, and Serena studied the shot again. Her simpering expression in the picture made her groan out loud. Had she really been staring at Travis Holden with that moronic look of adoration, or was it a trick of light and the camera that made her appear so utterly mindless? How many people were looking at this same picture this morning and chuckling over it? Even her own father thought it amusing.

Well, it wasn't amusing to her. It was an invasion of her privacy, and she had a mind to call Kathleen Osterman and tell her so. But knowing how Kathleen functioned, tomorrow's headlines could very well read Serena Fanon Strenuously Objects To Her Published Photo, followed by a detailed account of the phone call. A public brouhaha was not the most beneficial way to begin her law practice. It was best to ignore the whole thing, just act as though it had never happened. Again Serena tossed the paper to the table.

Charlie bent over to kiss little Ron's blond curls, then left the kitchen to return to the front part of the large house and his business.

"Travis Holden looks like a very attractive man," Candace said then. She had a soft Southern accent and a sweet disposition, and Serena knew the remark was not intended to irritate her.

But she felt irritated—*very* irritated. "He's a crass opportunist, Candy. I listened to Kathleen's interview with him, and he insisted she mention his business in the article at least twice."

"Maybe so, but he saved two people's lives," Candace said softly.

She was spooning oatmeal into her son's rosy little mouth and made a lovely picture of caring motherhood. She was a beautiful woman, petite with a fantastic figure and pale blond hair that she wore in a straight, shoulder-length bob, often tied back from her face with a ribbon at her nape.

Until this summer, Serena had just barely known her sister-in-law, but anyone would like Candace and her gentle ways. Since her husband's death, she had dedicated herself to her son and the Fanon family. Having no family of her own, she seemed very content living with Charlie, and

Charlie was certainly pleased about having Candace and his grandson living with him, just as he was elated to have Serena home again.

"Yes, he did do that," Serena agreed, recalling how impressed she had been with Holden's courage yesterday. But then he had ruined the whole thing by coming on to her. That particular incident had been omitted from the story she'd told Charlie and Candace about the fire. It still unnerved her, and she wasn't going to talk about it. But she couldn't deny Trav's heroic deed yesterday, nor tarnish it with unkind remarks.

Candace smiled across the table, a gentle, completely guileless smile. "And he does come across as very attractive in the photo. But so do you, Serena. I wouldn't be upset about it if I were you." Her smile became a little shy. "You're so pretty, and I'm very proud to see your picture on the front page of the newspaper."

Serena sighed inwardly. Candace was the kindest person she'd ever known, but she was a bit naive. Serena knew that she herself had a temper. It didn't flare often, but it was there, inside of her. Not Candace. Since Serena had gotten to know her, Candace had never raised her voice in anger or irritability even once. They got along very well, but there was no question about the two of them having completely different personalities.

"Thank you," Serena murmured, deciding to let Candace think what she wanted about the photo without further comment.

But privately she despised the damned thing. She especially despised the fact that she'd been caught by the camera looking at Trav Holden with such a simpering expression. Pictures were forever. Years from now, when she was a successful, well-to-do attorney and a respected member of Montana's law community—her uppermost goal at the present—this photo could come back to haunt her. Kathleen's newspaper wasn't an important publication in the news world, but it was widely read in this area, and people had long memories.

Serena heaved another inner sigh. What was she going to do today? She'd help around the house, of course, but Candace was a natural-born homemaker and always seemed to be two steps ahead of her in the cooking-and-cleaning department. The Fanon home had never been so perfectly kept, nor had meals been as imaginative and delicious as they were with Candace at the helm.

Charlie had mentioned this to Serena when she had first come home. "Candace seems to enjoy taking care of the house and the cooking, honey, and it gives her something to do besides grieve for Ron." His eyes had teared for a moment, because he, too, was grieving for his son. They all were. But Charlie's concern was more for his deceased son's widow than for himself, and he liked it when Candace smiled or laughed about something. Serena knew that her father wanted all of his kids to be happy, and Candace had become one his kids when she'd married Ron.

As for little Ron, the boy was the apple of Charlie's eye. He was an adorable child, with almost white blond hair and huge brown eyes. What's more, he was a happy child, a good child. He never threw tantrums and usually was chortling and laughing. Everyone in the family loved him, and many of Charlie's customers and friends enjoyed seeing little Ron when they dropped in for coffee or their morning newspaper.

Serena smiled across the table at her tiny nephew, and he promptly smiled back. Then he looked at his mother. "Go pay, Mommy."

"Yes, darling, you may go play," Candace said, wiping the remnants of breakfast from his face with her napkin. She got up and lifted him out of his high chair.

"Go see Gampy," Ronnie said, and took off for the front of the house.

Candace smiled. "He has to go and see Gampy about fifty times a day."

"And Gampy loves it," Serena said with a smile.

Candace began clearing the table. "Yes, he does. They're great pals." Serena got up to help. "Now that you have your office, are you going to begin furnishing it?" Candace asked.

"Um, not yet, Candy. I'm going to wait until I hear from the bar association." She caught Candace's curious expression and added lightly, "Furniture and equipment will be costly, and it just seems wiser to me to wait until I hear from the bar before buying it." She was speaking in contradictions and uncomfortable with it. After all, she had put out a lot of money for the office without receiving confirmation from the bar. If she was confident enough to do that, why wouldn't she furnish the office?

"Hmm," Candace murmured, appearing to have turned her concentration to the dishes she was rinsing for the dishwasher at the kitchen sink.

The phone rang, but neither woman rushed to pick up the kitchen extension. The house had only one line, with the number listed under Charlie's Place in the phone book. Most incoming calls were for Charlie, so they always let him answer when he was around.

In a few minutes, he appeared in the kitchen doorway. "Serena, Lola's on the line for you."

"Okay, Dad, thanks." Serena laid down the dishcloth with which she'd been wiping the table and walked over to the phone. "Hi, Lola."

"Hi, yourself. How does it feel to see yourself on the front page of the newspaper?" There was a chuckle in Lola's voice.

"I can see right now that that picture is going to ruin my day," Serena said with a groan.

"Hey, it's a great picture. I was only teasing. Even Duke said it was a great picture of you. Why would it ruin your day?"

"It's not great, Lola. I look like a . . . a moron."

"You most certainly do not. Why would you think that? By the way, that Holden guy's a hunk. Is he taken?"

"I wouldn't know." *Was* he taken? Serena gritted her teeth. For a painful moment, Edward's perfidy came to mind, his smooth and disarming lies about his single status when he'd been married with two children all the time he'd been romancing her. Discovering the truth had been the most staggering emotional blow of her life. The thought of Trav Holden flirting with her yesterday with a wife in the background heightened the painful sensation. Would she ever be able to trust a man again?

"There's no mention of a Mrs. Holden in Kathleen's article," Lola said.

"Which proves nothing," Serena retorted. She had told Lola the whole sordid story about Edward when she returned to Montana, so her cousin would understand the bitter tone of her voice.

"No, I suppose not. Anyway, whether you think so or not, it's a good picture of you, and I liked seeing it on the front page of the paper."

"I'm sure it's the talk of the town," Serena said dryly.

"Oh, it is not. Well, maybe a little. But tomorrow they'll be talking about something else. Don't let it bother you so much, coz. Listen, I've got to run. Drop in at the store when you can."

"Will do. Maybe even sometime today."

"Great. See ya, coz. Bye."

Sighing, Serena put down the phone and picked up the dishcloth to finish wiping the table and counters.

Trav was at the car lot when the paper was delivered. He was in his small office going over the sales and contracts that had been generated since his last visit to Rocky Ford when one of the salespeople brought it in.

"Hey, Trav, you're front-page news," the man exclaimed.

Trav took the paper and sat back in his chair to grin at the photo of himself on the front page. Serena Fanon being in the shot was unexpected and exciting. *Damn, she's pretty,* he thought while studying the picture. And from the way she was looking at him, it appeared that she thought he was kind of pretty, too. His grin broadened. She'd been a little cool over his flirtatious remarks, but some women couldn't help playing hard to get. Would she still be cool if he called her?

Grabbing the Rocky Ford phone book, he looked for her name. The only Fanon listed was Charlie. "Hmm," he grunted, surprised that Serena wouldn't be in the book. Thinking about it, he decided she must have an unlisted number.

But after dialing information and learning that Serena Fanon had no number at all, he sat back perplexed. Everyone with a house or apartment had a phone, didn't they? This was odd. She had said herself that she lived in Rocky Ford, so why wouldn't she have a telephone?

Then he snapped his fingers. She must live with someone else. Charlie, maybe? To be honest, she hadn't struck him as the sort of woman to still be living with a parent, but then he'd really only talked to her for a few minutes.

Opening the telephone book again, he dialed Charlie's number. A man answered, "Charlie's Place."

"Is this Charlie?"

"Yep. What can I do for you?"

"Charlie, this is Trav Holden. We met about a year ago when you bought that Ford pickup from my lot. By the way, how's it running?"

"It's a crackerjack, Trav. Sure, I remember meeting you, and I also saw your picture in today's paper. Great what you did yesterday. Everyone I've seen this morning is talking about it."

"It was no more than anyone would have done, Charlie. Listen, I met your daughter, Serena, yesterday and I'd like to talk to her again. But she doesn't seem to have a phone. Would you know how I could reach her?"

Charlie chuckled. "You can reach her right here, Trav. Hold on a minute and I'll get her." Charlie laid down the phone and went to the kitchen again. "Serena, honey, you've got another phone call."

Serena was drying her hands on a paper towel. "Who is it this time?"

"Trav Holden."

Serena's mouth dropped open. "You have got to be kidding." Quickly she recovered. "Dad, listen, I don't want to talk to Mr. Holden. Tell him . . . tell him I'm not here."

"But I already told him you were, honey. I can't go back and lie to the man now."

Both Charlie and Candace were looking at her with unmistakable curiosity. There was no way to get out of taking this call, Serena realized, not without a convoluted explanation she wasn't prepared to make.

"All right, I'll talk to him." Reluctantly she went to the phone and picked it up. Before she had placed it to her ear, Charlie had gone in one direction and Candace in another. It was obvious they were each trying to be discreet, which Serena appreciated. There was no telling where this conversation might go, and she didn't particularly want her family overhearing it.

"Hello," she finally said.

"Hi, doll. Great photo on the front page of the newspaper, don't you think?"

She cringed at his ridiculous choice of endearments. She was not the "doll" type and never would be. "No, I most certainly do not," she said icily, adding immediately, "Why are you calling me?"

"You don't like our picture? I think it's great."

"You would."

"Now, just how do you know that? Or are you basing your opinion of my taste in photographs on female intuition? You shouldn't do that, babe. Intuition isn't always accurate."

"And *you* shouldn't be calling me 'doll' and 'babe.' Believe me, I am neither."

"No? Do those loving terms offend you?"

Loving? Serena winced. "They're not only offensive, they're insulting."

Trav laughed. "Well, I sure never meant to insult you, sweetheart. Oops. Maybe 'sweetheart' is insulting, too. Sorry about that. I'll call you, um, let me think a minute. How about...'princess'? Or 'darling'? I always thought 'darling' was kind of classy."

"How about calling me Serena?" she snapped. "If you must call me anything, that is. Which brings me back to the question I asked you right away. Why did you phone me?"

"How come you don't have your own phone number? Are you living with your dad? Took me about ten minutes to figure out how to find you."

"That was ten extremely wasted minutes out of your life, Mr. Holden."

"That's where you're wrong, sweetheart. I mean, Serena. I would have gladly given up the entire day to track you down."

"Why?"

"Because of our date tonight."

Serena heaved an exasperated sigh. "Different day, same line. A one-line man. How sad for you. You must lead a very lonely life if that's the best you can do." She shook her head when he let out a whoop of laughter in her ear. "Did I say something funny?" she asked in a dry drawl.

"Hilarious, babe, absolutely hilarious. Listen, about tonight. I'd love to take you to the Horizon Resort for dinner. Ever eaten there?"

"No, but I don't intend to visit the place for the first time tonight. Nor with you."

"Hey, I promise to be on my very best behavior. I'll eat with my knife and fork instead of my fingers, and I'll try real hard not to spill." He dropped his voice to a sensual level. "Say yes, Serena. We could have a very good time."

A shiver went up Serena's spine. Holden's bedroom voice had caused the startling physical reaction, surprising her. It was time to break this off. "I strongly suspect that your idea of a good time and mine are worlds apart. I guess I'm going to have to be blunt, Mr. Holden. I'm not interested, not in you and not in spending an evening *with* you."

Trav became very still in his chair. Women didn't turn him down in this blunt, coldhearted fashion. "That's it, then? You're just not interested?" he said quietly.

"That's it," she confirmed. "Goodbye."

"If you change your mind, I'm at the car lot."

"I won't. Goodbye." Serena put the phone down with a heavy sigh. She didn't like being rude to anyone, but there'd been no other way to make Trav Holden finally accept the fact that she was not going out with him.

She wasn't two steps away from the phone when it rang again. Her eyes narrowed with sudden anger. Not even considering that Charlie would answer and positive that Holden had immediately called again, she grabbed the instrument and snapped, "What part of 'no' don't you understand?"

"Pardon?"

Serena's knees gave out. The male voice in her ear wasn't Holden's, it was Edward's!

"Serena, is that you?"

She sank into the nearest chair. "Yes, it's me," she said weakly.

"Sweetness, I miss you so much. Why did you run off the way you did? I've been going crazy. At first I thought you merely went away to collect yourself. But then I found out you gave up your apartment and quit your job. Darling, you're not intending to stay in Montana, are you? You love Washington, and you love me. How can you do this?"

She licked her dry lips. "How do *you* have the nerve to call me? I told you it was over."

"Yes, my love, I know what you said. But surely you didn't mean it."

"I meant it, Edward—every word. I never want to see you again, and neither do I want to talk to you on the phone. Don't call me again!" She slammed down the phone, then sat there trembling.

Pity for his wife nearly overwhelmed her. How horrible it must be to be married to a cheat and a liar. And how could a wife not know? There had to be signs. Maybe Edward *always* had a woman on the side, and his wife had come to accept it. Serena had probably only been one of many.

Groaning, she covered her face with her hands. Edward had cheapened and degraded her, turning her into the "other woman," someone she would never knowingly be. And he probably thought she was grieving away her life, hiding in Montana, seeing no one, brooding and suffering over him.

The bastard, she thought with sudden vehemence, because in a way, suffering and brooding were exactly what she'd been doing since she'd come home.

Well, she didn't have to live that way. Not when there was a man calling her and all but begging for a date!

With unsteady hands, she searched the phone book for the number of Holden's Used Car Lot. A strange voice answered.

"Trav Holden, please," she said without preamble.

"Hold on a minute, ma'am."

She was put on hold, and some annoying music blared in her ear while she waited.

Then the music died, and she heard, "Trav Holden speaking."

She cleared her throat. "This is Serena Fanon. You said if I changed my mind to call. I have two questions."

Delighted to hear her voice, Trav grinned. "Ask me anything, babe, anything at all."

His cocky tone made Serena grit her teeth, but backing down now would feel as though she had just given Edward the upper hand. He might never know it, but she would, and in no way was Edward ever going to influence her life again.

"First are you married?" she asked flatly.

"Married! Where'd you get that idea? No, Serena, I'm not married. Never have been. What's your second question?"

"Is your offer of dinner at the Horizon Resort still open?"

Trav could hardly believe his ears. "Damned right it's open, sweetheart. I'll make reservations for eight and pick you up at seven."

"I'll be ready. Goodbye."

"Bye," Trav returned. After hanging up, he sat there, pondered Serena's speedy change of heart, then chuckled under his breath. He might not ever know why she had changed her mind so quickly, but did it matter? He was going to see her tonight!

"Hell's bells," he said out loud, mystified in a most pleasing manner. If there was anything he liked more than a pretty woman, it was a pretty woman with a touch of mystery and a lot of brass.

Serena Fanon had it all.

Chapter Three

*T*he occupant of room 116 of the Sundowner Motel neatly clipped the photo of Trav Holden and Serena Fanon from the newspaper. Seated at the small table near the window of her room, she pasted it onto a page in a notebook, which contained every published reference to a Fanon, and many of her own handwritten notes, since her arrival in Rocky Ford.

The morning was warm and the room stuffy, so she got up and slid the window open. Voices immediately drifted in...the maids working in the next room, chatting about their families. Obviously they had opened the window in there, as well.

The woman sat again and slowly started going through her notebook. Rocky Ford's gossipy little newspaper had provided a great deal of information about the Fanons. From it, she had learned the name and status of each member of the Fanon family. She had come to Rocky Ford to find Charles Fanon and had been startled to discover he had

grown children. *Apparently he had no wife. Until her marriage to Duke Sheridan, Charlie's niece, Lola, had lived with
him. Now, at the present, his daughter, Serena, and his
daughter-in-law and grandson, Candace and Ronnie, lived
in Charlie's big house with him.*

*Flipping pages, she came to the small article regarding
Serena's homecoming.*

Serena Fanon, daughter of Charlie Fanon, has returned to Rocky Ford to set up a law practice. Serena
is a graduate of Georgetown University in Washington, D.C., where she also worked part-time in a senator's office. Welcome home, Serena. Rocky Ford is
proud of you.

*Sighing, the woman closed the notebook. When was she
going to do it? Her procrastination was nerve-racking. She
had come to Rocky Ford with a specific goal in mind, and
she had only herself to blame for the long delay.*

*She should have done it immediately, the moment she'd
unearthed Charlie's address, she thought gloomily. Every
day that passed made her goal seem more difficult. And she
had started out many times determined to do it on a particular day only to find her courage slipping as she drove from
the motel toward Charlie's home. It was maddening and
frustrating.*

The voices in the next room broke through her thoughts.

"I can't imagine myself living in a motel for so long," one
woman said. *"Can you?"*

*"Good grief, no. And think of the money she's spent on
that room. If I had that kind of money and intended to live
in a motel, I'd certainly be somewhere besides Rocky Ford."*

"I'd be in Las Vegas," the first woman said. *The two
maids giggled.*

*The woman in room 116 stiffened. They were talking
about her. She had stayed at the Sundowner too long,*

thereby drawing attention to herself. If she did nothing else, she had to move to another motel.

Better yet, she thought, she should find an apartment to rent. She was tired of motel living, anyway, tired of restaurant food. Yes, renting an apartment or a small house was her best course. She should have thought of it weeks ago.

Either that or broach Charlie Fanon today.

A shiver went up her spine, instantly followed by a surge of self-denunciation. Was she ever going to follow through with her plans? Was she going to grow old in Rocky Ford waiting for a probably nonexistent perfect moment?

A tear formed in the corner of her eye, and she brushed it away. She'd already indulged in enough self-pity to last a lifetime. But it hurt that she was so ambivalent. She knew what had to be done, so why didn't she just do it and get it over with? And if she wasn't going to do it, why keep staying in Rocky Ford?

Angry and disgusted with herself again—it was happening more and more—she flipped the pages of the newspaper open to the want-ad section. There were two possibilities in the rental column. She picked up the phone to call the numbers listed in the ads to get more information on the properties.

Serena and Lola were having lunch in a restaurant about six blocks from Lola's store.

"And so I called him back and agreed to the date," Serena said, finishing her story about Trav Holden's overbearing gall and Edward's bloody nerve. "Men," she said in disgust. "They could drive a woman to drink."

"Or into the arms of another man?" Lola said, making a question out of her remark.

Serena looked stunned. "My God, that's exactly what I let Edward's call do to me, isn't it?" Sitting back, she heaved an irritated sigh. "There I was, thinking that he wasn't going to run my life by long-distance. I pictured him visualizing me as brooding and suffering over him, not dating, not doing anything, and I got angry and called Trav. I can't believe my own stupidity."

"You're not stupid," Lola chided. "You were hurt badly in Washington and you're not going to get over it in a few weeks. Maybe you weren't thinking clearly this morning, but Edward's call was bound to shake you up. Don't be so hard on yourself."

"But I don't want to go out with Trav Holden. I don't want to go out with anyone." After a moment, she added, "Him, especially. He's so damned cocky, Lola. So sure of himself."

"Conceited? Egotistical?"

"The worst."

"Well, he is very good-looking."

"Good looks and a quarter will buy you a phone call," Serena retorted. She grimaced. "And he's a used-car salesman. I don't want to date a used-car salesman."

"That's not fair, coz. Trav Holden owns a string of car lots all over Montana. He's much more than a salesman, although if he were a salesman, I can't see anything wrong with that. And don't forget what he did yesterday. How many people do you know would risk their own hide to save two strangers the way he did? Going into a burning house twice? That takes guts, Serena."

Serena sighed. "I admire what he did yesterday, Lola, but that's as far as it goes for me. I never should have talked to him afterward," she added glumly. "It's my own darned fault that he even noticed me. Then there was that awful picture in this morning's paper. I'd like to wring Kathleen's neck. That picture gave him an excuse to call, you know. Without that, I probably never would have heard another word from him."

"Maybe, maybe not," Lola murmured. "If the idea of going out with him bothers you that much, call him and cancel."

Frowning slightly, Serena nodded. "That's exactly what I should do."

Lola sipped from her glass of ice tea. "Of course, you have to start getting out again, and this is a very good opportunity. There's nothing wrong with dating a man you're not crazy about, you know. Trav Holden could turn out to be a friend, and we all need friends."

Serena suspiciously eyed her cousin across the table. "I suppose you dated men strictly for friendship before you met Duke?"

"Actually..." Lola stopped. "Not often," she admitted with some reluctance, then looked thoughtful. "Aren't people strange? Friendship is as valuable as romance, and yet men and women are rarely friends. True friends, I'm talking about."

Her expression cleared. "But that's not to say it couldn't or doesn't happen. Right now you're shying away from Trav because of your bad experience with Edward. No one could blame you. He was a stinker of the first order and obviously didn't care if you got hurt in his furtive little arrangement as long as he was happy. But, Serena, not all men are like that. You've got to get out there and mix and mingle to really get over Edward. Trav Holden's a good start."

Serena was frowning, but she couldn't deny the wisdom of her cousin's opinion. "I suppose so."

Lola smiled. "My advice is to look pretty tonight and have a good time." She checked her watch and reached for the check. "My treat. I've got to get back to the store now. Call me tomorrow and tell me all about what happens tonight, okay?"

"Okay," Serena agreed. "I'll take care of the tip." She laid two dollars next to her plate.

They got up from the table and, after Lola paid for their lunch, they walked out together.

The mail was delivered to Charlie's Place around three in the afternoon, and every day Serena waited for the mailman with a knot in her stomach. Even though she was confident about having passed the bar exam, confirmation hung

over her head like a dark cloud, and doubts would sometimes tear her apart. What if she only thought she'd done
well? It hadn't been an easy test—far from it—and what if
she had failed the theory section, for instance? It was possible to pass some segments of the exam and fail in others,
which meant, of course, taking the failed segments again.
The exam was given at specific times of the year, and if she
had failed any portion of it, she would have to wait for the
next scheduled date. The prospect was abhorrent, especially in light of the lease she had signed for that office
space, which had to be paid for whether she used it or not.

After lunch with Lola, she drove to the Ridgeport Building and inspected her two rooms again. Mentally she placed
furniture and equipment. She really should hire a secretary
before she opened for business, but what if business was so
slow she wouldn't have the money to pay anyone a salary?

There was so much to worry about, so darned much.
Frowning, Serena stood at a window and looked out. She
couldn't help thinking of the opportunities she had dismissed by leaving Washington. Several firms had requested
interviews and presented her with good offers. She had left
it all behind because of Edward, and now here she was
worrying herself sick about money.

At the same time, it felt good to be home, and planning
her own one-woman law practice definitely prompted some
excitement. She wasn't sorry she had returned to Rocky
Ford, but there were moments when she rued the hasty way
she had left Washington. After all, she had as much right to
live and work there as Edward Redding did. And if they had
run into each other on occasion, so what?

It was just that she'd been so emotionally wounded and
confused, and the only thing that had made any sense at all
was to get as far away from Edward as she could.

Serena sighed at the window of her empty office. She
might not have taken the wisest course where Edward was
concerned, but she had made her bed, so to speak, and now
must lie in it.

"I can do it," she whispered with a defiant tilt of her head. "I *will* do it." Someway, somehow, she would manage to furnish this office and get her practice underway.

If she ever heard from the Montana bar, that is, she thought wryly.

Serena had an innate sense of what colors and styles were right for her in clothes. Her dress for the evening was taupe with gold threads woven into the fabric—a sleeveless, scooped-neck, cotton-knit dress that fell from her shoulders nearly to her ankles in one long, smooth line. There was a slit in the left side of the dress that went from the hem to just above her knee. Her accessories were midheeled, taupe sandals and a small taupe clutch bag.

She walked into the living room at a quarter to seven, ready to go. Charlie whistled. "Honey, you look like a million bucks."

Candace smiled. "You look very nice, Serena. That dress is perfect for you."

Serena sank on to the couch. "Thanks. I've worn it a dozen times and will probably wear it a dozen more. And it was on sale, to boot. Very good buy." All of her clothes were good buys. She had lived very thriftily during college and law school, earning what she could to help pay her living expenses. Charlie had paid for her tuition and books, and had also taken up the slack between what she earned herself and her actual cost of living. She had kept track of every penny he'd spent on her through the years and was completely sincere in her vow to repay him.

The TV was on; Candace and Charlie were watching a show. Little Ron was already in bed for the night. Serena had been home long enough to know that this was their evening routine. Candace bathed her son and put him to bed shortly after dinner, then she and Charlie would watch TV together until their own bedtimes.

She eyed her sister-in-law, so young, so pretty, and wondered if she was content. She seemed to be, but how long could a young woman live without entertainment, other than television? The mere thought made Serena shudder. In Washington she had been on the go almost constantly, what with school, friends, her job and Edward. But even before Edward, every day had been crammed with activity.

This waiting to hear from the bar association was beginning to get her down, she realized grimly. She never had been a person who enjoyed doing nothing. She would choose chaos over doing nothing any day of the week. Maybe dinner with Trav Holden wouldn't be so bad; at least she wouldn't be sitting here all night.

Sighing silently, she stared blankly at the TV screen.

Trav had looked up Charlie's address in the phone book and had no trouble finding the place. It wasn't until he saw it, however, that he remembered Charlie's operating a little coffeehouse type of business in his home. He grinned when he spotted the pickup he'd sold Charlie well over a year ago parked in the driveway. Next to it was the white sedan that Serena had been driving the day of the fire. And there was a third vehicle, a small yellow car, this year's model, parked in front of Charlie's pickup. He wondered whom the new car belonged to.

Because Charlie's property was so spacious, there was still room in the driveway for Trav to park his own car. He pulled in, turned off the ignition and got out. The sun, though sinking in the western sky, was still bright and warm. All of a sudden, without even a moment's warning, he felt nervous.

He almost laughed. Him, nervous over a date? Serena Fanon was a looker, all right, but had he ever dated a woman who wasn't? He was a sucker for pretty women and wasn't ashamed to admit it, either.

So why did he feel nervous about this date?

"Ridiculous," he mumbled under his breath. Since the front of the house was Charlie's place of business, which was closed for the day, it was only logical to head for the back. Passing an open window, Trav heard what sounded like a television program. Drawing a deep breath in an attempt to allay the peculiar quiver in his belly, he continued around the house and climbed the few steps to the back porch.

He looked for a doorbell and saw none, so he knocked. No more than a minute later, the door opened, and there was Serena.

"Hello," she said with an inscrutable expression.

Trav grinned. "Hi. I'm right on time, in case you didn't notice." His gaze moved down her dress and back up to her face. She looked fantastic, and that unfamiliar sensation in his gut intensified.

"I noticed," she said coolly. Their eyes met in a long look that neither seemed inclined to break. It felt like a silent challenge to Serena, but who really was challenging whom? In her own heart was a hands-off attitude, and maybe that was her challenge to this cocky man. But what was his to her?

Damn, he was handsome! Handsome enough to make any woman squirm. Serena nearly broke eye contact, and only stubbornness kept her gaze steady. She experienced a great deal of satisfaction when Trav looked away first, shifting his weight as though he was suddenly uncomfortable. She smiled then, positive she could control their relationship, however flirtatious, handsome and brash Trav Holden might be. "Please come in."

"Uh, sure." He really hadn't expected to be invited in, not when it was so obvious that Serena was ready to go.

"This way," she said, preceding him through the kitchen. Walking behind her, he thoroughly enjoyed the graceful movements of her body in that chic, delightfully feminine dress.

The sound of the TV set grew more distinct as she brought him to the living room. Charlie immediately turned down the volume with a remote control and got to his feet.

"Hello, Trav. How are you?"

"Fine, Charlie, just fine." They shook hands.

Serena spoke. "Candace, I'd like you to meet Travis Holden. Trav, Candace is my sister-in-law."

Candace smiled shyly. "Nice meeting you, Mr. Holden."

"Very nice meeting you, ma'am." He wasn't sure what name to call her. Was she married to a Fanon? There was a lot he didn't know about the Fanon family, and it was quite likely that Charlie had sons, or at least one son. The only other way Serena would have a sister-in-law was if she was married herself, which he knew wasn't the case.

But he'd bet anything that Candace was the owner of that little yellow car, and the way it was parked in front of Charlie's and Serena's vehicles indicated that Candace also lived in this big old house. So... where was her husband?

Serena picked up her purse from a table, then moved to her father and kissed his cheek. "See you later, Dad." She turned her gaze to Candace. "You, too, Candy." Finally she looked at Trav. "I'm ready when you are."

Trav nodded and smiled at Charlie and Candace. "Guess we're off, then. Good night."

The one thing Trav had sensed in that brief interlude was the affection the Fanons felt for each other. As always happened whenever he witnessed closeness and warmth within a family, he felt a pang of envy. He'd grown up with neither affection nor warmth. Hell, he'd grown up knowing he was no more important to his mother or anyone else than a piece of furniture.

Thinking of his childhood never failed to put a bad taste in his mouth, so he quickly buried all remnants of his past and concentrated on the present.

Politely he opened the passenger door of his car for Serena to get in. She said, "Thank you," and then he loped around the front of the car to the driver's side.

Serena took note of his clothing, a soft, summery white shirt and dark blue pants that fit his perfect body as though constructed solely for him. His dark hair was straight and combed back from his face without a part, and Serena recalled how mussed and intriguingly disarrayed it had been after he'd rescued the Bracks.

Trav got in and sent her a smile while starting the engine. "Nice evening."

She hooked her seat belt. "Yes, it is."

"I like your dress." He was looking at her instead of backing out of the driveway. "And your hair, your eyes, your..." He laughed. "I think it's safe to say I like everything about you."

"You must form opinions on a very shallow basis," she said. "You couldn't possibly like *everything* about me when you just barely know me."

"All right, then I like everything I see. Does that suit you better?" Trav backed the car out of the Fanon driveway and started down the street.

"It's a lot more honest, at least," Serena said evenly.

"I'm an honest man, honey."

"I wouldn't know about that, would I?"

Trav chuckled. "Maybe not, but try to believe it, okay?"

She turned her head to look at him and was struck again by his good looks. In the golden light of the setting sun, his tawny skin positively glowed against the white of his shirt. He sat behind the wheel with a lazy grace that was completely masculine. Looking at him made her uneasy, she realized, and faced front again.

"You were on the verge of saying something," Trav said.

She hesitated a moment to regroup her thoughts, to put aside his good looks. In the long run, good looks weren't important. Honesty was, though, incredibly so, and he wanted her to believe in his.

"I was going to ask why I should believe that you're an honest man."

Taking his eyes from the road, he cocked an eyebrow at her. "Would you rather believe I'm not?"

"When two people just barely know each other, believing anything about each other is a fool's game." *Even after you think you know someone enough to worship the ground he walks on, you should be careful about what you believe.*

"Other than what one can see with his or her own eyes?" Trav said.

"That pretty much sums it up, yes." Serena paused as Edward invaded her mind. "Even then, it's possible for one person to be deluded by another," she added.

"You know, there's a lot of bitterness in your voice. Surely you're not bitter over anything I've done. As you've said—twice, I believe—we barely know each other. Where'd that bitterness come from, sweetheart? Some guy tromp all over you?"

She stiffened. "That is none of your business."

Trav nodded knowingly. "Damned fool, whoever he was. Serena—" he turned his head to look at her "—I could really go for you in a big way."

Her frozen face slowly turned his way. "That sounds like you're offering a consolation prize for my being 'tromped' on by another man. Mr. Holden, I'm not sure you're a prize of any kind."

"Ouch," he said with a grimace. "First please don't revert back to that 'mister' business. And second I just might be the biggest prize you could ever win. At least give me a chance."

"A chance to prove what a marvelous human being you are," Serena drawled. "You do have nerve, don't you?"

"I think I already admitted that, babe." He peered at her. "Didn't I?"

"Yes," she said tersely. "Look, I agreed to this dinner date. At this point, I will not make any further agreements or promises. What happens happens, okay?"

Trav's grin was completely confident. "Okay. That's an agreement in itself, isn't it?"

"You're impossible." Serena stared out the side window, wishing that she were anywhere but in this car with the most egotistical man she'd ever met. Who cared if he was also the most handsome man she'd ever met? She didn't trust anything he said, and why should she? He sure didn't come across as honest and sincere.

"We're going to have a great time tonight," Trav said. Serena sniffed. *Yeah, right.*

Chapter Four

The one portion of the evening that Serena was truly looking forward to was seeing the Horizon Resort. It had been constructed four or five years ago, but during her brief trips home there had been no opportunity to go there. It was a good fifty miles from Rocky Ford, but she had heard people say—Lola, for one—that the resort was a wonderful place to have dinner or spend a weekend. "It has great hiking trails and spectacular scenery," Lola had told her.

It also had the area's most expensive restaurant. "But it's well worth the cost," had been Lola's opinion.

Serena was thinking about all of that when Trav asked, "So, what do you do?"

"Do?" She cocked an eyebrow at him, even though it was perfectly obvious what he was asking.

"Yeah, do. As in work...a job...a profession. You know what I mean. I'm sure you *do* something."

"Actually I don't."

Trav sent her a doubtful glance. "Really?"

Serena sighed. "Right now I'm doing nothing. Unless you can construe waiting as a career."

"Waiting for what?"

"A letter."

Trav stiffened slightly. Serena was being deliberately evasive, deliberately snotty. Why? Wasn't he good enough for her to relax and enjoy herself with? Good enough to talk to without that attitude? Okay, maybe some guy *had* tromped on her, but she shouldn't dislike him for some other man's sins. She had a glowing beauty, and he hated thinking that it might be only skin-deep. But it was possible. He'd met beautiful women before who'd had lousy personalities.

Still, he found it hard to believe that Charlie Fanon's daughter would have a lousy personality; Charlie was one of the nicest, most friendly guys he'd ever met. No, there was more to Serena's chilly attitude than that. Maybe she'd been hurt real bad by some joker and really was having a hard time getting over it.

Driving along, he tried conversation again. "Must be an important letter."

"It is." Shame suddenly surged through Serena. Trav might be too sure of himself for her taste, but did he deserve disdain? There were only two people to blame for that fiasco in Washington—Edward and herself. She couldn't go around taking out her pain and anger on every man she met. Well, she could, but what would that earn her besides a nose-in-the-air reputation that certainly wouldn't help her law practice? Rocky Ford was a typical small town; information and gossip spread like wildfire. She had to be nice to people if she expected them to seek legal advice from her.

What hurt was that she had never before had to think about being nice to anyone; it had just come naturally. Now she was wary, guarded and defensive around men, and God only knew how long that aberration would last.

Feeling chagrined over her own behavior, she spoke quietly. "The letter I'm waiting for is from the Montana Bar Association."

That was the last thing Trav had expected to hear. "You're a lawyer?" he said incredulously.

"Almost."

"And you're going to be practicing in Rocky Ford?"

"Yes."

"Well, I'll be damned," Trav mumbled. She sure didn't look like any lawyer he'd ever seen. And yet he had sensed something special about her—beyond her striking face and sexy body. Now he knew what it was: education. His own education wasn't anything to brag about, and he greatly admired those people he met who had taken years out of their lives to get a college degree. Serena wasn't your run-of-the-mill pretty woman; she was a lawyer! He was so impressed that he didn't know what to say, and speechlessness was not a common affliction for him.

Because Trav was so silent, surprising Serena, she found herself talking to fill the gap. "I leased office space in the Ridgeport Building. Do you know where that is?"

Trav swallowed. "Yeah, I do. I . . . I'm really impressed, Serena."

She turned startled eyes on him, probably because he truly sounded impressed. And sincere.

But the second that thought formed, another took its place: Edward had been a master at false sincerity. And why would her being a lawyer impress Trav so much? In his business, he must deal with professional people—both accountants and attorneys—all the time.

Still, there was something different about Travis. His brashness wasn't hitting her in the face, and in fact he seemed rather subdued.

Well, she certainly didn't know how to read Trav Holden, she thought with some annoyance. Maybe he didn't like professional women, women with brains; maybe he felt threatened by them.

It was possible they simply didn't like each other at all, she thought next and then frowned at the idea, wondering at the same time why it should bother her. Did she want Trav

Holden to like her? Lord knew she'd done nothing to encourage his interest.

She could only blame her peculiar ambiguity toward Trav on confusion about men in general, she decided uneasily. She sneaked a glance at him, and her frown deepened. No man should be that handsome. He probably had women by the score chasing after him. Did she want to join those ranks?

"We're almost there," Trav announced after a right turn onto a secondary road.

Serena had seen several signs advertising the resort as being just ahead, so his announcement was completely unnecessary. But suddenly it seemed he didn't know how to talk to her now that he'd learned of her profession. How strange.

The Horizon Resort was as attractive as Lola had proclaimed, Serena saw as they drove nearer to it. The sprawling, two-story building had a rustic appearance and was constructed of native rock and wood that had been stained several shades of brown. Whoever had designed the Horizon Resort had admirably blended it with the environment. There were dozens of cars in the parking area, and people were going in and coming out through the large double doors of the entrance.

"Very nice," Serena murmured.

"Yes, it is," Trav agreed. "I come here a lot. When I'm visiting Rocky Ford, of course. The food is terrific."

"So I've heard."

Trav pulled into a parking space and turned off the engine. He turned his head and looked at her with intense admiration. She really was too pretty to be believed. And she was a lawyer. That had really knocked him for a loop.

He cleared his throat. "Uh, I know Jack Houston, the owner. I'll introduce you, if he's around."

Serena nodded calmly, although she was very much aware of Trav's eyes on her. Actually she'd like to stare back, and it took great effort not to do so.

And then again, maybe I won't, Trav thought, still thinking of that introduction. Jack Houston was young, good-
looking and single, and Trav didn't need the competition.

"Wait a sec and I'll get your door," he said gruffly before hopping out of the car.

Startled by his tone, Serena wondered what was going on
in his head now. This was not an ordinary date. But why
wasn't it? What made it different from the other dates she'd
been on?

Trav, of course, she thought with a sigh. He was different than anyone she'd ever known, so naturally the date
would feel different.

He escorted her into the building and to the restaurant.
The hostess, an attractive young woman, greeted him like an
old friend. "Trav, how are you?"

"Couldn't be better, Connie. How are things with you?"

"Just fine, thank you. I have your favorite table all
ready," Connie said. "Follow me."

Trav took Serena's arm as they wound through the tables
of diners to one by a wall of window glass. Connie laid
down menus. "Here you are."

"Thanks, Connie." Trav pressed a five-dollar bill into her
hand.

"Thank you," Connie said, then added, "I read about
your saving the Bracks from that fire, Trav." She blinked at
Serena, as though just now recognizing her. "You're the
woman in the photo with Trav."

"Serena Fanon, Connie Bergmen," Trav said.

Serena smiled, albeit weakly. "Hello. Nice meeting you."

"You saw the fire?"

"Yes, I saw it." Trav pulled out a chair for Serena, and
she sank onto it. Connie wasn't only friendly; she was curious. Maybe *nosy* was a better word, Serena thought,
wondering if she and Trav had been together before the fire.
"Quite by accident," Serena added to clear up that point,
"I just happened to be driving by."

Trav took his own seat across the small table. "Serena's a lawyer, Connie. She'll be open for business any day now, in the Ridgeport Building, so remember her if you need any legal work done."

Connie's eyes widened. "No kidding? Hey, that's great. So Rocky Ford is finally going to have a full-time attorney. About time, I say. Do you have a card, Serena?"

Serena smiled, again wanly. "No, I'm sorry, I don't."

"Oh. Well, I guess I can remember the Ridgeport Building. You two enjoy your dinner. I'd better get back to work."

The minute Connie was out of earshot, Serena sent Trav a dirty look. "Did I ask you to drum up business for me? I told you I was waiting to hear from the bar association. It could be weeks yet, and Connie asking for a card when I don't have any was embarrassing."

"You don't have your business cards yet?" Trav couldn't conceal his disapproval. "You should be handing them out left and right. How else are people going to know that Rocky Ford is finally going to have a full-time lawyer? Advertising is a must, Serena."

"Ethical attorneys do not advertise," she retorted.

"I've seen lots of ads on TV and in newspapers for attorneys. Are you telling me those guys aren't ethical?"

"Most of them are personal-injury attorneys."

"So? Aren't they ethical?"

This was a subject that caused many an argument among attorneys. Some believed that advertising tainted their profession. Others felt that advertising was the backbone of any business, and how else would the public know of their existence?

Serena was torn on the matter. She had been planning to put a sedate, formal announcement in the newspaper when she was ready to start her practice, and certainly there was nothing wrong with handing out business cards, especially when a person asked for one.

But Trav had jumped the gun tonight—without her permission—and it irritated her.

"Even if I intended to advertise, which I don't," she said coldly, "it's too soon to do so. Passing out business cards stating I'm an attorney would not only be in bad taste, it would be an infraction of the rules. Please don't do that to me again." Picking up her menu, she began studying it.

Trav drew a deep, slightly annoyed breath. He had stepped on her toes, or, at least, *she* thought he had. But one would think she would be so proud of what she'd accomplished that she would be telling everyone about it herself.

Apparently not. His lips flattened into a thin line while he read his own menu, although he practically knew it by heart.

"Trav!"

Serena looked up to see a young, shapely woman with long blond hair, wearing a very short white leather skirt and very high heels, bearing down on them.

Trav grinned. "Hi, Ava. How's tricks?"

Serena felt as if she had suddenly become invisible. Ava's full attention, including a dazzling smile, was focused entirely on Trav. "Oh, you know me, Trav. I always enjoy myself. Want a cocktail before dinner, hon?" she asked.

Oh, she's a cocktail waitress, Serena thought, giving that short skirt an extremely cool appraisal. A very *friendly* cocktail waitress. Obviously she and Trav shared the same views on advertising, because Ava's clothing, or lack thereof, advertised every curve she had. Her hot pink peasant blouse was perfect for leaning forward and giving a man a good look at her ample bosom.

Folding her arms, Serena sat back to watch this little tableau. Trav wasn't the least put off by Ava's gushing personality. In fact he seemed to be enjoying it. Serena gritted her teeth.

"Yes, I think we'll have something," Trav said. "Serena, what would you like?"

At long last, Ava's gaze turned to Serena, who felt as though she'd just been discovered.

"A glass of white wine," she said stonily.

"And I'll have a glass of red," Trav said.

Ava laughed. "No Scotch tonight, hon?"

"Nope, not tonight, Ava."

"Be back in a flash," Ava said with a little-girl giggle that raised the hair on the back of Serena's neck.

"Well," she said when Ava had tripped away on her three-inch heels. "Looks like you're on very friendly terms with the help in this place."

"I told you I come here often." His lips twitched into a half smile. Was Miss Frosty Fanon just a little bit jealous? Now, wasn't that an interesting concept? Maybe there was hope for the evening, after all. If he could just get her to unbend, to relax, she might be a dynamite gal. Actually she *was* dynamite, only she didn't seem particularly fond of him. That was what he had to work on. There wasn't a reason in the world why she shouldn't like him.

He realized in the next heartbeat that he wanted her to like him. Do more than just like him. In fact what he really wanted was . . . her. Blood suddenly rushed to his groin, intensifying that thought.

He cleared his throat. "Have you decided what you'd like for dinner?"

"The trout," Serena said.

"Good choice."

"I'm so glad you approve."

He laughed. "What's the matter, babe? Why do you try so hard to keep me at a safe distance?"

"Is that what your ego is telling you?" Serena gave a short, brittle laugh. "Believe me, I'm not worried about distance, Mr. Holden."

He leaned forward. "Oh, yes, you are. A man can tell when a woman is attracted and doesn't want to be."

"And you're an expert on women." She glanced pointedly at the bar, where Ava was chatting with a customer. "With some women, I'm sure you are an expert. Women of a certain nature," she added with obvious distaste.

"Most women have similar natures. Some of them merely dress it differently," Trav said casually.

"That's absurd," she said with her chin tilted at a disdainful angle. "Really—"

She was interrupted by Ava's chirping voice. "Here we go, hon," she said to Trav while setting the glasses of wine down on the table. It was obvious that she finally really saw Serena. "Say, aren't you the gal in the newspaper picture of Trav?"

Serena groaned inwardly. But Ava's interest in her was already spent. "Trav, that was the bravest thing I've ever heard of," she said breathily. "My goodness, weren't you scared out of your wits? No, you wouldn't be. Not you."

Picking up her glass of wine, Serena took a huge swallow. Ava's mincing and prancing was getting nauseating. How could some women make such complete fools of themselves?

An agonizing truth jolted through Serena. How did she have the nerve to think of Ava or any other woman as a fool when she'd proved herself to be the biggest fool of all with Edward? She was never again going to be the same carefree young woman she'd been before meeting Edward, and that knowledge was painful. Tears suddenly clogged her throat, and she got rid of them by finishing off the wine in her glass.

Trav noticed. "Better bring another glass of white wine, Ava," he said with a chuckle.

Dinner took several hours. People kept stopping by the table to say hello to Trav, and then he would introduce them to Serena and they would all talk until the person or couple would wander off. Jack Houston, the owner of the resort, actually pulled a chair over to their table and sat with them for about twenty minutes. Houston was a tall, thin man with an incredible smile, friendly as all outdoors and obviously glad to see Trav.

That was what Serena kept picking up from the parade of Trav's friends: they liked him. Over and over she heard,

"When will you be back in Rocky Ford again, Trav? You really must let us know so we can plan something." He was jolly and joking with both the men and women, but when he talked to a woman, there was also a bit of roguish charm thrown in. He was a natural-born flirt, and since he was doing it right in front of his date for the evening, he obviously saw nothing wrong with his devilish smiles and outrageous flattery.

Serena's opinion of Trav Holden fluctuated so much during that long, drawn-out meal, she felt confused. She had always admired gregarious people, but Trav's friendliness, while encompassing both men and women, was definitely slanted in favor of the fairer sex. It might be perfectly normal, but it was also disturbing. He could be the biggest heartbreaker in the state of Montana, and the last thing she needed these days was another man who thought he was God's greatest gift to womankind. Another who believed the rules of fair play didn't apply to him.

As they were leaving—much to Serena's relief—a whole slew of people came in. Immediately they were surrounded while Trav was slapped on the back by the men and smiled at and hugged by the women.

Again Serena went through introductions. Her mind swam from so many names. To her dismay, she and Trav were swept along by the newcomers to the resort's lounge. Tables were pushed together, chairs repositioned. There were other people in the lounge, and a jukebox—colorful, old-fashioned and charming—was playing a country song.

This was a noisy group, laughing, teasing one another and telling jokes. They sat down willy-nilly, and Serena found herself squeezed between a man and a woman whose names had already fled her mind. Trav was at the other end of the throng, talking and laughing with his friends.

Serena really didn't mind this interlude. In fact it reminded her of the many times she and her college or law-school friends would congregate in some restaurant or tavern, have a beer or two and talk and laugh about everything from professors to their personal lives. Sometimes they had gotten into serious discussions, and the conversation was quick and intelligent. Debates and arguments occurred on occasion, sometimes lasting for hours.

But those particular sessions were not what she was comparing to this gathering. This was a fun group with nothing serious or important on their minds. Trav was enjoying himself, she could see, and there was no reason why she shouldn't do the same.

A waitress, attractive but definitely not another Ava, took their orders, and it was a very mixed order, indeed, consisting of beer, soft drinks and coffee. Serena noted that Trav ordered coffee, but she wasn't doing the driving so she asked for another glass of white wine.

The woman on her right began talking to her. "I'm not from around here. I'm visiting my cousin. That's her over there, the gal with the long dark hair. Would you believe all of those curls are natural? Karen's so lucky. She's never had to have a perm in her life."

Serena smiled. Her own hair was naturally curly, but boasting wasn't her style. "Yes," she said. "Your cousin is very lucky. And she's also very pretty."

The woman lowered her voice. "That's not her husband she's with."

"Oh?" Serena's revulsion toward infidelity kicked in. Apparently the man hanging on Karen was... what? A boyfriend? And Karen had a husband. Serena could feel her stomach muscles tighten.

"I don't blame her one bit," the woman continued. "Larry—that's her husband—is such a jerk. He beat her so badly a month ago she ended up in the hospital. They're separated now, and I expect Karen to file for a divorce any day. I really don't know why she hasn't already done it."

Serena didn't know how to reply to that, so she merely nodded in mute understanding. This gal was as chatty as they came, and apparently her cousin's unhappy situation was uppermost in her mind.

The man on her left said, "I know the Fanon name. Are you related to Charlie?"

"He's my father."

"Is that a fact? Great guy, old Charlie."

"Yes, he is. But he's really not that old, you know." She was happy to recite Charlie's true age and then explain his youthful outlook on everything from soup to nuts.

The drinks were delivered. Some of the people at the table got up to dance. Serena sipped her wine and talked to anyone who said something to her. As the boisterous conversation went on around her, she began assigning names to faces. She was enjoying herself, she realized. Most of these people lived in Rocky Ford or nearby, and most were around her age. It was a good group, and she was glad to have met them.

Then she heard the word *lawyer* being passed around the tables. She looked at Trav, who was grinning at her. He'd done it again, apparently—announced her profession without her permission. He was an incorrigible big-mouth, she thought with a sigh, even though this time she felt no annoyance over it.

She was suddenly the center of attention. Both men and women dug out and passed her their business cards and asked for hers.

"I'm sorry," she said to one and all, tucking the cards into her bag. "I'm not open for business yet and I haven't had my cards printed up."

"But her office is in the Ridgeport Building," Trav said over the din.

"When *will* you be open?" Karen called out.

Serena had the discomfiting premonition that her first client was going to be a divorce case. Given a choice, she would avoid divorces completely, but she was in no position to be choosy, just starting out and all.

And she could only guess at the timing. Nevertheless she answered as though she weren't a bundle of nerves waiting to hear from the bar association. "Probably in a couple of weeks."

The party went on. The lounge gradually emptied, until only their group remained. Serena peered at her watch and saw that it was almost midnight.

She felt a tap on her shoulder and turned her head to see Trav standing behind her.

"Let's dance, sweetheart," he said, not loudly, but it seemed to Serena that everyone had heard.

There was no one else on the dance floor. Serena's first impulse was to refuse. But these were Trav's friends, and she had no desire to embarrass him, even if he had called her "sweetheart" in a possessive way and she wished he hadn't.

"All right," she said, pushing her chair back to get up.

He led her to the dance floor. The music was a slow number. He put his arm around her waist and took her right hand, but before moving one step, he looked into her eyes.

Serena's breath caught in her throat. Being this close to Trav was an unexpected and extremely disturbing thrill. Oh, those dark, dark eyes, she thought nervously. His aftershave—obviously used very sparingly, of which she heartily approved as she had never liked strong perfumes on either men or women—assailed her senses. His hair, combed so smoothly at the start of the evening, had tumbled slightly so that a lock of it draped over one side of his forehead. He was, in a word, gorgeous. And her body knew and felt it, even if her mind was trying desperately to cling to her own reality.

"Damn, you're beautiful," he whispered huskily. Pulling her closer, he began moving with the slow, sensual beat of the music.

"We're being watched." Serena pushed herself back from him, putting space between their bodies. Her overfast heartbeat was not welcome. She wasn't seeking romance and even if she were, it wouldn't be the reason she had come out with Trav tonight. He wasn't her type. She didn't trust him. He was incredibly good-looking and knew it. She could have extended that list ad infinitum, but it all boiled down to the same conclusion: she was not interested in Trav Holden on a personal level.

Trav glanced at his pals and grinned. "So we are." His eyes met Serena's. "Does other people's curiosity really matter to you?"

"Not always."

"But in my case, it does."

"You have a lot of friends. I suspect you're quite the ladies' man, so yes, in your case it matters."

"Don't you like my friends?"

"I like them just fine. What I don't like is giving them the impression that you and I are an item."

"An item. Interesting term. Do you consider it a polite substitute for the word *lovers?*"

She was glad the lounge was dimly lit, because her cheeks were suddenly hot and had to be red. "Perhaps we should clarify our date tonight," she said. "One evening together does not constitute a relationship, and you and I are never going to be lovers."

His grin seemed to penetrate her skin and arrow straight to the core of her. "A debatable point, sweetheart."

"No, it is not a debatable point," she retorted.

In the next instant, he had pulled her close again and was breathing into her hair. "Sure it is," he whispered.

He was not a great dancer. In fact he barely moved his feet. They had to be a spectacle, the only couple standing in the middle of the dance floor, swaying seductively to the music.

Serena again pushed away from him. "It's late. I'd like to go home now."

Trav looked at her for a long moment, then nodded. "Sure, if that's what you want. We'll say good-night to the gang." They returned to the conglomeration of tables, where Trav announced, "We're leaving, my friends."

A chorus of protests ensued, but Trav merely joked with his friends while Serena retrieved her purse from where she'd left it and said good-night to everyone. With Trav's hand on her elbow, they walked out of the lounge and then went through the resort's double doors to the outdoors.

The night air was fresh, cool and bracing. Serena breathed deeply and admitted relief at finally calling a halt to the evening. It would take them about an hour to drive back to town, Trav would drop her off and that would be that.

Settled in the car, she hid a yawn behind her hand. In her mind, the evening was already over. It was merely a matter of getting home now.

She would be very glad to crawl into bed and give in to the weariness she was feeling.

Chapter Five

During the drive, Trav talked about the people Serena had met tonight. She said "Hmm" and "Really?" at appropriate moments, but actually contributed very little to the conversation. Her reticence didn't seem to bother Trav, and he kept up a steady stream of patter for miles and miles. There was very little traffic; it was late, and most of the area's residents were home in bed, which was where Serena wanted to be.

Then, about five miles from town, there was a muffled bang and the car began to wobble.

"Oh-oh," Trav muttered. "Feels like we've got a flat tire."

Serena groaned inwardly—simply over another delay in getting home—as he guided the car to the side of the road. He turned off the engine and, in an appeasing gesture, patted her arm. "It'll only take a few minutes to put on the spare. Stay put. I'll handle everything."

Indeed you will, Serena thought dryly. She'd never changed a tire in her life and certainly wasn't going to start now. Besides, there was the tiniest spark of suspicion coming to life in the back of her mind: was he playing the old "running out of gas" game, being slightly more inventive by substituting a flat tire for a supposedly empty gas tank? She could only wait and see on that score. If he made a pass . . . Well, he'd just better not!

Trav took the keys and got out. Serena sighed and put her head back. She was thinking about the evening—all in all, quite unusual—when Trav returned to the car and got in.

"Um, there isn't a spare in the trunk," he said in a subdued, apologetic tone of voice.

Serena bolted upright. "What do you mean there isn't a spare? *Every* car has a spare. Isn't this your car? Why wouldn't you have a spare?"

"Yes, this is my car, but I took it off the lot without checking with any of my salespeople. It never occurred to me it might not have a spare tire."

"Don't you own a car that isn't for sale?" she asked with heavy sarcasm.

"Actually, no."

She glared at him in the dark. "I can't believe this. We're still a good five miles from town with a flat tire and no spare. What do you suggest we do, or do you even have a suggestion?"

"Don't get ticked, Serena. We're both in the same canoe without a paddle. Okay, here's our options. I can walk to town and hope someone will come along and pick me up, thus speeding up the process. And you can go along or stay here until I get back with a new tire. I guess I should have said *your* options, because I'm going one way or the other."

"Your options stink."

"But they're the only ones we've got. So . . . what do you want to do, go with me or stay here?"

"Well, I'm certainly not going to sit alongside the road in the middle of the night for God knows how long!"

"Okay, then it's settled. Let's get started. We might have to hike the entire five miles, and it really is getting late now."

Fuming, Serena got out her side of the car while Trav got out of his side. He pushed the automatic-door-lock button, then closed his door. Serena gave hers a push to close it. They met at the front of the car and started walking.

After a few minutes, her suspicions would no longer remain contained. "It wouldn't surprise me in the least if you had planned this... this fiasco."

"I planned to walk five miles in the middle of the night? What do you think I am, nuts? I don't mind a good hike now and then. In fact I *like* to hike. But not at one in the morning and certainly not with a complaining woman."

"I have every right to complain. I can't believe you didn't check the trunk for a spare."

"Neither can I, but that's the way the old ball bounced, kiddo. Save your energy for walking and stop giving me hell, okay?"

As upset and distraught as Serena felt, she was noticing where they were and recalling old memories of the area. The moon was bright, thank goodness, and she could see everything—trees, fence lines and the road—quite well.

Abruptly she announced, "I know a shortcut. It's up ahead a little farther. All we have to do is cut through the Johnson ranch and pick up a back road that will eliminate at least two miles from this miserable trek."

"Are you sure?"

"Yes, I'm sure. I grew up in Rocky Ford, in case you've forgotten."

"Then you know exactly where we are?"

"Exactly."

"All right, then, we'll take your shortcut."

Serena was wishing her sandals didn't have skinny little heels. They were only about an inch in height, certainly not too high for ordinary walking, but they kept catching on pebbles and weren't altogether steady. Flats would have been so much better for a middle-of-the-night hike, but why on earth would she have dressed for a hike when she'd been invited to the nicest restaurant around?

And truly the food at the Horizon Resort had been as good as reputed. There were a lot of things about the long evening that could be labeled good, to be honest.

This, she thought with sudden venom, was not one of them. Hiking along a dark road was not her idea of how best to end an evening. And she blamed Trav for it. Not checking an unfamiliar car for a spare tire was unthinkable in her book. So he might be handsome, charming, courageous *and* just a doll, she thought drolly, recalling Ava's simpering behavior around him, but he was also careless.

"*I* would never have taken a strange car on a fifty-mile drive without checking the spare," she said coldly.

Trav scowled at her. "Not all of us mortals are perfect, though."

"Your insult is duly noted. Regardless of mortal imperfections, I never would have—"

"I know, I know. Stop with the lecture, all right? I'm not any more thrilled with this than you are."

Silent and seething, Serena trudged on. Then she squinted across the field on their right. A tall, bulky form, what she remembered as the Johnsons' water tank, was the landmark she'd been watching for.

"Here's where we go through the fence," she said coolly.

"Are you sure this is all right?" Trav asked. "The owner won't mind us trespassing?"

"The Johnsons happen to be very nice people, and it's only a grazing field for their cattle. Why would they mind? Come on." Serena started toward the barbed-wire fence.

Trav hesitated while he checked the road in both directions and saw not a trace of traffic. But some of the people they'd left at the resort had to use this road to get home, and they could be coming along any minute.

"Serena, I'm not sure leaving the road is a good idea," he said, raising his voice as she was already to the fence.

Walking over to her, he explained his logic. "In mere minutes from now, there could be several cars going past here."

She was tired, getting chilled from the night air on her sleeveless arms, and her feet hurt. All she wanted was to get home by the fastest route, crawl into her warm bed and shut her eyes.

"And supposing your friends decide to party till dawn?" She cocked an eyebrow. "Is that possible?"

He shifted his weight from one foot to the other. "Anything's possible, but—"

"I'm taking the shortcut," she said, cutting him off in midsentence. "You do what you want." Turning, she sized up the three strands of barbed wire. "If you'd hold the wire apart for me to crawl through, I'd appreciate it."

"Then you're going to head across that field all alone in the dark," he said gruffly.

"I'm not afraid of the dark, for pity's sake."

"Then why didn't you wait in the car?"

"Because it's parked on the road, of course." She lifted her chin. "Anyone could come along, see it and stop. At least out here there's only cattle to contend with, and they certainly won't bother me." She waited. "Well? Are you going to hold the wire or not?"

"Damn, you're an irritating woman," he muttered. "Yes, I'm going to hold the wire, and I'm also going where you go. I picked you up at your house tonight, and it's my responsibility to see that you get back there in one piece."

She scoffed. "It most certainly is *not* your responsibility. I can take care of myself."

He merely shook his head in disgust, placed his foot on the bottom strand of barbed wire and held the middle strand up. "The door's open, Your Highness."

"And you have the bloody gall to call *me* irritating." Bending over, Serena slipped through the gap in the fence. Then she held down the bottom strand of wire with her foot and lifted the middle strand for him. Trav came through it as easily as she had.

She took off walking. "Are you positive you know where you're going?" Trav asked, falling in step with her.

"Yes, I know where I'm going. See that big black thing over there? It's the Johnsons' water tank. This is a huge field, and we'll lose sight of that tank before we come to the road I told you about. But once on that road, it's only a short distance to the edge of town."

Trav gave up. "Okay, I guess you know what you're doing."

Serena had started frowning, and not over the conversation, either. They were walking on sharp, dry stubble of some sort, and to her knowledge, the Johnsons had never planted anything in this field. Her sandals were very poor protection against the stubble, and she had to bite her lip from crying out whenever a stalk pierced her hose—ruining it, of course—and scratched the skin of her ankles.

Then she began spotting the shocks. The field was heavily dotted with loosely stacked mounds of something—it looked like hay or straw—and there wasn't a cow or a steer anywhere to be seen. All right, fine, she told herself. Sometime in the past several years, the Johnsons had changed this from grazing ground to a planted field. But what difference did that make? It certainly didn't alter the route to town, did it?

"Damn," Trav said, looking up at the sky. "There're clouds over the moon."

Serena's heart skipped a beat. In the space of a very few minutes, it had grown about ten times darker than before.

"Here, take my hand," Trav told her.

She did it because she had already tripped over something unseen and nearly fallen. If she fell facefirst in this sharp stubble, she could receive some awful cuts and scratches.

"Now that it's so dark, do you still know the way?" Trav asked.

She knew the way, but could she find it in such dense darkness? Looking behind them, she couldn't make out the water tank anymore, but surely if they kept to a fairly straight line they would come to the old road. Besides, she didn't want to appear incompetent after insisting they take this shortcut.

"The way hasn't changed just because it's darker than it was," she retorted.

She seemed so confident that Trav had no choice but to trust her, although he still wished they had stayed on the highway. Even so, holding her hand was a pleasant sensation. He was suddenly feeling very guilty about putting her through this.

"Serena, I'm really sorry about this," he said quietly.

"You should be."

Her rebuff cut deeply. She didn't like him any better now than she had at the start of the evening, and he might as well admit failure, he thought grimly. There were moments during dinner and afterward in the lounge that he'd sensed warmth from her, but that could have been his imagination. Or a hope for more than just one date with her.

They trudged along, skirting what appeared in the darkness to be stacks of hay. The moon was suddenly bright again, and Serena stopped in her tracks.

"Um, I . . . I'm not sure we're still going in the right direction," she said reluctantly, hating having to make such an admission. She looked up at the moon and realized that it was in a different place in the sky than when they'd left the car, which was only natural but certainly didn't help her directional bearings.

Trav glanced around. The landscape looked the same in every direction, stacks of hay or some kind of grain and nothing else. Dammit, they should have stayed on the road!

Releasing her hand, he headed for the nearest haystack and sat down. Blinking in surprise, Serena followed.

"What *are* you doing?" she asked with an irate expression.

"Thinking," he said grumpily. She was standing there glaring at him. "You may as well sit down, too. This could take a while."

Sitting for a few minutes didn't seem like such a bad idea to Serena. Wearily she plopped down onto the hay. They should have stayed on the road. Why had she recalled an old shortcut that she really didn't remember at all? Lying back, she studied the moon and another bank of clouds that was beginning to move across its face. Had she been leading Trav in circles? Shouldn't they have come to that old road by now?

She sighed heavily and heard the crackle of hay or straw as Trav changed positions. In the next heartbeat, he was leaning over her, looking into her face.

"Do you know where we are?" he asked. "I'm talking about precise location."

She inhaled slowly, uneasy with his nearness. Obviously they were in an immense field, but she knew what he meant by "precise location."

"No," she had to admit. "I... I don't think we kept to a straight line when it was so dark."

"So we've probably been bearing one way or the other in the wrong direction."

She couldn't see his eyes clearly. What remained of the moon was behind his head, and his face was heavily shadowed. It stunned her that she was feeling something very physical because of his proximity, a stirring of blood that she knew very well was sexual.

"You have every right to be angry with me," she said, noting the unusual breathiness of her voice, another symptom of sexual attraction she couldn't help recognizing. She knew them all quite well because of Edward, who'd taught her much more about men, women and lovemaking than he'd had any right to teach anyone when he had a wife at home.

But she wasn't thinking of Edward now, except in the most distant, vague way. The man looming over her—not touching her but much too close to pretend he wasn't there or to feel total nonchalance about it—was causing the most delicious languor to spread throughout her body. In a way, she'd been waiting for a pass all evening, fully prepared to put Mr. Holden in his place when he tried something.

The thing was, he wasn't really trying anything. He was merely lying next to her—with no part of him touching any part of her—and leaning on his elbow to peer into her face in the dark.

"I'm not angry with you," he said, speaking quietly. "You sound as though you wish I were."

"I was angry with you over the tire," she qualified.

"Your prerogative. The truth is, sweetheart, we're all just plain old human beings trying to get through life without making too many mistakes. Every so often we trip up. I did it today by not checking the trunk for a spare. Tonight you thought you could find an old shortcut, and you probably would have if—"

"That's too kind," she interrupted. "It's been so many years since I was out here that everything's changed. I never should have dragged you into this field."

"You hardly dragged me," Trav said gently. She was so pretty lying there in the dim moonlight that he was talking about one thing and thinking of another. The subject making him feel so softhearted and kindly toward this beautiful woman was kissing. The way her luscious lips moved when she spoke was utterly fascinating, and he just knew her mouth would feel incredible under his.

Slowly he brought his head down, and it truly surprised him when she didn't say or do something to stop him. Instead he saw her lips part seductively, as though she was anticipating a kiss as much as he. His pulse went a little crazy even before they actually kissed, and it became wilder still when his mouth was caressing hers.

Dare he hope that she really did like him? Maybe she appeared standoffish and sharp-tongued with every man she was attracted to. Some women were like that, leery of getting involved, especially when some yokel had just walked all over them.

Her response seemed like permission to Trav—an invitation—and he gathered her into his arms to kiss her the way he really wanted to, thoroughly, possessively and with all his heart and soul. His tongue slid into her mouth. Her arms went around his waist. They kept wriggling closer and closer to each other, until he could feel her breasts against his chest and the exciting curve of her lower belly against his arousal.

Serena's head was spinning, and she had not expected to get dizzy from a mere kiss. Of course, one could hardly construe rolling around in the hay with a man as a mere kiss. Trav's mouth, tongue and hands were sinfully knowledgeable, and she was reveling in the sensations that could only be caused by a sexually experienced man who knew where and how to touch a woman.

And his kisses. Oh, dear God, his kisses. One second his lips pressed hard and rough against hers, and the next they were gentle as a summer breeze. He nibbled at her mouth, stroking and teasing it with the tip of his tongue. Was there nothing about kissing that he did not know? All the while, his body moved against hers.

Serena knew she was sinking fast, but she couldn't seem to pull herself out of the steamy storm of emotions he was causing, not when they were so enjoyable, so desirable. Had she even desired Edward this much? Surely she had, but . . .

Well, it just didn't seem important. In fact, right at the moment, Edward was only the vaguest of memories. Trav was what was real—real and alive, big and potent. Warm. Exciting. Utterly male.

Had the whole evening been leading up to this mad exchange of kisses? Had she looked at his mouth while they were eating, while he was grinning or talking, and thought of kisses? Had he thought of kissing her?

Yes, he had, she decided adamantly. She would bet on it.

But who cared right now? As she writhed against him, the question repeated in her mind . . . who cared?

Trav stroked her breasts through her dress and bra. Her responsive whimpers and sexy movements kept telling him to take the next step.

But her dress didn't have an opening...no buttons, no zipper, nothing. It was one of those chic little knit numbers that could only be gotten into by a woman dropping it over her head and shimmying it down her body. Taking it off would be a reverse of that process, sliding it up to her neck and over her head. It just wasn't a convenient dress for seduction, although Trav had his doubts about just how far Serena would permit this extremely exciting interlude to go, anyway.

He decided to find out. Even if he hadn't wanted her from the moment he'd set eyes on her, her own prim, priggish and downright snotty attitude made him very curious about her passionate response now. Bottom line—if she didn't like him, why was she kissing him back as though she couldn't get enough? Surprising. *Very* surprising.

She felt incredible to him, soft and womanly. And while kissing her was a pastime he could indulge in for a good long spell, it was definitely arousing him to more-adult ideas. Arousing him to new heights, he thought with a silent chuckle. Yes, it would be very interesting to see at exactly which point Serena would put on the brakes. It would be even more interesting, of course, if she completely forgot about those brakes.

That thought caused his blood to roar in his ears. Having her here, now, would be really wild. She had to know what was in his mind. His kisses were hot and heavy. His hands were everywhere, albeit on the outside of her dress. Her own hands weren't entirely innocent and inactive, either. She had unbuttoned his shirt and gone into it!

That was when he began working up the skirt of her dress. Breathing hard, kissing her delectable mouth, teasing her nipples through her clothing, he could think of only one thing: reaching her panties, shoving them aside and touch-

ing the part of her that had the power to send both of them
over the edge.

She didn't mumble an objection. She didn't turn her face
from his kisses and say no. In fact she opened her legs—just
a little—to make his sensual journey easier for him. His
fingertips slowly danced up her thigh; he couldn't believe
she wasn't protesting.

And yet why shouldn't he believe it? She was as ready for
lovemaking as any woman he'd ever observed. Her eyes,
when he caught a glimpse of them, appeared glazed with
desire. Her lips were pouty and swollen from kiss after kiss.
Her hair was completely disheveled and strewed with bits of
hay. She looked wanton and she felt wanton.

She felt to him like a woman in need, and God knew he
was a man in need.

"Serena...sweetheart," he whispered raggedly, pluck-
ing at the narrow band of silk that separated her woman's
secrets from his ravenously hungry hand.

"Oh, Trav," she moaned when the narrow band was no
longer there and she felt his hand and fingers caressing the
very essence of her femininity. She needed it so badly. She
arched her back, raising her hips higher for his touch,
opening her legs wider, giving him...giving him...

My God, what was she doing? Reality blasted her in a
breath-stealing explosion. Pushing against him, she rolled
away.

"Hey, what's wrong?" Trav said in a not-very-thrilled
voice.

Serena sat up and worked on catching her breath. "What
do you think is wrong?" she managed to get out while hoping she sounded insulted and enraged.

Trav wasn't entirely convinced by her supposed anger. She
looked beautiful, adorable, and Trav wasn't having a whole
lot of luck with the sudden shock of having to settle down
his libido.

He sat up, too, sidling close enough to her to pluck a piece
of hay from her hair. She recoiled. "Don't do that."

"Honey, we're awfully good together," he said hoarsely, willing to beg, borrow or steal to get her back under him.

"And how many times in your life have you said that to a woman?" Serena began sliding down the hay mound so she could get to her feet.

"Why would you think I'd said it at all?"

She was standing. "Whatever else you may think of me, don't believe I'm a fool. I saw how you behave around women tonight."

"You included?" Trav maneuvered himself to his feet.

"Yes, me included."

He flicked some hay from her shoulder. "Ah, but you're different, babe." The moment he said it, he knew it was true. What had been intended as a flippant remark was *true!* Serena Fanon meant something to him. She wasn't just another woman, another date, and this wasn't just another night of fun and games.

He suddenly wasn't so sure of himself. This had never happened to him before. One pretty woman had never been any more important than the next pretty woman.

He wanted Serena to know how he felt. Taking the back of her head in his hand, he stepped closer and peered into her eyes. "You are different, Serena. I'm different because of you. You have to believe me. I think we've got something—"

She'd been startled by his nervy advance, but she'd finally gotten herself together. Interrupting him, she wrested herself free of his hand. "Cool down, Holden. You and I have *nothing.* Do you understand? We have nothing. Don't make a mountain out of a molehill. So we kissed each other a little."

"A little?" he echoed incredulously. They had been kissing like two sex-starved creatures until she'd stopped the whole thing. "We kissed each other a little?"

"That subject is closed," she said abruptly, wishing to God her own heartbeat would return to normal. "Which way do you think we should go to get back to the highway?''

He folded his arms across his chest in a belligerent stance, not at all happy at the way she'd turned off on him. ''You know so much. You tell me,'' he said gruffly.

She walked off in a huff. ''Why does every man take no from a woman as a personal insult? I don't know if I'm going the right way, but I'm not going to stand around and argue with you for the rest of the night.''

Trav watched her for a minute, knowing full well her direction would never take her back to the highway.

Jogging, he caught her arm and turned her around. ''Come on. The highway is this way.''

''How do you know?''

''I just know.''

''Then we were never lost at all?''

''Hell, yes, we were lost. We were trying to find an old road, if you'd care to remember. But if we're going back to the highway, I know which direction to go to get there.''

''Built-in compass?'' she said sweetly, stung that he knew more about their location than she did.

''One of my better traits,'' he retorted.

''Oh. I didn't know you had any.''

''You're only ticked off because you loved kissing me.''

They were hiking along. Her feet were hurting again, but now so was her ego. He was right; she *had* loved kissing him. In fact she had gotten lost in his kisses.

And she didn't even like him.

Tears stung her eyes. How could she love a man's kisses when she didn't like *him?*

''Serena?'' Trav tried to see her face in the dark.

''Why don't you just walk and shut up?'' she snapped.

His lips flattened into an angry line. ''Babe, you've got it,'' he said with all the sarcasm and cynicism he could muster. Who needed her and her smart mouth? He might be part fool, but he sure as hell wasn't *all* fool.

Not yet, he wasn't.

Chapter Six

The silence Serena deliberately maintained as they trudged along felt oppressive even to herself. How it felt to Trav she could only guess at, and it surprised her that she would give even two seconds of her time to what he thought or felt about anything.

Yet she had kissed him with a shockingly voracious hunger. How could she have lowered herself to such amoral behavior? She barely knew him, and she wasn't overly impressed with those insights she had gained into his personality during this date from hell that seemed destined to go on forever.

Trav was thinking similar thoughts. Who in hell did Serena Fanon think she was? What a nasty disposition. Had he ever met anyone before who looked good enough to eat and then verbally clawed your eyes out if you got close enough to try a nibble? Dammit, she'd kissed him back! She'd done more than kiss. She had moved her body against his, her breasts, her thighs, and she'd touched him with her

hands. Just thinking about their frenetic groping on tha
stack of hay had him aroused and straining the seams of his
pants again.

Okay, he thought, *so she's one sexy number, and you'*
like to take her to bed. It's probably what she needs, any
way.

But maybe she knew she needed a man. Maybe that wa
the reason she had backed off. He didn't doubt that she wa
a woman of morals and personal ethics, and maybe she
hadn't expected such fireworks from a kiss.

Of course, that first kiss had led to another and then an
other, and if she hadn't stopped him he would have gone o
and on and taken them both to the gates of paradise.

Travis gulped uncomfortably. Trying desperately to pusl
from his mind the arousing image of himself sprawled or
Serena, joined in passion, he told himself to forget the whole
damned thing. She was not his kind of woman. Everything
was serious with her. She barely laughed, and even he
smiles were doled out as though they were too precious t
squander on ordinary men.

Well, that's what he was—a common, very ordinary man
Except for his financial success with his chain of used-ca
lots, he couldn't boast of even one small claim to fame. Se
rena was a lawyer, just at the beginning of her career. In hi:
heart, he knew she would make it big in some way, maybe
leaving Rocky Ford for a real city with more opportunity, o
maybe getting into Montana politics. Possibly even aiming
for national politics. There was just something special abou
her and something big in her future; he knew it as sure as he
knew anything.

So what kind of nitwit was he to fall for a woman who
was not only beautiful, intelligent and sexy, but had a ca
reer and an undoubtedly exciting future to look forward to?

The phrase *fall for a woman* got stuck in his mind. He'
never really been in love. Oh, he'd said it plenty of times
whenever he'd been passionate over some little cutie for a

week or two. But instinct told him now that the feelings Serena aroused were a whole other ball game.

It wasn't too late to stop what was happening, he told himself grimly. Damned if he'd chase after a woman who made it crystal clear that she wasn't interested.

Though she'd been plenty interested for a while in that stack of hay.

Trav was still puzzling over the evening, going first one way with Serena's behavior toward him and then another, when he spotted the highway.

"There's the road," he announced gruffly.

Serena wanted to shout her relief. Her feet were scratched and aching, her hosiery was in shreds and even the bottom few inches of her dress had some pulls and snags.

She was ready to call her lengthy silence off, and this was a good opportunity to start talking again. Still, she spoke a little superciliously. After all, he had presumed far too much with her tonight, putting his hands wherever he liked, making her want... Her mind stumbled over the word *sex,* although it was the one that fit what had nearly happened between them, no question about it.

"So you did know the right direction back to the highway."

Her nose was a bit in the air, which irked Trav. "Told you I did," he said bluntly.

"Obviously you have a better sense of direction than I do."

"Obviously."

He sounded belligerent and argumentative. Serena realized that she was too tired for even friendly conversation, let alone an argument. She had never been so happy to see a fence in her life. Going through it, however, with Trav holding the strands of barbed wire apart, she frowned.

"Where's your car?" she said.

"It's somewhere on this road. We just didn't come out of the field at the same place we went into it."

"Oh." Serena checked the road in both directions. "Well, there's still no traffic. I only hope Charlie didn't wake up for some reason, realize I wasn't home yet and call the police."

"Would he do that?"

Serena sighed. "I don't know. He would have when we were teenagers."

"Come on. We'd better get moving." Trav took her arm in his hand and urged her to start walking. Her exhaustion was in every line of her body, and anger at his own careless-ness surged through him. There was no excuse for driving around without a spare tire, no *forgivable* excuse for put-ting Serena through this, even if she was a first-class pain in the butt.

Then again, she could have either waited in the car for him to bring back a tire from town or stayed on the high-way with him, hoping someone would come along and give them a lift. That shortcut idea had been hers, and a damned foolish mistake it had been in the middle of the night, too. So she was no more perfect than he was. He almost said so, but another glance at Serena squelched the notion. Why say something that would only cause more hard feelings be-tween them? For them, it was over before it had really be-gun, only he'd been too thickheaded to see it.

Still, how come a woman who hadn't liked a man from the moment they met had not only gone out with him but damned near had sex with him? That was where their kisses had been heading before she'd called a halt.

Trudging along, he shook his head. He'd probably never understand Serena Fanon. Most gals he knew were as easy to read as a book. Not Serena.

"There's a car up ahead," Serena said. She stopped as embarrassment caught up with her. My God, she thought, her "shortcut" had lost them at least two hours' time and put them *behind* Trav's car on the highway.

"I think this time you'd better wait in the car." Trav didn't sound as if he intended to argue about it. Pulling the keys from his pocket, he inserted one into the door lock.

Just then they heard the unmistakable sound of an approaching vehicle.

"A car!" Serena exclaimed. Trav breathed a relieved sigh. They watched it coming closer. Trav stood in the middle of the road and waved his arms. It slowed and then pulled to a stop right next to Trav's car at the side of the road.

A window was rolled down, and a gushing female voice giggled. "Are you out of gas, Trav?"

Serena's heart sank. It was Ava of the white leather skirt and three-inch heels.

Trav bent over to peer through Ava's window. "How about a lift to town? I've got a flat and no spare."

"Well, of course you can have a lift to town. Get in, hon."

"Come on, Serena," Trav called.

She slowly and reluctantly ambled to Ava's car and heard the woman sing out gaily, "You can ride in back, Serena. My car has bucket seats, so there's only room for two in the front."

Lola had been listening to Serena's tale of the previous night for a good ten minutes on the phone.

"The shortcut idea was mine, so I can't blame hiking around in the middle of the night on him. But everything else..." Serena shook her head in anger and disgust. "The final straw was climbing out of that...that person's car, insisting to Trav that I did not need an escort to the door of the house, then catching my shoe on a crack in the sidewalk and knocking off its heel. No one laughed, believe me, but I was totally mortified. I managed to muster some dignity from the shambles of my pride, pick up the heel and march on into the house. But it was the worst evening of my life, Lola, the absolute worst."

"Sounds like it," Lola agreed. "Do you think Trav feels the same?"

"How could he not?"

"Well, there were those kisses in the hay...."

"They meant nothing, Lola."

"Oh, I can tell. From your point of view, that is. What I was wondering was how Trav felt about necking in—"

"We weren't necking! It was only a few kisses. Not that it couldn't have gotten out of hand if I hadn't kept my head."

"That Trav sounds like a real jerk to me. If he ever calls again, I bet you'll give him what for with both barrels." Lola waited a moment for Serena's answer. "Won't you?"

"Uh, yes. Yes, of course." You bet she would give him "what for." Why had she hesitated in answering Lola for even a second?

But she had a gnawing, not altogether relieved premonition that she was not going to get the chance to tell him anything. Deep down she suspected that Trav wasn't going to call her again. He was in and out of Rocky Ford on an informal, erratic schedule. Avoiding her wouldn't be at all difficult, merely because she had no way of knowing when he'd be in town again. For that matter, she had no idea if he had left the area or was staying for a month.

Another thing that was a complete unknown to her was where he stayed when he *was* in Rocky Ford. So even if she decided to look him up for some reason, she'd have to start at the car lot, which seemed too embarrassing to consider.

She grimaced. Good God, she certainly wasn't going to look Trav Holden up for *any* reason. What on earth was wrong with her?

"Anyway, Lola, that's the whole dismal story," she said to her cousin. "I've told some of it to Candace and Dad, as well as to you, and now I just want to forget the whole miserable evening."

"And Trav, too."

"Pardon?"

"You want to forget Trav as much as the evening."

"Um, I guess that goes without saying. Well, I know you're busy, Lola, so I won't keep you on the phone any longer. Talk to you later, okay?"

"Okay. Bye, coz."

Serena put the phone down with a long-suffering sigh. What in heaven's name was she going to do all day? If she didn't hear from the Montana bar soon, she was apt to tear out her own hair in frustration.

Maybe that all-important letter would be in today's mail, she told herself, praying for it to be true. *And if it is, how are you going to finance your office furniture and equipment?*

Totally unnerved over that topic, Serena went to find her sister-in-law. "Candace, I'm sure you have some chores or cooking planned for today. Will you let me help, even if I am pretty much all thumbs in the kitchen? I *have* to stay busy today. I honestly feel as though I'm going to explode."

It didn't seem possible, but several hours later, Serena was finally holding an envelope from the Montana Bar Association in her hands. Her stomach churned; she was afraid to open it.

Charlie walked in. "Mail come yet?" He saw the pallor of his daughter's face and the envelope she was gripping so tightly that her knuckles were white. "That's it, isn't it?" he said quietly.

Serena nodded. Wondering if she could speak at all, given the enormous lump in her throat, she sank onto the nearest chair.

"Do you want to be alone?" Charlie asked gently.

She shook her head. Her voice did work, because she managed to croak, "Stay, Dad. If I passed, you deserve a great deal of the credit." She paused to draw a nervous breath. "And you certainly deserve to be the first to know."

Charlie sank to a chair. "You passed, honey. I've never doubted it for a minute."

Serena smiled, albeit weakly. "Even though none of us kids were born with wings, you always thought we should be able to fly."

Charlie laughed. "Guess you've got my number, all right. Well, open it up, honey. Stop torturing yourself."

She nodded. "That's exactly what I'm doing, isn't it? Well, here goes."

A minute later, she was in her father's arms, laughing and shedding a few tears while they hugged.

"Told you so," Charlie said smugly. "It never entered my mind even one time that you hadn't passed."

"Dad, there's not another person in the world like you." Serena kissed Charlie's cheek. "I've got to tell Candace." She started from the room.

"And call Lola and tell her, too," Charlie said. He was already thinking of the people *he* was going to call a little later on, after Serena had made her calls—old friends who would genuinely welcome the news and a few smart alecks who thought their kids were the only ones who ever did anything right.

"Hey," he said to himself after Serena had left the room. "This calls for a celebration." He took off after his daughter to tell her so.

The second Lola was told the good news, she insisted that the family come to the ranch for dinner that night. "We'll do something simple...probably barbecued chicken. Oh, Serena, I'm so proud of you I could burst."

Candace had said virtually the same thing, and certainly Charlie's feelings were obvious. The Fanon family was united in their pride in Serena, and she, in turn, was filled with love and gratitude that she had such a caring family. If only her brother, Ron, were alive and here with his wife and son, everything would be perfect, she thought with a sudden spate of searing emotions.

But Ron wasn't alive, and all Serena could do about that was to spend a few minutes alone in her room until her emotions settled down.

Serena liked the Sheridan Ranch and she liked Duke, the man Lola had married. Duke was popular with Charlie and Candace, as well, so the evening promised to be enjoyable.

At five-thirty they piled into Serena's car for the drive to Duke's ranch, choosing her vehicle because it had the most passenger space. Little Ron was strapped into his car seat in the back, and Charlie sat next to him. Candace rode in the front with Serena, and the adults chatted and laughed all the way to the ranch. Even Ronnie seemed to sense something special about the outing, because he, too, did a lot of laughing. And, of course, he talked to his "Gampy."

Charlie couldn't seem to look at his grandson enough. Several times Serena glanced into the rearview mirror and saw her father watching little Ron with an expression of utter adoration; these were precious moments that warmed her heart.

Beneath the jokes, giggles and titters in the car while she drove, however, Serena was doing some heavy-duty worrying. Other than a little red tape—licenses and the swearing-in ceremony—she was now legally ready to open her law office. She was going to have to ask Charlie for the money in order to purchase office equipment; there really was no other way, and the idea really bothered her. Actually, if she had to get the money from Charlie, she preferred opening the subject before he did so she could set the tone of their conversation and discuss it as a loan. So far, apparently office furniture and equipment hadn't crossed his mind, but they would. Something would click, and he would realize that her two leased rooms were useless as they were.

They were almost to the ranch, driving on Gibson Road. Candace stared in awe at the beauty of the area—field upon field of grass, meandering creeks, scores of cattle and the grandeur of distant mountains. "The scenery out here is fantastic. You know, I think I'd like to live on a ranch. Especially if it were in country like this. How about you, Serena?"

Serena shook her head. "I like living in town, Candy. Lola sure has taken to ranch life, though."

"She really has, hasn't she?" Candace said in a pleased tone of voice. "Of course, she's very much in love with her husband, so she'd probably be happy anywhere if Duke was there."

"That's true, but I think she genuinely likes ranch life." Slowing for the turn onto the mile-long Sheridan driveway, Serena gave a nostalgic laugh. "With Lola's advanced case of wanderlust, it's a wonder she settled anywhere."

"But that's what love does to a person," Candace said.

"Lola returned to Rocky Ford and settled down before she met Duke," Serena reminded her sister-in-law. "Starting her business and all."

"Why, yes, that's true, isn't it?" Candace hadn't been around then, so she had momentarily forgotten Lola's history. "But given her hunger to roam, maybe we should be asking ourselves if she would have remained content without Duke in the picture."

Serena sent her sister-in-law a slightly surprised glance. "I never thought of that, Candy."

Candace sighed. "There's nothing else in the world like falling in love, Serena." Candace turned to see Charlie. "Don't you agree, Charlie?"

"Yes, indeed," Charlie said with a broad grin.

"You experienced it with Serena and Ron's mother," Candace said softly.

Serena was watching her dad's face in the rearview mirror, and the speed with which his grin vanished startled her. He didn't even attempt to answer Candace. Instead he ignored her completely and started playing peek-a-boo with Ronnie.

Candy quickly turned around and sent Serena a puzzled, questioning look. All Serena could do was shrug, because she had no idea why Charlie had suddenly clammed up. Had he ever done that before? She was still wondering about it, when they reached the buildings of the ranch.

Parking near the house, they got out. Both Lola and Duke came outside to greet them. After a few words, Duke picked up Ronnie and swung him up to his shoulders, much to the child's delight. Lola watched her husband cavort with the little boy with a smile of complete adulation, and Serena watched Lola's supremely happy face.

For some crazy reason, Trav Holden was suddenly in her mind. She drew an uneasy breath. Trav hadn't called, and she should be glad.

Why, instead, did she feel as though something crucial was missing from her person? As though she was no longer a whole, complete woman? What had he taken from her, and how would she get it back when she didn't even know what it was?

Or where he was?

The main topic of conversation throughout the evening was Serena's admirable accomplishment. There was no doubt in anyone's mind that she would be a tremendous success, doing the family proud and making scads of money. There were a lot of good-natured jokes about all the money she would make as an attorney, in fact, which she kept laughing off. The sad truth, which felt as though it were written in concrete in her brain and she was very careful to keep from coloring anything she said or did, was that without clients she wouldn't make any money. And she couldn't take clients without furniture and equipment. Even then, once that hurdle was passed in one way or another, she should be practical enough to admit that few lawyers ever got rich in a small town and surrounding rural area. If all they did was practice their craft, that is.

She remembered the ethics discussions and debates among her classmates in law school. *If you had a client with nothing to his name but a piece of property worth three times your normal fee, would you take the property as payment? Assuming the client offered it and never mentioned actual value, would you accept the property as payment in full and keep your own mouth shut about actual value?*

They would debate for hours on questions like that. Sometimes it was a fictional question, sometimes one taken directly from a law book. Even though she had lost interest

in debates of that nature about the middle of her second
year in law school, the point was that there were ways for a
lawyer to get rich that had very little to do with the actual
practice of law. A sharp eye, a keen ear and a shrewd mind
were probably necessary to anyone's financial success, but
a lawyer, who was being fed privileged information anyway, was in a position to use those advantages better than
most.

It was an individual thing, Serena knew. Was she capable of using privileged information to make money above
and beyond the legal fee she would charge a client?

She didn't think so, but only time would tell what sort of
attorney she was going to be.

It was a very pleasant evening. Duke and Lola were great
hosts. June Hansen, who'd been the cook and housekeeper
on the Sheridan Ranch for many years, had prepared most
of the meal before Lola got home from work, leaving very
little beyond the grilling of the chicken to finish up. Then
June went home with her husband, Rufe, who also worked
at the ranch, although both Duke and Lola invited them to
stay.

"No, no," June had said adamantly. "This is a family
celebration, and we wouldn't dream of intruding."

Since everything was nearly ready, except for the chicken,
which Lola put on the outside grill and Duke said he would
watch, the three women and little Ron took a walk around
the ranch compound.

There were horses in one of the corrals, and they stopped
so Ronnie could look through the fence at the beautiful
animals.

"You're so happy living out here on the ranch with Duke,
aren't you?" Candace quietly asked Lola.

"I've never been so happy," Lola said. She glanced down
to Candace's small son. "Only one thing would make it
more perfect."

"A baby," Candace said.

"Do you really want a baby?" Serena asked, surprised because this was the first time her cousin had said anything about children. "But what about your store?"

Lola waved that question away as trivial. "Other working women have babies. I'm sure I could handle both." Her expression softened. "Besides, Duke wants children. He isn't pressuring me about it, but he's mentioned it and I can tell when he's around other people's kids."

"I think it's wonderful," Candace said. "There's nothing like a child of your own, Lola."

Lola was looking at her cousin. "You want children someday, don't you, Serena?"

"I...guess so," Serena said slowly. Then she laughed. "It's not a high-priority topic at the moment, you understand."

Lola and Candace laughed, too. "No, it wouldn't be, would it? Oh, it's so exciting, Serena. Being a lawyer, opening your own practice. You must be walking on air." The second Lola said that phrase, she winced. "I'm sorry. That's one expression you didn't need to hear."

Serena looked off into the distance and recalled how she had described herself as being so in love with Edward she felt as though she were walking on air.

"Don't apologize," she said to Lola. "Being such an utter fool was no one's fault but my own. And please let's not start talking about Edward. I really don't even want to hear his name."

"You're absolutely right," Lola said firmly. "So let's talk about when you're planning to open for business."

Serena drew a deep breath. They were leaning on the corral fence, with little Ron peering through the bottom two rails, totally mesmerized by the horses.

"I guess I can speak freely with you two," she said uneasily. "I'm going to have to ask Dad for another loan to furnish and equip the office. I hate the idea and have been putting it off."

Lola and Candace glanced at each other. "Charlie would give you anything," Lola said.

"Yes, but taking it is almost more than I can bear. I'm going to pay him back, but right now my promises aren't worth two cents."

"Your promises are worth the world," Lola retorted. "Listen, we should be getting back to the men now, but how about the three of us having lunch together tomorrow?"

"Great idea," Candace instantly agreed.

"Well...all right. If you want," Serena said, knowing she wasn't going to be very good company until she had that talk with Charlie. Maybe she'd talk to him tonight when they got home, she thought.

"Let's meet at the store around twelve and go from there," Lola said.

Duke called out then. "Honey, I think the chicken's getting done. You'd better come and check it."

Lola smiled. "Be right there, Duke."

They left the corral and started toward the house. Serena didn't see the conspiratorial look exchanged by Lola and Candace, but she wouldn't have understood it if she had. It seemed as though her mind was totally bogged down, what with one problem and another.

And lurking among all of those other problems was Trav Holden, which not only annoyed but angered her. He was not a part of her life and should not be sneaking into her thoughts.

She sighed just before they reached the patio and the men. It seemed as though she didn't have very much control over her thoughts these days. Maybe very little over her life, for that matter.

Was that Trav's doing or her own?

Then again it would be very easy to blame Edward for everything that went wrong for the rest of her life.

Sad to say, she wasn't very happy on this pleasant family occasion. Not deep down, she wasn't.

Chapter Seven

Serena awoke totally disoriented. It took what seemed forever, though it was probably only a minute, for her bedroom to become familiar in the dark and for her to get a grasp on reality.

Once she knew who and where she was, she sat up and turned on the bedside lamp. Stacking her pillows, she lay back against them and frowned at the ceiling. Waking in the night was no big deal, but suddenly finding yourself awake with your mind so fogged you couldn't even place yourself was just too bizarre.

Serena tried to piece it together. She must have been sleeping hard, dreaming probably, and then been awakened abruptly. Maybe by a sound. Something from outside, possibly, such as a car backfiring.

She sighed while thinking. At any rate, she hoped it didn't happen again. Another annoying aspect of the episode was that she was wide-awake at one-thirty in the morning, and she knew herself well enough to predict what was going to happen next.

Groaning, she turned off the light and squeezed her eyes shut, praying for sleep. But exactly as she had feared, her mind began nitpicking at every little thing that had happened to her since childhood.

Actually this time it went back farther than she could remember—to her mother. The family had no pictures of Sandra Fanon. Charlie had told her and Ron years and years ago—when they'd been old enough to ask—that all of his pictures and papers had been destroyed in a fire that had occurred shortly after Sandra's death. Serena had been about a year old and Ron two when their mother passed away; thus neither of them had grown up with any memories of her. For as long as she could remember, Serena had passionately wished for a picture of her mother. She recalled prying details out of Charlie when she'd been about thirteen.

What color was her hair, Dad?

Uh, red.

Like mine?

Darker than yours, honey. Lighter than Ron's but darker than yours.

Was she tall? Short? Thin? Plump?

She was a pretty woman, on the small side. That's enough questions, Serena. I have work to do.

She had tried talking about her mother several other times during her teens, but Charlie had always cut the conversations short. It was, Serena realized now while lying in her bed in the middle of this unnerving night, the only subject that she had ever broached with her father that he hadn't been willing to discuss at great length.

But she could only lay Charlie's out-of-character reticence on grief. On losing the only woman he had ever loved—evidenced by the fact that not only had he never remarried but he'd never even had a real date that Serena knew of.

Thoughts of Serena's empty office suddenly displaced Charlie and the past in her mind. She hadn't talked to Charlie about a loan because they had gotten home from Duke and Lola's pretty late and he had carried little Ron from the car into the house for Candace. The youngster had fallen asleep during the drive and he was starting to get heavy for Candace to lift.

At any rate, everyone had scurried to bed, or so it seemed to Serena. It was disappointing, but she had gone to her own bedroom with nothing resolved. Now she thought of how best to approach Charlie in the morning.

Dad, I need to talk to you about furnishing my office. I'm talking strictly a loan here, so please don't just try to give me the money.

Serena's lips tensed. That was exactly what he would do, try to give her the money. If only there was some other way for her to get it. The bank was out of the question. Fresh from school, she had no credit of her own, and the bank would require a cosigner, which would put her right back to square one.

But maybe someone else. Wasn't there anyone she knew who might be willing to loan her enough money to get started?

Trav Holden suddenly popped into her mind. Appalled, she first thought, *Oh, I couldn't!*

But why couldn't she? He was a businessman and might even understand why she didn't want to go to Charlie with this. She would pay interest on the loan, of course, maybe even offer a few points higher than the going rate. What harm would asking him do?

She winced slightly. What if he agreed to loaning her the money and then used it to gain a personal advantage? Did she trust him to be the type of man who wouldn't behave so dishonorably?

No, she certainly did not, she decided vehemently. In fact she really didn't trust Trav Holden at all. And maybe—even though the idea was totally abhorrent—she didn't completely trust herself where he was concerned. How could she have kissed him so lustfully in that pile of hay? Thank God she'd come to her senses in time.

Still lying there restlessly in her bed an hour later, however, the idea of talking to Trav about a loan didn't seem so terrible. If he said no, that would be the end of it. And if he said yes, she could let him know in a concise, businesslike way that nothing personal would ever pass between them because she owed him money.

Well, that might be a little hard to get across without sounding a bit peculiar, but the right words, tactfully spoken, would come to her; she was sure of it.

Yes, she thought sleepily, she would call Trav in the morning. Since she had no idea where he was staying, she would again call the car lot.

It seemed like a sane and sensible plan, and she fell asleep feeling much better than when she'd awakened.

"Holden's Used Cars, Darrel Endicott speaking."

Serena hesitated. She had been hoping that Trav would answer himself. Instead she had this Darrel Endicott person to deal with, which didn't exactly thrill her.

"Is Mr. Holden in?" she asked.

"No, ma'am, but I'm sure someone else can help you. If you're calling about a car, that is."

She certainly wasn't going to explain her reason for this call to a stranger, and yet if she wasn't calling about a car, wouldn't Endicott automatically classify the call as personal?

"I am calling about a car," she lied. "But Mr. Holden told me to speak directly to him. What time do you expect him?"

Endicott chuckled in her ear. "Never know when to expect Trav, ma'am. He just comes and goes as he pleases. I think he was heading for Miles City when he left here, but—"

"You mean he's out of the area?" Without a goodbye or the slightest acknowledgment of her existence? A pain of surprising dimensions knifed through her body, immediately followed by an onslaught of anger. Just who did he think he was to leave town without even the common courtesy of a telephone call?

And then it hit her: she was nothing to him, no more important than last week's news. Now why would something that she'd known all along hurt so much? One woman among the myriad females of the world would never stand out for Trav, especially one who hadn't been particularly nice to him and then had made a total fool out of herself by insisting they take a shortcut she really couldn't remember.

Well, she didn't like him, either!

Before Darrel Endicott could say anything else, Serena said icily, "Never mind. It's nothing important."

"Wait! Won't you at least leave your name?"

"No. Goodbye, Mr. Endicott."

Hanging up, Serena glared at the phone. So much for *that* stupid idea!

The three women went to Tommy's Grill for lunch and ordered chef salads. Lola also ordered a small carafe of chilled white wine and sent Serena a smile while she did it.

Serena smiled back. She had suspected this was going to be another celebration for her passing the bar, a girls-only lunch. The wine proved she'd been right, as none of them drank wine in the middle of the day without a good reason.

It pleased Serena immensely. She regarded her sister-in-law and cousin around the little table with great affection. They were as close as any sisters could ever be, and, in fact, even though they looked nothing alike, there were people who thought they were sisters. Lola was a sultry brunette with gorgeous green eyes; Candace was a delicate, hazel-eyed blonde, very petite, very pretty; and Serena was tall, slender and had reddish gold hair and big blue eyes. Her brother, too, had been tall. Charlie was tall and since he'd told Serena that her mother had been on the small side, she and Ron had apparently gotten their height from him.

Lola's eyes twinkled as she raised her glass to her cousin. "Here's to the Fanon family's resident lawyer."

Serena and Candace laughed while touching their glasses to Lola's. They all took a sip.

"Here's to a very successful law practice," Candace said, making the second toast.

"Hear, hear," Lola said.

Serena made the third toast. "Here's to two really great relatives. Everyone should be so lucky."

Laughing, they clicked their glasses together and took a drink.

Lola picked up her purse and pulled out a blue envelope. Serena grinned happily. A card. How nice. Candace, too, had a card for her. Serena read them, and because they had verses that were mushy and sentimental, she got tears in her eyes.

"You two really are the best," she said huskily. "Thank you."

"We have something else, too," Candace said softly. "Lola?"

Lola produced another envelope from her purse and handed it to Serena.

An uneasy frown appeared between Serena's eyes. "What's this?"

"Open it," Candace said.

"Open it," Lola repeated.

Serena took a breath. "I have a feeling...."

"Quash it," Lola said in her inimitable take-charge way. "Come on, coz, quit stalling and open the envelope. It's not even sealed. All you have to do is slip the flap out from—"

"I can see that," Serena retorted. She hesitated another moment, then finally slid the flap free. From the envelope she withdrew two checks, made out to her, each for the sum of five thousand dollars, one signed by Candace, the other by Lola.

Taking a long breath, she sat back in her chair. "What do you two think you're doing?"

"Getting you started in the lawyering business," Lola said calmly. "Now, before you get all huffy and indignant, Candy and I both want you to know that we don't care how you look at this money. You can consider it a gift, a loan or anything else that makes you happy. It simply doesn't matter to either of us."

"That's true, Serena," Candace said. "I have all that insurance money from Ron...Ron's passing, and I think it would make him very happy to know some of it was going to his sister. The money is yours. You have to take it."

Lola was smiling impishly. "And everyone knows my husband's loaded. Besides that, I'm doing very well with the store."

Ten thousand dollars. More than enough money to furnish and equip her office. Tears filled Serena's eyes.

"It's a loan," she whispered hoarsely. "That's the only way I could take it." She dabbed at her eyes with her napkin. "And how can I ever thank the two of you?"

"I'm sure we'll think of something," Lola said drolly, which made them all laugh.

Their salads were delivered, and lunch turned out to be a rousing success.

Whenever Trav was in the Miles City area, he parked his forty-foot luxury motor home on the ranch of a friend who had poured a concrete pad and put in utilities about a quarter-mile from the main house, expressly for Trav's use. The friend, Bob Conroy, was a widower around forty-five years of age and he was always glad to see Trav come driving up. That motor home was Trav's pride and joy, and the only home he had, much to Bob's amusement.

The two men had become fast friends about five years before during a guided hunting trip into Canada. Bob's wife was alive then, and Trav had liked Sharon, too. He'd gone through some of the hell that Bob had during Sharon's long illness, and had felt some of the relief that Bob admitted to feeling after her death. "The relief is for her sake, Trav, not mine. She's no longer in pain," Bob had said.

"I know, old friend." They had left the cemetery together, returned to Bob's ranch and quietly gotten drunk. After Sharon's passing, they had grown even closer, and now there wasn't much that happened in either man's life that he couldn't talk about to the other.

Seated on Bob's patio with cold beers and the setting sun for a backdrop, Trav mentioned that he'd just spent four days in Rocky Ford.

"Business okay over there?" Bob asked.

"It's darned good for a small town. Of course, there are the outlying ranches and any number of other communities to draw upon, but I can't complain about business in Rocky Ford."

Bob grinned. "From the sound of things, you have no reason to complain about business in any of your locations."

Trav chuckled amicably and took a swallow of beer. It was true. Business was good in all present locations, and he had his eye on several towns for more car lots. He really wasn't thinking of business tonight, though.

"You know, I met a woman in Rocky Ford and I can't get her out of my mind." Trav cast his friend a deliberately woeful look. "And believe me, I've tried."

"You're kidding," Bob said. "In all the years I've known you, I've never heard you say something like that. This woman must be a goddess."

"She's a lawyer." Trav took another swallow from his bottle. "She's also haughty as hell, gorgeous to look at and, to be really honest, I don't know if she's a dream or a nightmare." He looked at his friend. "All I know is that I keep thinking about her. What d'ya think that means?"

Bob shrugged. "Could mean no more than that you want to sleep with her."

Trav grinned. "That's a given."

"Well, from your reputation, you don't have too much trouble getting women between the sheets," Bob said dryly.

"Except in Serena's case, there's more."

"More of what?"

"That's what I've been trying to figure out. God, she's a pain in the neck." Trav launched into the story of their ill-fated date. Bob laughed so hard a couple of times that tears ran down his cheeks.

"And this is the woman keeping you awake nights?" Bob said with another burst of laughter when Trav finished the tale with Serena stomping into her house after refusing his assistance and breaking the heel of her shoe.

Trav chuckled. "I know it sounds crazy."

"To put it mildly, yes." After a moment of silence, Bob sighed. "But then, who's to say? I'll tell you something, Trav. When the lovebug bites, there isn't a man alive who's strong enough to resist scratching that itch."

Trav looked startled. "Hey, I didn't say anything about falling in love, man."

"Not in so many words, no. But that's what's happening, old friend. You might as well save yourself a lot of misery and just go with the flow."

The last rays of the sun were coloring the western sky. Trav got up abruptly and set his empty bottle on the table. "Think I'm going to turn in early, Bob. See you in the morning."

Bob got to his feet. "G'night, Trav. Sleep well." There was a hint of laughter in his voice.

Trav ignored it and headed for his motor home. His heart was beating a mile a minute, and he didn't like the unsteady, almost sick sensation in his stomach. Falling in love? Bob was way off base. He was a good friend, maybe his best friend, but that didn't make his opinions infallible.

Scoffing, Trav went inside the motor home. Without turning on a light, he walked to the back of the unit, threw off his clothes and crawled into bed.

Hell, he'd been in love dozens of times, he thought irately as he moved around seeking a comfortable position. Bob's comments were no big deal. So why had he gotten all shook up over them?

Something in his own brain answered. *Because this thing with Serena is different, that's why.*

He muttered one explosive word. "Damn!"

But he knew in the back of his mind that he would be returning to Rocky Ford in the very near future, and it wasn't because his car lot needed attention, either.

Serena had most of her office furniture and equipment purchased and delivered very quickly. Mostly she'd called in orders from catalogs that she had been collecting for quite some time. Rocky Ford's only office-supply outlet took up one corner of the hardware store—a haphazard arrangement at best—but it carried the small items every office needed, such as paper clips, notepads, pens, pencils and file folders.

Knowing exactly what she wanted in her office, from computer equipment to the chair for her desk, was a big help in speeding up the furnishing process. Once the phone was in service, Serena spent every day in her two rooms at the Ridgeport Building taking deliveries as they came in, arranging things just so and uncrating her computer equipment when it arrived and getting it on line. Also Charlie had told her to take anything she could use from the stuff in his attic. He'd moved a lot of things up there when he'd remodeled the house for his business years ago, and she found several good chairs, a couple of occasional tables, some old paintings and two lamps that would work beautifully for the reception area of her office.

It was all very exciting. The complex provided the inset for the large sign in front of the building—at her cost, of course—but her name and profession were finally before the public. She went to the newspaper office and had a tasteful announcement designed for the next three publications.

She was, for all intents and purposes, ready for business.

Only there was no business. The only people who stuck their heads into her office were other occupants of the building who said hello and welcome. And her family, of course. Each one came by, looked everything over and praised her efforts.

But she wasn't dissatisfied or disturbed by the lack of clientele, since she hadn't expected a rush of business the minute the word was out that her office was open. This was not like opening a retail business where nearly everyone in town dropped in to see what kind of merchandise you were carrying. The only time people even thought of lawyers was when they had a legal problem. The problems would arise; the people would come. Serena was confident that it was only a matter of time.

All the same, she was darned grateful to have free room and board under Charlie's roof. She had spent wisely on her furniture and equipment and still had almost three thousand dollars in the bank, which would take care of the office rent and utility bills for several months. By then she was bound to have some money coming in.

Well, everything was done, she thought one morning after unlocking her office and going in. There were no more pictures to hang, nothing left for her to do except wait for someone to call or drop in with a problem that required the services of an attorney.

She dusted for something to do, then turned on the computer, which she had set up in the second office—her office. The first room was the reception area and where her secretary would work when she hired one. In the meantime, Serena kept the doors open so she could hear anyone who might come in.

Seated at her desk, she fiddled around with various computer programs for a while, then pulled up a game program, chose one of the numerous card games available and began playing. She'd noticed that the computer had come with these games already installed, but thus far she hadn't had the time or inclination to try them.

They were interesting, challenging and fun, and she became quite involved, using the mouse to move the cards around on the screen. When someone called "Hello, anybody here?" from the other room, she jumped a foot.

Before she could answer, Trav Holden was standing in the doorway connecting the two rooms. Her heart leapt into her throat. Getting caught playing solitaire on her office computer by Trav was downright humiliating.

In the next heartbeat, it occurred to her that he couldn't see the computer screen, thus he had no idea what she'd been doing. Getting to her feet, she turned down the brightness of the monitor until it was black.

He was looking at her, smiling at her with a light in his eyes she couldn't mistake for anything but elation at seeing her. And she was glad to see him, too. He looked wonderful, clean and crisp in dark blue jeans and a white shirt.

But glad to see him? Could this really be possible? Stunned by that idea, she nearly tripped over her own feet walking around the desk.

"Hello. I was busy and didn't hear you come in." Oh, Lord, was her voice really as husky and unnatural as it sounded to her own ears? She couldn't seem to do anything about the timbre of her voice, but maybe Trav wouldn't notice.

"You just opened for business and already you're busy," Trav murmured, filling his eyes with the sight of her. She was wearing a pale gray straight-line dress that buttoned up the front and matching pumps. She looked beautiful. As beautiful as he remembered. "You were concentrating so hard on that computer, you didn't even hear me come in, did you?"

"Um, I was concentrating, yes," she said weakly. She would die if he discovered that she'd been playing solitaire. She gestured toward the two chairs at the front of her desk. "Would you like to sit down?"

"Yes, thanks."

She resumed her chair behind the desk. "Give me a minute to clear this away," she murmured, and quickly brightened the screen to see her way through the speedy process of getting rid of the game program.

"I didn't mean to interrupt. I mean, if you're in the middle of something important..."

"No, it's all right." Serena pushed the combination of keyboard buttons to clear the screen and breathed a silent sigh of relief when it went blank. Her gaze returned to Trav while she turned off the computer. "So, what brings you back to Rocky Ford so soon?" A blush crept into her cheeks. "What a silly question," she said with a nervous little laugh. "Your car lot, of course. I guess I didn't realize you checked on it so often."

"I don't. Not usually," Trav said quietly. "My normal routine would have been to come back to Rocky Ford in about a month. Actually my visits to any of my lots range in the three- to six-week category."

"I see." She was getting more nervous by the second. Not only was there some ridiculously traitorous portion of herself glad to see this crude skirt-chaser, but she was feeling much too warm because of him.

"Do you?" Leaning forward, Trav's eyes bored into her. "Do you really see?"

"Um, I'm not sure to what you're referring. What should I be seeing?"

"Serena, when I said I ordinarily wouldn't return to Rocky Ford for another month, you said 'I see.' I merely asked if you really knew what I meant or were just being polite."

"Oh. Well, I guess I was just being polite."

"That's what I thought." Trav paused for a moment and stared at her.

Startled, Serena couldn't help staring back. He was too handsome, too sure of himself, and she wished he weren't sitting there across her desk. She wished he hadn't come here at all. What could come of it? Surely he didn't have personal ideas about the two of them. Wasn't that one awful date of theirs enough evidence that they weren't meant to be more than casual acquaintances?

"I came back so soon to see you," he said then.

Oh, my God, she thought, swallowing hard. "Um, in what capacity? Do you need a lawyer?"

Trav nearly laughed. His lips twitched. "Yeah," he said. "I guess you could say I need a lawyer."

She knew he wasn't talking about the law. He was flirting, letting her know he wanted her. When in heaven's name had that happened? After all, he'd left town without so much as a phone call.

Her eyes narrowed in speculation of what might have occurred between him and the glamorous if overdone Ava after dropping her off to conclude their fiasco of a date.

But that was something she wasn't comfortable thinking about, and she quickly banished it from her mind, the same as she'd done every time that image had attempted to suck her into a morass of unnerving conjecture.

The truth was, this man sitting across her desk annoyed the heck out of her. In many ways, to be truthful. She didn't want to think him handsome, but she did; she didn't want to feel fluttery and female just because he was making googoo eyes at her, but she did; and last but certainly not least, she couldn't let him get away with blunt innuendo about "needing" a lawyer.

Her expression, voice and posture became noticeably less friendly. "If you need some legal work done, then you and I might have something to talk about. But if your only reason for coming here was to badger me with sexual innuendo, I'm going to have to ask you to leave."

She meant it. The bottom fell out of Trav's stomach. How could she be so beautiful and give off vibes that he could only interpret as receptive, then turn on him like this?

And how could he like her enough to keep coming back for more?

His spine stiffened, and his own voice became cooler as he automatically went into a defensive mode that would also greatly diminish his embarrassment. It was all lies, but he personally didn't give a damn at this point.

"You're badly mistaken if you think I came here with anything sexual in mind, innuendo or otherwise," he said flatly. "I need a lawyer. If you don't want my business, I can easily take it elsewhere."

Serena froze. Had her imagination been playing tricks with her mind? Had he really come here because he needed legal advice? How could she turn away business? Anyone's business? She couldn't. Not in her financial situation.

She drew a shaky breath and strove for composure. "Oh. Well, um, yes, of course. You need a lawyer and I'm a lawyer. Why else would you be here?"

Sitting back in his chair, Trav folded his arms across his chest. "Shall we get down to business?"

"Yes . . . yes." Serena opened a drawer and pulled out a yellow pad. Then she tried very hard to look him in the eye and at the same time appear to be an efficient, capable, knowledgeable attorney.

With pen poised, ready for use, she asked, "Now, just what is the nature of your problem?"

Chapter Eight

Trav had gotten himself into this situation and only he could get himself out of it. He wasn't blaming Serena, who was looking very serious while she waited to hear what legal problem had brought him to her office. But all he'd wanted to do was see her. How had a normal urge come to this?

The unnerving truth was that he didn't understand Serena, who reacted so differently to him than any woman he'd ever known. Did she like him or didn't she? There were moments when he felt something so hot and vital from her he got dizzy. Then there were the expressions and gestures from her that made his blood run cold.

Right now she was all business. He cleared his throat. "Uh, my legal work is scattered all over the state, in the hands of at least a dozen different lawyers."

Serena took a moment to absorb that information, then laid down her pen with a decisive sort of finality. "In that case, why would you need another?"

Trav's mind had started percolating, and an idea took shape. Yes, he thought. Why not? What better excuse could he have for seeing Serena often? For calling her when he was out of the area, every day if he felt like it?

He sat up straighter. "For some time now, I've been thinking of consolidating all of the legal work for the car lots, putting everything in the hands of one attorney." It wasn't a lie; the idea of assigning everything to one attorney had occurred to him off and on for several years.

Maybe he'd done nothing about it because all of his lawyers seemed cut from the same cloth, none better or worse than the others. It would have been tough to pick one, which might have denoted superiority in the pack when there was none. It wasn't at all tough to decide on Serena, which was strange when he knew nothing of her legal ability. Yet he still had all the faith in the world in her.

Serena's pulse took a wild jump. Apparently Trav had quite a few used-car lots, which could translate into a small mountain of legal work. A client of his stature would be an incredible start for any independent attorney. She would, of course, have to hire a secretary at once.

But... she was getting ahead of herself. Ahead of Trav, for that matter. Attempting to appear interested but not voracious, she said almost cautiously, "It does make sense to have all of your legal work in one place." *But why Rocky Ford? And why choose me over experienced lawyers?* Did she dare pretend those questions didn't exist or weren't important? Was he playing some kind of game with her? Was she as guilty of game playing as him?

Her mind raced, searching for answers. Was he doing this to get close to her? In a way, he would be her boss. Only where his own work was concerned, of course, but it sounded as though he had quite a lot of legal work scattered around the state. How much of her time would his work require? More importantly how much of her time would he demand?

She had to keep this arrangement—should they come to one—strictly business. And in perspective.

Clearing her throat, she picked up her pen again. "If you're seriously considering putting your legal work in my hands, then I need some particulars."

"I'm serious," Trav answered. "What do you want to know?" He was still thinking about having so much faith in her and wondering if he wasn't making a business decision on a personal basis. If so, it would be a first for him, and he wasn't altogether comfortable with the idea. Yet there was something so strong and real in this pleasant little office with him and Serena that he couldn't ignore its presence. Did she feel it, too?

"First your home address and telephone number," Serena said.

Trav chuckled, knowing his answer was going to startle her. "No home address, no home phone number."

He *was* playing with her, damn him! She felt like throwing the pen in her hand right into his cocky face.

Instead she glared across the desk. "You may think that's funny. I do not."

"Funny?" Trav gave another little laugh. "I wasn't trying to be funny. I live in a motor home. The only address I have is whichever car lot I'm visiting at a particular time. Same with a phone number. Although I do have a cell phone, and that number is 555-8811."

She jotted down the number. "You don't carry it with you. At least I haven't seen it."

"I don't take it everywhere I go, no. Mostly I leave it in the motor home because that's where I need and use it."

She was trying to envision a person living without one specific, permanent address. Lola had done an enormous amount of traveling for quite a long time, but home had still been Charlie's address. What Trav was telling her seemed entirely different. "A motor home," she said slowly, almost to herself. "I never would have guessed that. So, how do the lawyers you now have handling your legal work reach you?"

"They usually have a general idea where I am, so they call the local car lot, and the manager or one of the salespeople runs me down. And, of course, they often reach me on the cell phone. It's never hard to do, Serena." He grinned. "Believe me, you wouldn't have the slightest problem getting hold of me anytime you needed to talk about something."

He really did seem serious about this. Serena felt her excitement mounting. Trav Holden, intrusion on her private life or not, would be an astonishing first client. Was this a stroke of luck or was this a stroke of luck? God, how *should* she look at this?

Again she put down her pen. This time when Trav stared across the desk, she stared back.

"I'm not sure how I feel about this," she finally said, evenly and without inflection. After all, he really didn't need to know she was having difficulty accepting what could turn out to be the best financial offer she might ever run into while practicing law in Rocky Ford. The truth was that her own ambiguity confused even her. What would it do to Trav? It wasn't unthinkable to imagine him laughing at her. Here she was, supposedly a professional businesswoman, and she was hedging on accepting a client that she strongly suspected could and would pay her quite a lot of money in legal fees.

"I don't think I understand," Trav said in reply. "What aren't you sure of?"

Why in the world *would* he understand? She inhaled a deep breath. "Sorry. Of course I'm interested in your offer." Her fingers crept to the pen again. "Do you have the time now to talk about what sort of legal work you require?"

Trav thought for a second. "Tell you what. I have several boxes of files in the motor home. Why don't I run and get them?" He paused briefly, then went on. "Better yet, why don't you come with me? There's not much sense in bringing those boxes back here when you'll need only some of the files in them. We could go through them together."

"Oh . . . well, I suppose . . ." Serena was suddenly befuddled. Go with him? And yet, if she was going to be his attorney, there might be many occasions when she would have to go someplace with him. Why was she so damned wishy-washy where Trav was concerned?

It had to stop. That's all there was to it. Either she had to tell him she wasn't interested in working for him or start behaving like an adult.

Pushing her chair back, she got to her feet. "Let's go and get those files."

They went down to Trav's car and drove away from the Ridgeport Building. "Where is your motor home parked?" Serena asked. She knew of one RV park in the immediate area, but it was small and not very attractive. Somehow she couldn't picture Trav staying there.

"About three years ago, I bought five acres on Access Creek. That's where I park when I'm in Rocky Ford."

Serena frowned slightly. "Do you have utilities out there?" Access Creek didn't touch on the town at all. The local RV park might not be nearly as pretty as the creek area, but at least it had the benefit of utilities.

"There's electricity," Trav said. "It's only recently that anyone started building on their land along the creek, so I'm sure it won't be long before all utilities are available. I bought that acreage for investment purposes, and it's doubled in value in just three years."

"Really? Sounds like it turned out to be a wise investment."

"I'd say so. Sometimes I wish I'd bought three or four of those five-acre parcels. Hard to tell, though. Some developments turn out junky. This one has covenants, so only certain types of structures can be put up."

"Sensible. That's probably one of the reasons it's gone up in value." Serena could tell they were heading for Access Road, which led to Access Creek.

"I'm sure it is. 'Course, most Montana real estate has increased in value in the past few years."

"Has it? That's something I haven't kept abreast of," Serena murmured.

"Understandable when you weren't living here." Trav sent her a glance. "Where did you go to school?"

"Georgetown University in Washington, D.C. For both college and law school."

"Why'd you choose a college and law school so far from home?"

Serena smiled. "Because I was eighteen and impressed that good schools—several, to be factual—would accept me. And I was always fascinated with politics. That was probably the factor that most influenced my decision to choose Georgetown University." Her voice took on a wistful note. "I love Washington, D.C."

Trav cast another glance in her direction, this one containing intense curiosity and a touch of alarm. If she loved Washington, D.C., so much, what was there to stop her from going back?

"And yet you returned to Rocky Ford," he said, swallowing the panic that progression of thoughts caused.

She was silent a moment, thinking, remembering. Then she spoke briskly. "Yes, I came home."

Trav knew then. It was as though the clouds had suddenly parted and everything had become clear as a bell: the guy who'd trampled her heart lived in Washington! Or he had when she was there. Maybe she'd met him in school. Another student. A professor. Maybe someone in the political arena.

That fool, whoever he was, was the reason Serena was leery of another personal involvement. So it wasn't him, Trav Holden, that she was shying from; she was simply afraid of getting hurt again.

What an eye-opener, Trav thought with a monumental sense of relief. He had to stop worrying about her liking him. Hadn't she already proved that she couldn't help responding to him with some very hot kisses in that stack of hay? If that didn't indicate affection, what could?

His pulse sped up at the memory of touching her delectable body, and he had to take a deep breath to try to slow his racing blood. But his libido had started running on high, and he couldn't think of Serena as anything but the most desirable, sensuous woman he'd ever known. Certainly the fact that she was now his one and only lawyer—or would be once the others were notified—was secondary in his mind. Barely discernible, for that matter. She was beautiful, she was sexy and whatever perfume she was wearing was making him dizzy with erotic thoughts and images.

Serena didn't suspect in the least what was going on in Trav's mind. She was picturing Washington, D.C., and Edward just naturally crept into her thoughts. It wasn't that she still loved Edward, God forbid, but there were moments when memories of some of the special times they'd had together would control her emotions. It wasn't difficult to evade such moments; all she had to do was think of his lies and deceit. The only problem then was the resentment she couldn't help feeling.

So Serena's mood as they arrived at Access Creek was one of deeply embedded resentment, completely and precisely aimed at Edward Redding. She had learned all about forgiveness in Sunday school as a child, church when she was older and from her own father, and maybe someday she would be able to forgive Edward and remember him as merely a part of her past.

But not yet, she thought with pursed lips. Not yet.

Trav pulled up next to his motor home and turned off the ignition. He looked at Serena. "This is it."

She blinked, as though coming awake. Peering out the window, her eyes opened wider. "This is your motor home?"

"Sure is. Come on. Let's go in."

Trav's gleaming blue-and-silver motor home was one of those units that resembled a bus on the outside. Serena recalled Charlie saying something about these particular models costing in the hundreds of thousands of dollars. It wasn't what she had expected, and she couldn't help showing her surprise.

"I had no idea you were talking about this kind of motor home," she said as they got out of the car.

"No?" There was a glimmer of amusement in Trav's eyes, but it was vastly overpowered by the personal feelings he was enduring because Serena was here with him. They were going to be alone in his motor home. That thought caused his chest to tighten and created a sudden sensation of needing air.

Stealing a big breath as quietly as he could manage, he led the way to the main door of the motor home. Taking a ring of keys from his pants pocket, he unlocked the door and pulled it open.

Then he stepped back. "You first."

There were three steps up into the huge vehicle. With a small smile at Trav, Serena took the stairs and found herself surrounded by utter elegance.

Trav was right behind her. "It's a little messy. I wasn't expecting company." His gaze stayed on her, hot and heavy. She didn't seem to notice because she was so busy looking at everything.

"It's very beautiful," she finally murmured. "When you said motor home, I guess I anticipated an ordinary model. This is not ordinary."

"No, guess it's not." Trav walked to the refrigerator. "How about something cold to drink?"

"Sure. Whatever you have is fine."

Trav pulled out two bottles of a fruit drink. "Would you like a glass?" He undid the caps of both bottles.

"No, the bottle's fine. Thank you," Serena said, accepting the drink.

"I'll get those boxes of files. Go ahead and sit down." He hesitated. "Unless you'd rather look at the rest of the unit."

"Would you mind? I've never been in a motor home like this before." She could tell Charlie all about it tonight, she thought. He had mentioned buying an RV of one kind or another a couple of different times. Of course, it would be nothing like this one, but he would enjoy hearing about Trav's luxury unit all the same.

"Look all you want," Trav told her. He leaned his hips against the sink counter, drank from his bottle and watched Serena move through the motor home. When she was way in back, in the bedroom, he set down his empty bottle and followed.

She was looking genuinely astonished. "I can't believe you have a king-size bed. And your bathroom is...well, I've never seen a prettier bathroom. It's really quite incredible, Trav."

"I like it. I also like having you in it."

Serena's eyes jerked to his. "Pardon?"

"I'm sure you heard me." He began moving toward her.

As large as this unit was in the world of motor homes, walking space was still limited. So it only took a few steps to put him right in front of her. Behind her was that king-size bed. In fact she had automatically taken a backward step and could feel it against her legs.

There was a look in his eyes that any woman would recognize. Serena swallowed. "Tell me you didn't bring me here to make a pass."

"I brought you here to look at those files." His hand rose to toy with the burnished curls on her left shoulder. "And you know something? Kissing you doesn't seem like a pass to me."

"Well, what does it seem like to you?" Her voice was much too breathy, probably because her heart was beating ridiculously fast.

"A pass happens between two people who don't give a damn about each other beyond a little momentary pleasure."

"Oh, really? Wherever did you get that idea?"

"It's original. It's how I look at passes." His hand crept under her hair to the back of her neck, sending quivering, shivering thrills up and down her spine. "With you, everything's different. Don't ask me why 'cause I don't know why."

She couldn't tear her eyes from his—so dark, so deep and intense, so masculinely mysterious. And she knew he was going to kiss her. What she didn't know was what she was going to do about it. He wouldn't force her into anything; he wasn't that kind of man. But he was outrageously handsome and obviously aroused because of her—incredibly influencing—and he wasn't a pauper. Not that she had ever measured a person's true value by his net worth. But she had always admired ambition and she herself hoped to someday have a respectable net worth. It was too bad he was only in the used-car business instead of connected in some way to her own profession, but she wasn't going to marry the man, for crying out loud. He only wanted to kiss her.

And maybe she wanted to kiss him. The way her blood was racing around in her veins, maybe she wanted more than a kiss. Maybe she *needed* more. She was, after all, a mere mortal and a woman with the normal amount of hormones.

Involuntarily, so it seemed, the tip of her tongue slowly circled her lips, making them glisten with moisture.

As he watched her mouth, Trav's heart nearly stopped. She knew how to tease a man, and it was damned exciting that she would bother. Knowing now that she wouldn't stop him from kissing her, he slowly urged her forward, at the same time lowering his head.

He was already breathing hard, and when his lips were finally on hers, his desire went crazy. The kiss instantly deepened and evolved into hot and straining passion. Her

hands were moving as frantically as his, leaving no doubt in
his befuddled mind about her response.

For Trav, their kisses weren't only sexually thrilling and
exciting; they were emotionally exhilarating. She liked him.
However peculiar their relationship had been at the onset,
Serena liked him. And *peculiar* definitely described their
first date.

It was okay, he thought in the midst of another kiss that
had his heart exploding in his chest. Someday they would
laugh together about that first date. At the present, he didn't
feel at all like laughing.

His mouth drifted over her face, dropping kisses as it
went. "Serena ... Serena."

Her small gasps were all he heard from her. But the
snuggling of her body against his and the way her hands
kept sliding over his chest, shoulders and neck, could only
be interpreted as a feminine plea for more.

Yes, he thought dimly, so aroused he could barely think.
More ... they both needed more. He skimmed his hands
down her back to her bottom, cupped it and brought her
forward to nestle his engorged manhood into the V of her
legs. Her breath caught in her throat—he heard it and felt
it—but she didn't pull away.

Their kisses were becoming shorter, rougher, hungrier.
His fingers felt clumsy on the buttons of her dress, but he
realized that she was just as awkwardly fumbling with the
buttons on his shirt.

Their gazes crossed accidentally, and then he couldn't
look away. What was in the dark blue depths of her beautiful eyes made his blood pressure soar. She wanted it all; she
was not going to suddenly call a halt.

Well, he wanted it all, too. Everything. Having her naked and in his bed. His hands on her silky skin. His mouth
on every part of her. *Every* part.

Finally her dress was unbuttoned. He didn't want to appear totally out of control—no easy feat when he felt so
driven—so he forced himself to push the dress from her

shoulders without haste. The thing was, Serena was doing the same with his shirt, and she, too, seemed to be holding back.

It was damned silly; that's what it was. They both wanted the same thing, and each of them was trying to act much too civilized about it.

He quit being polite and gentlemanly and kissed her hard and long, grinding her lips with his, pushing his tongue deep into her mouth. She groaned hoarsely and kissed him back, just as hard, just as needful.

Serena knew she shouldn't be here and behaving like some sex-starved creature, but she couldn't stop either herself or Trav. A question flew through her mind: *was* she sex starved? Another immediately followed: would just any man do, or was Trav especially sexy?

When he buried his face in the curve of her throat, she admitted with a moan that he was especially sexy. Edward might have taught her the finer points of making love, but Trav had a potent brand of charisma that few women would be able to resist.

Her mind cleared momentarily. "My dress," she whispered, realizing that she would have to put it on again and she didn't want it wrinkled. Trav let go of her so she could bend down and pick it up off the carpet.

"Give it to me," he said in a thick, unnatural voice. "I'll hang it in the closet."

Silently she handed it over. Not only would she have to put it on again, but she would have to return to her office. Probably go through the files Trav had talked about.

But work and everything else seemed so far away right now. She was in a man's bedroom—even if it was on wheels—and every cell in her body demanded his touch. Ached for it.

He returned to undo the clasp of her bra and then, with her naked to the waist, all he could do was stare.

"Serena, you're so beautiful," he whispered raggedly. He was in awe of this lady for more than one reason, even if all he could think of at the moment was her physical beauty.

She took his hands and lifted them to her breasts. That was when he forgot there was a world beyond this room and brought her down on the bed. Arms and legs tangled, they kissed passionately and managed to finish undressing each other in the process.

When they were both completely nude, Trav became very still—looking at her, just looking. Serena watched his eyes with her heart in her throat. His expression was one of adoration, but she didn't want to believe it.

Quickly she pulled his head down to lavish kisses on his mouth. Then she whispered huskily, "Use protection."

Trav's senses went flying. Stretching to reach the drawer in the bedside table, he pulled out a small packet. Serena watched while he put on the condom because he had a remarkably beautiful body and she was forced to admit—if only to herself—that she loved looking at it.

He was back with her in moments, fitting himself on top of her, lying between her open thighs. Her face was feverish and flushed, her hair disheveled, her lips swollen and sensuous looking from their many kisses. He took one more kiss while he guided himself into the heated opening of her body.

A moan built in her throat, and she tore her mouth from his to take in air. But then she urged him on, arching her hips up from the bed to meet his thrusts, nipping at his mouth with her teeth, rubbing her breasts against his chest.

She was one hot number—hadn't he sensed this about her all along?—and Trav knew he wasn't going to last very long.

But neither could he slow himself down. Never had he needed a woman more. How did she have so much power over his feelings? All she had to do was to move a fraction of an inch, move anything—an arm, a leg, her head—and it affected him so strongly he couldn't see straight or even think.

He wanted her satisfaction before his own, but he couldn't guarantee it. All he could do was hope that she was as worked up with him as she seemed to be. Her whimpers and moans filled his brain. Her body was soft and yielding under his. They moved together in an erotic rhythm that seemed too perfect to be real.

And yet it was the most real thing that had ever happened to Trav, and he wondered if he would ever get enough of Serena's incredible body and unique brand of lovemaking.

Her breath was coming in short gasps. "Oh...oh...oh. Yes...yes...yes. Trav...Trav...*Trav!*"

He shouted one word, "Serena," and collapsed on her, suddenly as weak as a newborn babe.

Chapter Nine

Minutes passed before Trav came back to life. Serena had been completely still for a long time. Maybe a little too still? What was she thinking about? He ardently hoped she wasn't regretting their lovemaking.

Slowly he raised his head and saw that her eyes were closed. "Serena?" he asked softly.

Her lashes lifted, and she looked into the seemingly bottomless depths of his dark eyes with a whispered "Yes?"

He didn't know what to make of Serena Fanon. Their lovemaking had been off the charts, incredible, fantastic.

But those were his feelings. What were hers?

He cleared his throat. "Uh, did you . . . you know?"

She couldn't believe he had to ask. Actually she couldn't believe he had the gall to ask. If he really didn't know, one would think that tact or pride or something would have kept that embarrassing question buried.

"Did I what?" she said, acting as though she couldn't imagine what he was talking about.

Dipping his head, he kissed her cheek. Then he whispered into her ear, "It's kind of hard to tell sometimes. I mean, I got pretty carried away at the end, and—"

"Oh, please," she interrupted, no longer able to pretend that she didn't catch his drift. "I see no good reason to talk about it." She didn't feel nearly as friendly toward him as she had only a few minutes ago. Why didn't he know how good it had been for her? Was he so selfishly wrapped up in his own pleasure that he hadn't given hers a thought until the whole thing was over? How fortunate for her that her body had functioned so well.

She turned her head slightly to think about that. *Why* had her body functioned in such a wanton manner? Never before had she made love with a man for whom she hadn't felt something important. Did she feel anything for Trav that could be labeled as important?

Oh, damn, she thought with a surge of self-disgust. She had just slept with a client. Her *first* client. And now she was in a great situation, just great. She was in Trav's motor home, miles from her office and car. If he was going to be her client, she had to get his files, which meant some normal and impersonal conversation between them. Was that even possible after such wild, uninhibited lovemaking? Good Lord, she was still in his bed, still under him! And the final straw—if she was going back to the office, which she definitely should do, she needed a shower.

She groaned right out loud.

Trav's head jerked up. "What's the matter?"

"About fifty zillion things," she mumbled. "Let me up."

Mutely he moved. She was ticked about something, and he wasn't sure he wanted to hear what it was.

Hauling the top sheet with her, Serena got off the bed. Coolly she glanced at Trav. "May I use your shower?"

"Use anything you want."

"Thank you." Gathering up her clothes, she entered the bathroom and firmly closed the door behind her.

Drawing the light blanket up to his waist, Trav lay back on the pillows. After a heavy sigh, he pondered the past few minutes. Serena didn't seem regretful, and for that he was glad. But she did seem upset or maybe angry. Apparently he'd done something to irritate her.

On the other hand, she could be annoyed with herself. Some women were like that, hot as pistols until it was over, then madder than hell at themselves because they'd given in to the demands of their own bodies. Then there was the independent type who hated needing anything from anyone, even sex. Serena seemed independent, but not to that extreme.

The truth, he finally had to admit, was that he didn't understand the woman who'd just given him such bliss. Hell, did she understand herself?

A frown furrowed his forehead. In this case, did *he* understand *himself?* Had a woman ever confused him to this extent before? Had he ever cared enough about any woman to really worry about her feelings? Why was he so drawn to Serena? His favorite type of female cracked jokes, laughed a lot, smelled good, looked good and wasn't stingy with her charms. Other than looking and smelling good, Serena really didn't fit that mold. Wasn't she too damned serious for his taste?

Hell, if she didn't like what had happened here today, maybe he didn't, either.

Throwing back the blanket, Trav got up. He could hear Serena in the bathroom and wasn't about to interrupt her. Quickly he washed up at the kitchen sink and got dressed.

When she came out of the bathroom ten minutes later, he was sitting on the couch going through the cardboard box of file folders on the floor at his feet.

"Almost done here," he told her with barely a glance in her direction.

His cocky nonchalance was crushing. She'd expected...what? Certainly not what she was picking up from him.

"Fine," she said evenly, taking one of the chairs opposite the sofa. There were two other boxes pushed toward the other end of the sofa, she saw, and a growing stack of file folders on the cushion next to Trav. Apparently he'd been working fast.

Well, why wouldn't he? she thought peevishly. What was he if not a fast worker?

Finally he put the remaining files from the box he was working with into the two other boxes, then took the folders from the sofa and stuck them in the empty box.

"All set," he told her, getting to his feet. "I think it's best if you go through these on your own, then we'll have a meeting so I can answer any questions you might have." He bent over to pick up the box.

Serena stood. "Very well."

In minutes they were in his car. The box of files was in the trunk, and they were on their way back to her office. Serena was both shocked and numb. How dare he act as if nothing personal had happened in his motor home? *Why* was he acting that way? Was this the way he treated any woman stupid enough to go to bed with him?

Her lips flattened into a thin, grim line as she mentally berated herself. After her awful experience with Edward, how could she act like such a fool with another man—particularly Trav Holden?

This was not something she would easily get over or forget. And God help her, it was not going to happen again. It wasn't! What she'd like to do—oh, if only she could—was to tell this arrogant jerk to shove each and every one of his files up his nose.

Someday, she thought. Someday she would be in a position to turn down any business that displeased her.

That day was not today, dammit! She *couldn't* tell Trav to get out of her life; she dare not refuse any client.

Trav's files were in surprisingly good shape. There were letters, legal documents and notes of telephone calls in each one that pretty much told Serena what was going on. She jotted down questions as she scrupulously went through the files, but the list was neither long nor cumbersome.

Reading through those files was not a pleasant chore. Trav's name was almost constantly in sight, and too many times Serena stopped dead to think about the morning. It occurred to her that Trav could have planned the whole thing—dropping in, talking about hiring her and suggesting with a straight face while thinking of seduction that they go to his motor home and get his files. If that was the case, she'd fallen for his sneaky manipulation hook, line and sinker.

On the other hand, it was possible that he'd planned nothing. Except to hire her, of course. But she still couldn't figure out why he would put so much business into the hands of a totally green attorney. He *had* to have an ulterior motive, and she was pretty darned positive that she'd already found out what it was.

She just felt so stupid about it. So gullible.

And then, in the blink of an eye, her thoughts would change, and she would be reliving the incident. If Trav Holden knew nothing else in this confusing world, he knew how to make love to a woman. Her skin all but quivered every time she thought of his hands and mouth on it. And his body. "Flawless," she muttered unhappily. "Absolutely flawless."

But putting everything else aside—it wasn't impossible to do, just difficult—she was most bothered about Trav's eyes. She'd never known anyone with eyes like his.

Serena was completely immersed in the unique shape, color, emotion and quality of Trav's eyes when someone rapped on the doorframe.

"Hello?" a female voice called. "Serena?"

Serena jumped up and hurried to the outer office. The woman was wearing jeans, a hot pink T-shirt and sandals. Her hair was long, dark and curly. She looked familiar, someone Serena knew she should know by name, and yet...

"You don't remember me," the woman said with a breezy smile. "I'm Karen Breen. We met the other night at the Horizon Resort. You were with Trav...."

"Yes, of course," Serena said as memory came flooding in. She offered her right hand. "How are you?"

Over the handshake, Karen's expression sobered. "I'm here for a divorce, Serena, and it's not a pretty story. Actually I'm so glad you're a woman. I know you'll understand my situation much better than a man would."

Serena's heart sank. A divorce. Well, just as in Trav's case, she couldn't turn down business.

"Come into the other office, Karen. This one is going to be for my secretary, as soon as I find one."

"You're looking for a secretary? My God, is this fate or what? Serena, I'm looking for a job." Karen jabbered on while Serena stared. "I haven't worked for an attorney before, but I'm an excellent typist and a fast learner. To tell you the truth, Serena, you're not going to find anyone in Rocky Ford with any real legal experience. Oh, I wish I'd dressed up today. I've got some real nice clothes. And—"

Serena finally got her bearings and held up her hand. "One thing at a time, Karen, please. You've got my head spinning."

Karen laughed. "Sorry. Sometimes I do rattle on." Her smile vanished. "But I promise not to do that if you hire me. I really need a job, and there are so few secretarial positions in Rocky Ford. I was thinking I was going to have to move and live somewhere else. Maybe to Billings or Missoula. And I don't want to leave Rocky Ford. What family I have lives around here, and I would hate living off by myself, even though Billings and Missoula aren't completely unfamiliar. But you know how it is, moving and all can be a real pain. Anyway..."

Serena gave up and started toward her own office. Karen followed, as Serena had known she would. The woman was a talking machine. The funny thing was, Serena really didn't find Karen's chatter all that annoying. And certainly a woman with her gift of gab wouldn't have any trouble making clients feel at ease.

"Have a seat," Serena said, gesturing to the chairs in front of her desk. She walked around it and sat down.

"Oh, my goodness," Karen exclaimed at the sight of the stacks of files on Serena's desk. "You've only been open for business a short time, and look at the work that's already piled up. You really do need a secretary, don't you?"

Serena couldn't help laughing. "Yes, Karen, I really do need a secretary. What should we talk about first, your divorce or your qualifications for the job?"

Serena had another visitor that afternoon. It was a little after four, and she was thinking of calling it a day. She'd read through Trav's files until she was bleary-eyed, and there were still about a half dozen to go. Standing up, she was stretching the kinks out of her back when a man's voice called, "Hello? Anybody here?"

It was a totally unknown voice, deep and resonant. Another client maybe? What an unusual day it had turned out to be. Wincing over a stabbing jolt of memory of the morning, Serena rounded her desk and headed for the other office.

"Yes, I'm here." She stopped at the doorway.

"Well, now, I sure didn't expect my competition to look like a New York model," the man said with a broad smile. He was impeccably dressed in a dark suit and had graying black hair and a craggy face. A nice-looking man, actually. Around fifty years old, Serena estimated.

"Competition?"

"I'm Tom Powers. Perhaps you've heard of me."

Serena nodded. "Yes, I have. You're a lawyer in Billings and maintain a part-time office here in Rocky Ford." She stepped forward and they shook hands. "Nice of you to stop in, Mr. Powers."

He smiled. "Well, I had to take a look at you, Miss Fanon. Curiosity, you know. You know something else, young woman? You're going to take most of the local business away from me. You'll be here all of the time, and I wouldn't be even if I could. Yes, indeed, you'll soon be king of the hill in the legal department around here.''

Serena felt her face getting pink. "You must have known a full-time lawyer would appear on the scene sooner or later."

Tom Powers laughed. "It was always a possibility, of course. Oh, don't worry about it. I've had a good long run here in Rocky Ford with no competition whatsoever. There are always some that leave their home ground for legal advice, of course, no matter where they live or how many attorneys are available. They think distance gives them more privacy, I guess, and they're probably right. At any rate, I welcome you to town, Miss Fanon, and I wish you every success."

"Thank you, but I'm not new to Rocky Ford, Mr. Powers. I've lived here almost all of my life."

"Is that a fact? Did you go to school in Montana?"

Apparently Tom Powers wanted to chat, which Serena wasn't at all averse to doing. He might be an older man, but he was attractive, intelligent and charming. *And,* he was a lawyer.

"Would you like to sit down?" she asked.

Tom smiled. "Yes, thank you."

"And perhaps you'd enjoy a cold drink? I have a small refrigerator in my office and I can offer you a soda, lemonade or ice tea."

"A lemonade would be wonderful, Serena, thank you. Oh. Is it all right if I use your first name?"

"Quite all right, Tom." Smiling, Serena hurried away for the drinks. She returned with two frosty cans of lemonade and two napkins and passed one of each to Tom. "Sorry I don't have a glass to give you. I'm not a hundred percent organized yet."

"The can is fine, Serena, thank you."

They sat down, each taking one of the chairs in the reception area. Serena took a peek at Tom's left hand and was pleased to see no ring. A bare ring finger didn't guarantee bachelorhood, but it definitely opened the possibility.

This was the kind of man she had hoped to meet since she'd decided on the law many years ago. Suave, intelligent and involved in the law himself. He was older than her by quite a few years, but what did age matter? She gave him an inviting smile, and the one she received in return couldn't have been warmer.

"I believe we were talking about schools," Tom said.

"Yes, I believe we were. To answer your question, I got my law degree in the East. Georgetown."

A new respect entered Tom's eyes, which were almost as blue as Serena's own. She was glad they weren't dark like Trav's. In fact she was glad that nothing about Tom Powers reminded her of Trav.

The muscles of her jaws tightened in self-reproach. If nothing about Tom Powers reminded her of Trav, why was she thinking of him?

"Rocky Ford has to be pretty dull after Washington, D.C.," Tom said in quiet conversation. "I'm curious as to why you came home to practice independently. Surely you had other offers."

Serena took a sip from her can of lemonade and pretended that this topic didn't tear at the core of her. "Just homesick, Tom. My family is here, and I really needed to come home."

He nodded. "You know, that's similar to what happened to me. I'll tell you my story sometime, if you're interested. Maybe over dinner some evening." He got to his feet. "Much to my regret, I have to leave now. I have a dinner meeting in Billings tonight. But may I call you?"

"You may," she said softly. "I'll get you my card." Walking over to the desk, she set down her lemonade can, opened a drawer and extracted a business card, which she first wrote on and then handed to Tom. "That's my home number."

"Wonderful." Tom took her hand. "It's been a pleasure, Serena."

"Yes, it has, Tom."

"Goodbye for now."

"Goodbye."

When she was alone again, Serena closed the door to the hall and locked it. She didn't want to see anyone else today. Moving to the desk, she sat behind it and pondered the day from morning until this very moment.

It had been an unusual day, both disturbing and satisfying. What she had to ask herself was what phase of the day was so satisfying—meeting Tom Powers this afternoon or writhing under Trav Holden's superb body this morning?

She was suddenly trembling. Just thinking of making love with Trav had her shaking like a bowl of gelatin!

Jumping up, she grabbed her purse and left, hastily re-locking the door behind her.

She would discard the lemonade cans in the morning. Right now she needed some fresh air.

Finding a decent rental had not been easy. She should have foreseen the lack of rental units in a small town such as Rocky Ford, but the first day that she had even thought of getting out of the Sundowner Motel, two such units had been listed in the newspaper. It hadn't occurred to her that neither of them would fit her needs.

She had scoured the town and surrounding area for an apartment or house to rent. It wasn't that she was overly picky, either, but she needed something at least partially furnished. It didn't have to be immaculate, but it did have to be clean enough that she could wipe down cabinets and furniture and feel comfortable about it.

Now, standing in the tiny living room of a small house on the western perimeter of town, she realized that she had gotten lucky. This little place was perfect. She'd fallen in love with the yard at first sight. It had grass, wild rose-bushes and huge old trees that towered over the one-story house and shaded it completely from both the sun and the street. Privacy, she thought with an inner sigh. Blessed privacy.

And the house was fine. Very clean. Bright, shiny window panes. Glistening linoleum. Immaculate appliances. The furniture was sparse, a bed and small dresser in the bedroom, a table and two chairs in the kitchen and a small settee, one chair and a floor lamp in the living room.

She turned to the owner, who had graciously shown her the house. "I like it. I'll take it."

The woman nodded. "I'll need the first and last month's rent and a cleaning deposit."

"Yes, you mentioned that on the phone. The deposits are fine. I'll pay you in cash right now, as I'd like to move in today."

"I'll get my receipt book from my car." The woman walked out.

Alone in the little house, she walked to a front window and looked out. The street was visible through the trees and rosebushes, but just barely. No one would whisper about her living here for too long as the maids had done in the motel. She could stay for however long it took her to recognize the perfect moment to accomplish her goal in Rocky Ford.

It would happen. She just had to be patient.

A smile tipped the corners of her mouth. For the first time in months, her stomach wasn't churning and she felt calm.

It was the charm and quiet of this little house, she thought, turning to look at the living room again. With a few decorative touches, she would make it into a real home.

How lucky she was to have found it. How very lucky.

One of the salesmen yelled, "Trav, pick up line two. A woman wants to talk to you."

Trav cocked an eyebrow. A woman? Serena maybe? His pulse fluttered, and there was a tightening in his groin, which didn't thrill him. *Damn,* he thought irately, *just thinking of that woman causes me problems. Why in hell did I give her my files?*

All afternoon he'd been arguing with himself. In essence he'd hired her, but no money had exchanged hands. Legally he could pick up his files and tell her he'd changed his mind about assigning all of his legal work to one attorney. Not that he thought Serena would sue him or anything like that; she really didn't strike him as the type of person who sued people at the drop of a hat.

But that whole idea would no more than form in his mind when he'd tell himself to stop being a damn fool. He'd made a deal with Serena and he wasn't going to renege on it.

That didn't mean that he had to take her to bed again. But in Serena's case, maybe even once was too much. After all, she wasn't a woman to sleep with and then forget. Dammit, she was the kind of woman men married, and he didn't want to get married. She was, getting down to basics, a woman he should avoid at all costs.

Which, of course, led him back to the fact that he'd hired her this morning and there was no way she could do his legal work without seeing a lot of him.

It was damned peculiar how this morning's session in his bed had changed things. Before that, seeing Serena was all he'd been able to think about. Now he wanted to avoid her. What was wrong with him?

Snorting in disgust, he punched the button for line two and picked up the phone. "Trav Holden here."

"Trav, this is Kathleen Osterman. From the newspaper, remember?"

"Yes, I remember. How are you?"

"I'm very well, thank you. I think you'll be pleased about my reason for calling. The Rocky Ford Association for the Betterment of the Community—" Kathleen laughed. "Some title, huh? Anyway, our little group has decided to honor your courage with the Citizen of the Year award. Every August we hold a very nice dinner at the community center and award the citizen who has stood out during the year with some remarkable deed or accomplishment. I don't mind admitting that we haven't had the good fortune to honor someone of your caliber for quite some time now, but—"

"Whoa, Kathleen. Slow down a minute. First of all, I'm not a citizen of Rocky Ford. Doesn't that make a difference?"

"We discussed that. But since you own a business here, Trav, we decided that you qualify. Please say you'll accept the award. It really is an honor. We take it very seriously."

Trav rubbed his mouth. He wanted to refuse the whole thing. He hadn't run into that fire to get an award, and he would rather that everyone forgot about it. He had checked on the Bracks, and both mother and daughter were recovering. Wasn't that what was most important? Give *them* the award for living through a terrible ordeal.

But Kathleen had him over a barrel. He sold cars to the people of Rocky Ford; he sure as hell couldn't refuse their award.

"Of course I'll accept," he said into the phone. "When is the ceremony?"

"Saturday the nineteenth. It starts at six in the evening. I'll need to spend a few minutes with you before the festivities to familiarize you with the routine, so it would be best if you arrived at the center around five-thirty. And we'd like you to say a few words after receiving the award, so it might be best if you prepared a little speech."

"A speech. Fine," Trav said with a grimace. If there was anything he hated, it was making speeches.

"Well, that's about it," Kathleen said. "See you on the nineteenth."

"Right. See you then. Goodbye, Kathleen."

"Goodbye, Trav."

He put the phone down, leaned back in his chair and stared at the ceiling. It seemed lately that everything happening in his life was taking place in Rocky Ford.

The funny thing was, he didn't know how to change whatever it was that seemed to be controlling his destiny. His own libido was getting him in pretty darned deep with a woman lawyer, and now he was receiving an award that he didn't want for something that had been purely accidental.

Why did he suddenly feel as though he were on the outside looking in, watching himself from afar while someone or something mysterious and unseen pulled the strings?

With a snort of disgust, he got to his feet. That kind of thinking could drive a guy over the edge. He was the only one controlling his life. He could have said no to Kathleen and taken the consequences. It had been his decision to accept her little award, and he would live with it.

As for Serena, he would make the decisions there, too.

He wasn't a kid, after all. He'd been on his own for a good many years and done very well for himself. He'd fall in love when *he* decided and he'd marry when *he* decided to marry. That was the long and the short of it.

Telling the men he was leaving for the day, he got in the car he was using off the lot and headed for the motor home.

He needed, almost desperately, to be alone.

He was nearly to Access Creek and the motor home when he realized that he didn't know why he needed to be alone. Slamming the steering wheel with his palm, he muttered a string of curses.

Something or someone *was* pulling the strings, and he didn't like it one damned bit.

Chapter Ten

Serena walked into the house at a quarter to five. Charlie had the kitchen telephone in his right hand and was holding it out to her. "It's for you, honey."

Please don't let it be Trav, Serena thought, agonizing silently. She didn't want to talk to Trav again today. She probably wouldn't want to talk to him tomorrow, either, but she was going to have to. It could be embarrassing, depending on how he acted. There'd been a definite coolness in their attitudes when he'd driven her and the files to her office, a coolness that she had perpetuated as much as him. It was pretty obvious that he, too, regretted their loss of control in his bedroom this morning.

With an impatient sigh, she walked over to Charlie. Gingerly, a bit cautiously, she accepted the phone and brought it to her ear. "Hello?"

"Hello, Serena. Kathleen Osterman here. How are you, dear?"

Dear? Since when was she a "dear" to Kathleen? "I'm fine, Kathleen. And you?"

"Couldn't be better. I'm sure you're aware of Rocky Ford's little group of business people who are concerned with community betterment. Lola's a member."

"I've heard it mentioned." It seemed to Serena that she'd heard of the association, although she really couldn't pinpoint the time and place, or who may have done the mentioning. Since Lola was a member, it was probably her.

"Actually I tried calling your office first, Serena. What hours are you planning to keep in your law office, dear?"

Serena felt guilty as sin, as though she had done something unpardonable by leaving her office early. But letting Kathleen know how her little barb had pricked was unthinkable. She tilted her head at a defensive angle.

"My office hours are eight to five, Kathleen. Today was an unavoidable exception." Wincing because she really didn't owe Kathleen an explanation for anything she did, Serena clamped her lips tightly together.

"Well, that's neither here nor there and not the reason I called. I was thinking that you might be interested in joining the association, for one thing. I'll send you some literature about it. But my primary reason for calling is the honorary dinner the group is having for Travis Holden on the nineteenth of the month. Since you were with Trav the day he saved the Bracks, I was certain you'd enjoy attending the affair."

Serena's jaw dropped. "Kathleen, I was not with Travis Holden the day he saved the Bracks. I was passing by, saw the fire and stopped, the same as a dozen other people."

"Oh, really? I certainly received a much different impression."

"Inasmuch as you included me in your front-page photo of the near-tragedy, I'm sure you did."

"Then you don't know Mr. Holden at all?"

Serena's heart skipped a beat. "Um, only since the fire. I know him now, of course. But that was the day we met."

Kathleen gave a short little laugh. "Well, I certainly had the wrong idea, didn't I? Sorry about that. In any case, Serena, you still might enjoy the affair on the nineteenth. If nothing else, it would give you some idea of the goals and plans of our group, which we think are very important to the progress and development of Rocky Ford. I'll send you the data on time and place along with that literature I mentioned."

Serena glanced at her dad and wondered if he were a member. "I'll look everything over and let you know, Kathleen."

"Good. Say hello to the family for me. Bye for now."

"Goodbye, Kathleen." Serena put the phone down with a frown. Kathleen had really believed that she and Trav were together the day of the fire. After that photo in the paper, was the whole town under the same impression?

Not that a little gossip would hurt her, and it wasn't terrible gossip in the first place. She was single, after all, and unless Trav was lying—Serena shuddered at the thought—so was he. Single people had every right to see whomever they wanted.

It was just that . . . well, the whole idea made her uncomfortable. People talking, assuming things that weren't true.

Except . . . after this morning, anything that might be being said about her and Trav was more true than false, wasn't it?

Charlie had sat on the floor near the table to play with little Ron and his toy trucks and cars. Candace was at the stove and counter, cooking dinner. Each of them turned toward Serena with a questioning look.

"That was Kathleen Osterman," Serena said to both, even though they had to already know that. "Dad, are you a member of her group? Something about the betterment of the community? She said Lola is."

"No, I'm not, honey." Charlie got to his feet. "You know I've never been much for clubs and such. But I've donated money to Kathleen's group a couple of times because I thought they were working on what I considered a worthy cause. And yes, I believe Lola did join. Is Kathleen on a membership drive? I'm sure Lola could give you all of the particulars, if you're interested."

"I'm sure Kathleen is forever on a membership drive," Serena responded dryly. "But the main reason she called was to invite me to attend a dinner her group is giving to honor Travis Holden for rescuing the Bracks from that fire."

Charlie nodded his approval. "I'm glad of that, Serena. There should be some sort of public recognition for Trav's courage."

Candace murmured, "I heartily agree."

Serena didn't want to talk about this anymore, and she started from the room. "Do I have time for a shower before dinner?"

"Plenty of time," Candace answered, giving her sister-in-law a perplexed look. When Serena was gone, she said to Charlie, "Does Serena seem upset to you?"

Charlie thought for a second. "Yeah, she does. Maybe she had a bad day. Let's give her lots of space this evening. Sometimes that's what a person needs to work out a problem."

Candace nodded in mute agreement, but it seemed to her that Serena's mood had more to do with Kathleen's phone call than the possibility of a bad day. Serena had so obviously tensed up when Kathleen had presumed she was a good friend of Trav Holden's that Candace could only conclude that Mr. Holden was somehow responsible for her sister-in-law's blue funk.

"Hmm," Candace murmured quietly, returning to her cooking and privately considering the many possibilities where Trav Holden would be in a position to annoy or upset Serena.

Serena unlocked her office door very early the next morning. She hadn't slept well all night and, after waking up around four and struggling in vain to fall back asleep for at least an hour, she finally got up.

With a pot of coffee brewing, she got right to work on Trav's files. The pot finally stopped gurgling, and she poured herself a cup. She closed the last file a few minutes before eight and sat back to scan the list of questions she'd written pertaining to all of the files.

A sudden surge of self-condemnation made her chest feel tight. She had broken a sensible rule yesterday—to never get personally involved with a client. That he was her very first client made the incident reek with irony. And stupidity, she added with a bitter taste in her mouth.

Yesterday hadn't been a total bust, however. She had hired Karen Breen, who would start work on the following Monday, and she had met Tom Powers. Karen was also a paying client, Serena reminded herself. And more clients would dribble in. This office would soon be a busy place. She had to believe that.

Serena sighed in the present silence. She would be relieved and very grateful if she ever reached the stage of feeling swamped with ringing telephones and mountains of work.

"Fat chance," she mumbled, getting up to stare out the window. The one thing she should never kid herself about was the amount of legal work in and around Rocky Ford, certainly not enough that she would ever feel swamped.

After a minute or so of that sort of thinking, however, a determined expression came over her face. She was not going to stand around and rue past decisions. She was here, her office was pleasant, she already had two clients and the very best thing she could do with her extra time was to get involved in community affairs.

With that in mind, she returned to her desk and dialed Lola's store.

Lola herself answered, "Men's Western Wear. Lola speaking."

"Hi," Serena said. "Got a few minutes to talk?"

"Sure. What's up?"

"Lola, did you join the community-betterment group headed by Kathleen Osterman? At least I think it's headed by her. She acts as though it's her baby, at any rate. Anyway, are you a member?"

"Yes, I joined. It's a good group, Serena. Kathleen heads it. Democratically, I might add. The chairperson and those who head special committees are voted in by the members. What got me interested was their concern for the area's teenagers. You must remember that there was very little for teens to do around here when we were growing up. The group recognized the lack of entertainment for teenagers and did something about it. They arranged some steady activities, such as specially priced movies at the theater and teen dances on Friday nights, and they also set up a phone line for odd jobs for kids. In other words, if Mrs. Branson wants her lawn mowed, she can call that number and whoever's on phone duty that day will contact a teen on the list. It seems to be working quite well."

"I'm glad to hear it. Kathleen called me yesterday to invite me to the honorary dinner for Trav Holden."

"Wonderful! You can sit with Duke and me."

"I didn't say I was going, Lola."

"Oh, I forgot your disastrous date with the hero."

"It's not that . . . well, maybe it is. Lola, to tell you the truth, I'm going in circles. He . . . he's my client now." She had also confessed that disturbing fact to Charlie and Candace at the dinner table last night. Neither had asked questions, but there had been unmistakable curiosity in Candace's eyes.

"Pardon? Who's your client?"

"Trav. He gave me all of his legal files yesterday. I've been reading them ever since."

"He hired you to do his legal work? *All* of his legal work? Serena, that's wonderful!"

"Yes, I guess it is. But in the meantime, Kathleen is under the impression that we're an item and...and I think Trav is, too."

"You mean he hired you with an ulterior motive in mind? Like maybe he wants to get into your boxers?"

"You're laughing, Lola, and I don't think this is particularly funny."

"Sorry, coz. Look, I'm always here for you, you know that. But I really can't drum up any genuine sorrow because a handsome, ambitious man is interested in you. Maybe he has a shy side and is afraid to come right out and ask for another date. After the way the first one turned out, can you blame him? Maybe hiring you was the only thing he could think of to see you again."

Serena's shoulders slumped. She could tell Lola almost anything and, in fact, had for most of her life. But talking about yesterday morning with anyone just wasn't in the cards. She'd been such a pushover. A sucker for dark, romantic eyes. A slave to her own hormones. There were times when a woman simply could not confess her faults and flaws, and this was one of them.

"I can't begin to guess what motivates Trav Holden," she hedged.

"But you just said you were afraid that he could be thinking of the two of you as an item. Serena, maybe you'd best keep in mind that he's a pretty sharp businessman," Lola said. "Liking you personally probably has nothing to do with handing you his legal work. People usually don't become successful by thinking with their emotions, do they?"

"No, I suppose not," Serena mumbled. Her head was spinning. How could she possibly second-guess Trav's feelings and motives for doing anything? And hadn't she proved that her own emotions were still in a muddle over Edward by falling into bed with Trav yesterday morning? Why else would she have been so easy?

"So, then, are you going to attend the dinner honoring Trav?" Lola asked.

"Um, I'm not sure. Kathleen is sending me some literature on the group. I…I'll see what happens." Stuttering over any subject with Lola was like waving a red flag in front of a bull's nose, Serena knew. Her cousin was sharp minded and not at all averse to digging into anything that occurred within the family or even remotely touched upon it in any way. Serena groaned silently. Her own equivocation about Trav was bound to alert Lola to something unsaid.

But Lola surprised her by murmuring quietly, "It's your decision, Serena. Oh, I'm wanted out front. Talk to you later?"

"Yes, we'll talk again later," Serena agreed with relief. "Bye, Lola."

After hanging up, Serena weakly fell back in her chair. To do the best job possible, an attorney had to be objective about a client and his legal needs, which was one of the best arguments for staying personally distanced.

Her career was definitely getting off on the wrong foot when she had already slept with her first client.

Damn!

Trav arrived at the Ridgeport Building around ten. His stomach felt tied in knots. One part of his brain told him to retrieve his files from Serena and get the hell out of Rocky Ford. For some reason, he couldn't adhere to that advice without argument, which royally ticked him off. He walked into Serena's office, full of ambiguities and an expression as cold as a Montana winter day.

Serena saw the frost in his eyes and flushed with a sudden influx of anger. He was angry with her? For what, being too easy?

"I have a list of questions prepared," she said coolly. "If you'd care to sit down, we can get right to them."

Sit down. Answer her questions. Damn! It took a minute, but Trav finally lowered himself into the chair in front of her desk.

She, too, sat down. Her hands were steady only through intense effort. Inside she was a bundle of quaking nerves.

Watching her, Trav despised the flaw in his character that made him weak for this woman. Yes, she was beautiful. His jaw clenched tighter as he took in her smart white dress with navy piping around the sleeves and neckline. Her hair was up today, but those wispy, trailing curls around her face and ears were sinfully sexy.

His eyes narrowed on her. How could they have made such uninhibited love, then built a seemingly unbreachable barrier between them immediately after? Which of them had caused it, him, her or both? What was it he really felt from her? That haughty look on her face was hard to see through.

But maybe trying to see through that better-than-thou expression was what he was doing wrong. Maybe that's all there was. Trav's stomach lurched. God, she really didn't think she was better than him, did she? But if that was the whole painful truth, why had she melted in his arms yesterday morning?

Serena lowered the paper in her hands. "Did you understand the question?"

"Sorry. I was thinking about something else. Say it again."

It took about two hours to go through Serena's list of questions. She made written notes of Trav's answers and she also made a mental note that he hadn't smiled even once during this session.

But then, neither had she.

"Well, that does it," she announced, placing her list of questions and voluminous notes in a file folder. "It surprises me that most of your legal work consists of lawsuits."

Trav laid the ankle of his right foot over his left knee. "That's because people love to sue used-car dealers."

"Oh, really? More so than other types of businesses?"

"Can't speak for other types of businesses, Serena. But I learned from my very first car lot that there's always someone out there just waiting to sue the guy he bought an old car from." Dropping his foot to the floor, Trav leaned forward. "Look, it works like this. Even on old clunkers, my company has a warranty program. Sometimes it's thirty days, sometimes it's a year. Depends on the age and condition of the vehicle. In every case, that warranty eventually runs out. Most people accept the fact that my responsibility is finished at that point, but there are always some who jump at the chance to sue me because their vehicle broke down ten days, for example, after the warranty ran out."

"I see," she said.

"The funny thing is, if those same people would come in and talk to me or to the manager of whichever lot he bought from, we'd probably help him out with repairs. Or with another vehicle to replace the one that's giving him trouble. The last thing I want is for anyone to think I'm an unscrupulous car dealer. If I ever got the reputation of being a cheat, how long do you think I'd stay in business?"

"I'm sure that's a very good policy," Serena murmured, even though she was wondering whether or not to believe him. Used-car dealers *did* have a reputation; she'd heard tidbits along that line all of her life. If Trav was as honest and fair as he said, then he was a pretty rare bird.

Serena frowned because she didn't like her own thoughts. What did she really know about used-car dealers? Wasn't she being much too judgmental when she had no firsthand experience on which to base that judgment?

Looking at the man across her desk, she felt a hot, tingling sensation begin in her lower stomach and radiate outward from there. Like it or not, she was enormously attracted to Trav Holden. An affair with him was not out of the question. In fact, if he made a pass right now, she was apt to forget where they were.

Quickly she lowered her eyes and pretended genuine interest on a stack of forms. "I'll need your signature on each of these," she said rather breathlessly, pushing the stack forward. "They're notifications to the lawyers you've been dealing with, stating simply that I will be handling your work from now on."

Trav picked up one of the forms and read it. Behind a calm exterior, he felt like seething, molten lava. Wanting Serena was a persistent ache, one he damned well didn't deserve. Why her? Why was he falling for a woman who thought herself better than him? Maybe only career-wise, but how could any relationship endure if a woman sneered at her man's line of work?

All he had to do to eliminate the problem entirely was to say right now that he'd changed his mind. Just tell her that he wasn't signing these forms and ask how much he owed her for the time she'd put in thus far. He could write a check on the spot, leave with his files and that would be the end of it.

The words wouldn't come. Almost robotlike, he pulled the pen from his shirt pocket and began scrawling his signature.

Barely moving a muscle, Serena watched him. His good looks bombarded her senses, and the memory of yesterday morning's feverish sex in his bed made her mouth as dry as the Sahara Desert. Was what she was feeling merely a backlash from Edward's deceit, as she'd previously decided, or was something happening all on its own with Trav?

She inhaled a long, slow breath, keeping it as quiet as she could manage, not wanting to alert Trav to the disquietude and questions running amok in her system. For some reason, she couldn't be open and honest with him.

For some reason? Was this really the mystery she was trying to make it? Wasn't the "reason" named Edward, and would she ever openly and honestly risk her heart again?

"There you are," Trav announced, pushing the stack of forms back across the desk and returning his pen to his shirt pocket. Then he sat very still and looked at her.

She tried not to notice. More, she tried desperately not to squirm. His look was inquisitive. And personal, very personal, seemingly penetrating her clothes.

"So," he finally said softly. "Everything all right with you today?"

He was referring to what they'd done yesterday! Red stains crept into Serena's cheeks.

"Everything's fine," she replied, marveling that her voice was so steady.

"How about dinner tonight?" Something perverse was forcing him to test her, to push her into her true character, whatever that was. He knew he might not like it; she really might think he was no better than the dirt she walked on. But he had to know the truth, no matter how much it hurt.

Serena's heart skipped at least two full beats. Until she understood herself better, going anywhere with Trav was dangerous business. Look what had happened yesterday from a perfectly innocuous chore. No, she dare not risk dating him. Not yet.

"I ... I've been thinking—since yesterday—and I really feel that it's in both of our best interests if we keep our relationship impersonal."

His gaze bored into her. "You feel that, huh?"

"Uh, yes."

"The whole idea of you and I dating makes you uncomfortable. Why?" He leaned forward. "Why, Serena?"

"A lawyer shouldn't date her client, any more than a doctor should date his patient."

"Hogwash! In the first place, we've already moved past the formalities of impersonal dating. Considering what happened yesterday morning, I'd say we're about as involved as two people can get."

She mustered up an indignant expression. "Yesterday was a mistake that won't be repeated. I'd be eternally grateful if you'd forget it."

Trav sat back to ponder her remarks, ridiculous as they were. Did she honestly expect him to forget their lovemaking?

But then he remembered that he'd forgotten a lot of women, sometimes before the sheets had cooled down. Was that all yesterday had meant to Serena? A quick and easy tumble?

He didn't want to believe that. It was peculiar and irritating and heartrending all at the same time, that she could make him so confused about himself. After all, he'd always dated pretty, vivacious women strictly for laughs. For the first time, he wasn't laughing, and it hurt like hell to think that Serena might be.

She cleared her throat. "There are two lawsuits that need immediate attention. The Wycoff suit and...let me see..." Nervously Serena flipped through the file folders. "Oh, yes, the Saunders suit. In each case, motions must be filed with the district court in Helena. I plan to call the court secretary and ask for the first available space on her calendar for a civil-suit motion. Hopefully I'll get an appointment within a week."

"I could drive you there in the motor home," Trav said with a daring look on his face.

Her eyes jerked up to meet his. "You're not going to forget it, are you?"

Trav slowly got to his feet. "Nope. And you want to know something? I don't think you're going to forget it, either, even though you'd give your eye teeth to make me believe it meant nothing to you." It was a shot in the dark, all the ammunition he had. Her stunned expression was answer enough: he'd hit the bull's-eye. All of a sudden, he didn't feel quite so confused.

He walked to the door, where he stopped and turned. "See you tomorrow, babe. Oh, and if you change your mind about dinner tonight, just give me a call. And don't say it can't happen, 'cause that's exactly what you did on our first date.'' He sent her a brilliant smile. "See ya, beautiful.''

With her heart pounding like a hammer, Serena stared at the door long after he'd gone through it.

Then the anger set in. "Cocky SOB," she mumbled. "We'll see who has the last laugh, *Mr.* Holden!"

Chapter Eleven

"Oh, Dad, don't you wish Mother had lived to see Ron's precious son?" Serena spoke wistfully while watching her adorable little nephew running and playing on the grass of the backyard.

Candace had prepared a supper of cold ham and potato salad, and they had eaten outside at the old picnic table that had been a part of the Fanon backyard for as long as Serena could remember. Though the meal was over and the table cleared, the family had stayed outside to enjoy the cool evening air.

Serena caught the stiffening of her father's shoulders out of the corner of her eye and did a double take. "Dad?"

Charlie looked at her with a smile. Serena saw that in the blink of an eye he was himself again, although a perfectly normal reminder of her mother had caused him to react very strangely. And it had not been her imagination. He had physically recoiled from her question, and however much he smiled and pretended it hadn't happened, she had seen it with her own eyes.

She wanted to pursue the subject, to question him, adult to adult. To insist on talking about her mother and hearing every tiny detail that he could remember about her.

But she couldn't do it. Charlie was still her father, a man to respect, and she loved him. Still, the incident, which had apparently passed right over Candace's head, troubled Serena. It brought back some discomfiting old feelings and reinforced the questions she had wondered about during her teen years. Was there some sort of mystery connected to her mother's death? Charlie's long-ago story was that Sandra had become ill very suddenly with an uncommon heart ailment and had lived only a short time after the diagnosis.

But there was nothing mysterious about a heart attack or even a heart disease, so if she was looking for a mystery, wasn't she doubting her father's word?

Serena tensed at that thought. She had never known Charlie to lie about anything. There had never been a more honest, selfless person born. How dare she have the audacity to doubt him in any way?

"Did you see Mr. Holden today?" Candace asked.

It took Serena a moment to bring herself out of the past. When she caught up with the present, she nodded. "Yes, he came in."

"I think it's wonderful that your very first client is a person of his stature."

Serena couldn't discuss the actual work she would be doing for Trav—that was privileged information—but she had let her family know that her and Trav's business relationship had every chance of being long-term and quite lucrative. Actually she had only mentioned the possibility of good legal fees because she owed both Charlie and Candace so much money.

Now she wished she hadn't mentioned him at all. Having to see him—probably every day while he was in Rocky Ford this trip—was difficult enough to deal with; she certainly didn't want to discuss him with her family every evening.

But she couldn't be unkind to Candace and say so. Instead she said lightly, "Here's hoping he's only the first of many, Candy."

Candace smiled. "I'm sure that will be the case." Reaching out, she touched Serena's hand. "I'm so proud of you." Her expression became soft and loving. "And I'm especially proud to be a member of this family."

Charlie was sitting next to Candace and he put his arm around her shoulders, giving her a hug. "You're a nice girl, Candy, and we all love you."

The three of them sat at the picnic table for a long time, watching Ronnie at play, occasionally murmuring some remark but each mostly involved in his or her own thoughts.

Serena felt certain that Candace was thinking of her husband and that he should be here with his son. She was bound to have moments of bitterness over Ron's untimely death, although she never let them show. Her sister-in-law was quite a gal, Serena thought with admiration.

As for Charlie, Serena wondered if he weren't thinking of her mother. He might not be able to talk about his deceased wife, but Serena had firsthand experience with the impossibility of completely shutting out certain thoughts and memories. Yes, he was probably remembering Sandra and the tragedy of her death, the same as Candace felt about Ron.

Serena heaved a quiet sigh. When compared to her father's and Candace's losses, her romantic problems were trivial. How could she be so selfish as to moan and groan— if only to herself—about Edward's treachery and Trav's...Trav's...

Trav's what?

There was a sudden catch in her throat. There really was no logical excuse for her confusion over Trav, was there? Yes, he was cocky and irritating and too sure of himself.

And yes, she wasn't particularly impressed with his chosen career.

But he wasn't just another guy anymore, was he?

With her stomach suddenly tied in knots, Serena swung her legs from under the picnic table and got up.

"I think I'll call it a day." Determined to avoid the appearance of undue haste, which could cause Charlie and Candace some concern, she bent over to kiss Charlie's cheek. It was still early, after all, and she normally didn't go to bed while it was still light out. "Good night, Dad." She smiled at Candace. "'Night, Candy. Kiss Ronnie good-night for me."

"I will," Candace said. "We'll be going in shortly, too. Sleep well."

Charlie gave her a curious look. "You're okay, aren't you?"

"I'm fine, Dad. Just tired."

"Well, get a good night's sleep."

It was good advice, and Serena hoped she could do it. If Edward or Trav didn't float in and out of her dreams—or were they nightmares?—she would sleep just fine.

Sighing as she went into the house, she let the screen door close quietly behind her.

"Serena Fanon," she said into the phone on her desk.

"This is Trav, Serena. I'm driving to Great Falls today. A few days at the car lot there, and then I'll be going to Missoula. Is there anything you need to talk to me about before I leave?"

Serena was totally stunned. Was this the way he always lived? Never knowing from day to day where he'd be the next? What about roots? Didn't he ever want a traditional life, with a house and a family?

"I think we covered everything pretty well yesterday." During their question-and-answer session regarding his files, she had learned what action he wanted taken in each instance. "And I can reach you on your cellular if something unforeseen arises," she added.

"Good. And remember—Great Falls first, then Missoula. Did I give you a copy of my printed list of car lots with addresses and phone numbers?"

"No, I didn't know you had one."

"Well, I do. You won't have to be calling directory assistance every time you need to talk to me when I'm away from Rocky Ford. I'll drop one off on my way out of town. Are you going to be there all morning?"

"I plan to be, yes."

"I'll see you in an hour or so."

Serena put the phone down with a frown. So he was leaving town again. For how long this time? How could a man be both stable and unstable? Trav certainly seemed to be. He was successful in business, indicating stability, and at the same time, drifting around the state in that motor home like a vagabond, certainly a sign of instability to her.

Groaning, she put her elbow on the desk and her head in her hand. Lots of people lived in recreational vehicles. Why was she judging Trav so harshly? Granted, most of those who chose that carefree way of life were retired, older folks. And whoever said that a person had to live in a house to prove stability? Besides, did she even care how Trav Holden lived?

It struck her then: she didn't want Trav going off again! Startled, she sat up straighter and admitted shock over such a revelation. She was *not* falling in love with Trav; she wasn't!

All but leaping out of her chair, she paced her office with great agitation. Why did she permit men to turn her into a damned fool? First Edward, now Trav. Tears began stinging her eyes as a surge of self-pity nearly overwhelmed her.

It didn't last long, though. Edward was in the past, and she'd done enough crying about him. Trav was the one to worry about now, and while she'd succumbed to his charms and her own sexual appetite once with him, it didn't have to happen again.

He was not a man for any woman who had her own two feet firmly planted in one place to get involved with. Let him flit from woman to woman, and she would put him out of her mind once and for all. Except for their working relationship, of course.

Dammit, was she ever going to be happy with a man? Had Edward completely destroyed her ability to trust the male gender, to relax and believe what they said? All men were not liars and cheats, but would she recognize the genuine article even if she tripped over him?

Sighing despondently, she returned to her desk. Happiness just might be the most fleeting of human emotions. It came in bits and pieces, sometimes too brief and blurred to recognize until it was too late and one was living reality again.

No, she wasn't counting on any great happiness to suddenly come swooping down upon her. And certainly she would never look to Trav to make her happy. The way she felt right now, she would never look to any man to make her happy. So far in her personal life, the only things she'd gotten from men were some good sex, followed by confusion and misery.

She had to break that self-destructive pattern, even if it meant living without serious male companionship for the rest of her days.

Trav had called from the car lot's office. After hanging up the phone, he took from his briefcase a brochure listing the lots he owned. It was an attractive brochure, with color photos of a few of the lots and some low-key advertising. They had been designed expressly to pass out to bankers, chambers of commerce and business people. Customers rarely got one, as there was nothing in them that would interest the ordinary used-car buyer.

But Serena should have one because of the addresses and telephone numbers of each lot. Frowning, Trav stared down at the brochure in his hand. He should have told her he would put one in the mail rather than promising to deliver it in person. She'd upset his equilibrium so badly yesterday he'd hardly slept a wink last night. Not knowing what to do about a woman was a new experience for him, and he didn't like it. The thought of chasing a woman who didn't want him gave him chills. But at the same time that thought buried itself in his brain, he remembered how passionately she had responded to him in bed. What was a man to believe?

Anyway, he'd decided to get out of Rocky Ford again. This time he hoped for the good sense to stay away, at least until his normal schedule of visiting the lots brought him back. He never should have hired Serena, but it was done and he would live with it.

Living with it didn't mean he wanted to see her this morning, however. She had some sort of mystic power over him, extending even to their phone conversations. The only reason he'd called at all was to let her know he was leaving town and to make sure she didn't have some more questions that would only mean her having to track him down. Then he heard himself mention the brochure and tell her he'd bring one by within the hour.

"No way," he muttered, getting to his feet. "Darrel?" he yelled.

The office door was open, and Darrel promptly appeared in the doorway. "Yeah?"

Trav held out the brochure. "Do you know where the Ridgeport Building is?"

"Sure. Why?"

"I want you to do something for me. Take this brochure to Serena Fanon. Her office is in that building. Second floor. Incidentally she might be calling here from time to time, because she's the company attorney now. Anytime she calls, give her any information you might have about where I am."

Darrel nodded. "Okay, fine. I'll run that brochure over right away."

"Thanks."

"You all set to go now?"

Trav came around the desk. "All set. You know how to reach me. See you next time around. Or sooner if needed."

They shook hands, and Trav walked outside and on to his motor home, which was parked to the side of the building. What really ticked him off was that he didn't feel relieved about avoiding this morning's meeting with Serena.

She was really driving him crazy.

With a grim expression, he started the motor home's engine and drove away.

Lola telephoned Serena shortly after Trav's call. "So, how's the lawyering business, coz?" she asked brightly.

"Things are looking fairly good, Lola. I have two clients and I've hired a secretary. She starts work on Monday."

"A secretary? Anyone I know?"

"Her name is Karen Breen."

"Nope, don't know any Breens. Well, good for you. Two clients and the doors barely open. Good job, kiddo. Listen, the reason I called—you know that article about Travis Holden that Kathleen wrote and published? Well, it's been picked up by most of the Montana newspapers and published all over the state."

"Really? How do you know that?"

"Kathleen told me. She's very excited about it. But she said she should have anticipated the possibility when Holden is so well-known in Montana."

"I'm sure he'll appreciate the free advertising," Serena said dryly. "I can't say I'm thrilled about *my* less than flattering picture being spread across the state, however. My name, either."

"Serena, there's nothing wrong with that picture of you, and what's so terrible about your name getting around the state? You could use some free advertising, too. Anyone in business or a profession could."

"Neither the caption under that photo nor Kathleen's article mentioned my profession, Lola."

"Are you sure? Seems as though I remember..."

"I'm sure. What you're remembering is the announcement I put in the paper. A later edition, incidentally."

"Oh. Well, anyway, Kathleen expects some other repercussions from Holden's brave deed."

"What kind of repercussions?"

"Official recognition of Trav's courage in risking his own life to save people he didn't even know. On the county level, at least, although she's also thinking of something on the state level. She even told me about a national group who recognizes and rewards special achievements by ordinary citizens. It's called the American Institute for Public Service, with headquarters in Washington, D.C. Did you happen to hear about it while you lived there?"

"Yes, I believe I did," Serena said slowly. She couldn't pinpoint how, where, when or why she'd heard of the institute, but the name was familiar. "Surely Kathleen's sights aren't set that high."

"I think there's no limit to how high Kathleen's sights might go, coz. I have to agree that recognition on the national level would put Rocky Ford on the map."

"A fleeting moment of fame for our little town? Lola, you've never given two whits what anyone thought about anything. Has marriage changed you that much?"

To Serena's surprise, Lola sighed in her ear. And it didn't sound very much like an ecstatic sigh, either.

"Serena, you're probably the only person I can talk to about really personal things, and to tell you the truth, I wasn't going to mention it to you, either. The fact is...I...I have a problem. Could I come to your office?"

"Of course. Come right away."

"I will. Thanks, coz. See you in a few minutes."

It wasn't until Serena was hanging up that she remembered Trav was coming over with his car-lot brochure listing addresses and phone numbers.

But did it really matter if Lola was here at the same time?

Serena picked up a pen, then threw it down again with an exasperated grimace. Why on earth was she disappointed that she wouldn't be alone when Trav arrived?

Ten minutes later she looked up from her desk to see a balding, heavyset man with a wide grin walking in.

"Serena Fanon?" he said by way of a greeting.

Serena got to her feet. "Yes, I'm Serena. Can I do something for you, sir?"

"No, but I can do something for you." He chuckled at his own wit, then held out a glossy, folded paper. "Trav asked me to bring this to you. I'm Darrel Endicott, manager of Holden's Used Car Lot."

Serena stared as though struck dumb until she realized that Mr. Endicott was staring back. Somehow she regained enough composure to take the brochure from the man's very large hand.

"Should I assume that Trav has already left town?" Serena's voice sounded strained and not altogether steady, and she was glad that Mr. Endicott didn't know her well enough to tell that she wasn't speaking normally. But this felt like a personal affront. Trav had said he would drop off the brochure himself, then sent one of his employees to do it instead. It could only mean that he'd decided against seeing her.

"Already gone," Endicott confirmed jovially. "Well, hope to see you again, Serena. Trav said you could be calling the car lot, so we'll probably be talking to each other."

"It's possible," she said weakly, sinking back into her chair as Darrel Endicott walked out. "Oh! Thanks for the brochure," she called, then wondered if Endicott had heard her.

It didn't matter, she told herself with a spate of anger suddenly coursing through her veins. How dare Trav do this to her? She had every right to avoid a womanizer like him, but what had *she* done to annoy him? And if she did annoy him in some unimaginable way, why had he hired her? He was just too erratic to understand.

She was still muttering under her breath when Lola rapped on the doorframe. "You've only been open for business a few days and you're already talking to yourself?" Lola said teasingly.

Serena took a calming breath. "Just a little. Come in and sit down."

"Mind if I close the door?"

"Leave that one open. We'll sit in the other office. This is really the secretary's desk anyway."

Lola came in and looked around, though she had visited the office once before, as had the whole family. "It really is nice, Serena. Very pleasant."

"Thanks." Serena led the way to her own office. "Have a seat."

Lola chose a chair and sat down while studying her cousin across the desk. "You look harried. Anything you want to talk about?"

"You came here to tell me your problem. Let's deal with one at a time, okay?"

Lola's eyes narrowed slightly. It was obvious that she was wondering what Serena's problem was. "Agreed," she said evenly. "One problem at a time. Should I go first?"

"Please do. Oh, would you like some coffee?"

"Is it fresh?"

"Hours old, but I could make a fresh pot. It would only take a few minutes."

"Thanks, but I'll just have some water. Do you have any bottled water in that little fridge?"

"Sure do." Serena got up and returned to the desk with two small bottles of water. "Here you go." She handed one to Lola.

They twisted the caps off the bottles and drank. "Hmm, good," Lola said.

"Now, what's going on with you?" Serena asked. "You and Duke aren't having problems, are you?"

Lola looked aghast. "Lord, no. This problem is strictly my own. Duke's involved, of course, just as he's involved in every phase of my life. But I can't go to him with this, Serena. Let me explain."

She took another drink from her bottle, then set it on the edge of the desk. "When Duke and I were dating—well, I'm not sure you can call what we did dating. I mean, I think of dating as two people spending time together because they enjoy each other's company. We sort of danced around each other rather than dated in the traditional sense."

Sort of like Trav and me, Serena thought uneasily.

Lola continued. "Anyway, as things became more serious with us, Duke proposed. By then I was head over heels but apparently still looking for reasons to say no." Lola got up and walked to the window. "Not every detail of those days is clear in my mind, but I remember him saying something—more than once—about my selling the store. I told him I would never sell the store and if his 'courtship' was based on that assumption, then he could just forget the whole damned thing."

Serena was truly stunned. "Are you telling me that you and Duke had a stormy, uh, courtship?" It really was similar to what was happening to her and Trav. Good Lord, this was scary.

"Stormy, passionate and sometimes downright impossible," Lola replied. She returned to her chair, which she moved closer to the desk before sitting on it. Then she laid her forearms on the desk and looked her cousin in the eye. "Here's my problem. When Duke proposed in one breath and insisted I sell my store in the next, I turned him down flat. I'm not sure what changed his mind, but the next time I saw him, he said the store didn't matter and that I could keep it for the rest of my life. I was what mattered to him.

"Well, I was crazy in love with him, and all of our hurdles had suddenly vanished. We were married and I'm still crazy about him. The problem is, I think he likes my having the store now and I . . . I'd like to sell it." Her voice became softer. "Serena, I want to have a baby."

"And you think Duke would object to your selling the store? Lola, that man is so gone on you he wouldn't object to anything you wanted to do." Serena grinned wryly. "He especially wouldn't object to the two of you having a baby. I think you're making a mountain out of a molehill. Talk to him the minute you get home tonight. Tell him you've decided to sell the store. Tell him you want a baby. God, Lola, you don't have a problem. What you've got is a husband who worships you. You've got the world by the tail. What woman could ask for more?"

"You really think it's that simple?"

"Of course it's that simple."

"But won't he think I'm a little bit ridiculous. Serena, I fought like a tiger to keep my store. Now, out of the blue, I want to sell it. I don't want him thinking that I'm one of those women who doesn't know *what* she wants."

"I don't think he'd care if you were. He adores you, Lola. The love between you two is so obvious when you're together it's almost nauseating." Serena's smile told Lola she was only teasing and in truth was happy for her.

Lola sat back, taking her bottle of water with her. After a swallow, she smiled. "I feel a lot better. Now, let's see if I can solve your problem as easily as you solved mine."

"My . . . problem?" Uneasy again, Serena squirmed in her chair. She couldn't discuss Trav and confess how confused she felt about him, not even to Lola.

But she had indicated having a problem, so she thought fast. "Well, I'm not really sure this should be considered a problem—my problem, at least—but let me ask you something. Have you ever gotten the feeling that Dad is a little too reticent about my mother's death?"

A frown appeared between Lola's green eyes. "I'm not sure I understand."

"He won't talk about her, Lola. He never would. Were you ever there when Ron or I would ask him something about her? Ron didn't ask often that I knew of, but every so often, I tried to talk about her. Last night it happened again. This time all I did was mention her in a perfectly normal context, something about wishing she were alive to see Ron's adorable little son. Dad went absolutely rigid, Lola. It lasted for only a second, but I definitely saw it happen."

"What did he say?"

"He said nothing. He was stiff one second and as relaxed as Candy and myself the next." Serena released a long breath, as though she'd been holding it. After a moment, she added quietly, "I can't help feeling there's something about Mother's death that he hasn't told us. Am I crazy?"

"Well, you're not crazy, so you can eliminate that notion. Serena, how can I help you on this? When I came to live with you, my mind was on my own dead parents. I never knew your mother and, to tell you the truth, I only have a few memories of any of you mentioning her."

"I never knew her, either," Serena said in a low voice. "What I can't understand is why Dad won't tell me every minute detail of their life together. He must have lots of memories, Lola, wonderful memories."

"And sad memories, Serena. Many sad memories. Don't try to make him talk about it. Maybe he can't. He's lived alone except for us kids for so many years. He must have loved your mother too much to ever marry again. That's a special kind of love, Serena. Don't pressure him into talking about her."

Serena sat there for a long time thinking about it. Lola finished off the water in her bottle, and still Serena sat there.

Finally she drew a breath and nodded. "You're right. The last thing I would ever knowingly do is hurt Dad in any way. If he can't talk about Mother, then I just have to accept it. Maybe someday he'll feel differently."

Lola smiled in empathy. "Maybe he will."

Chapter Twelve

The literature Kathleen sent about the community-betterment association impressed Serena. The group appeared to have excellent goals: to maintain and expand leisure and job-related activities for teenagers, to finance a better-equipped and larger senior citizens' center, to provide organized sports and activities for young adults and to someday have an arts-and-crafts center for everyone's use. Also they were nudging local, county and state governments about poor street lighting in certain areas, zoning regulations, a new elementary school and the neglect of some of the city roads, which were in dire need of repair.

In the private sector, they were adamant about Rocky Ford needing an airstrip. Nothing large, certainly not for jumbo jets. But an airstrip to accommodate the smaller commuter planes would be of great benefit to the town's progress. According to Kathleen's data, there were several companies doing a feasibility study on a modest airport for Rocky Ford at the present time. It was explained that the group felt this project was not practical as a tax-related venture; thus they were dealing strictly with private industry on it.

And last but certainly not least, the group was determined that every person of legal age in the county be registered to vote. Serena heartily approved.

In fact she approved of it all. She decided there on the spot that she would join the association; she could see now why Lola had done so.

And, of course, she would attend the honorary dinner they were giving for Trav. Charlie was right. There should be some kind of formal recognition of Trav's courageous act, and she would not let personal feelings get in the way of the respect that she and everyone else in town owed him.

By the time the nineteenth of the month rolled around, her attitude toward Trav was different anyway. They had talked on the phone several times, and it had been strictly business between them. Obviously Trav wanted it that way as much as she did. That morning in his motor home had been a fluke, an error in judgment they both regretted.

Well, she could live with that. He was a valued client, and she would treat him as such. And if she awoke in the night at times to remember the wildness and passion between them that morning, who would ever know?

She suspected he was in town early in the day on the nineteenth but she had heard nothing from him by noon. Karen Breen was proving to be a capable secretary, but she didn't work Saturdays. Serena always went to the office on Saturday, as she was doing her own cleaning to save on the cost of a janitor. People were beginning to call. Her client list was growing. But money was going to be tight for a long time yet, and she didn't mind vacuuming, dusting and emptying wastebaskets in the least.

The two offices were spick-and-span and she was just getting ready to leave when someone knocked on the door. On Saturdays, Serena kept her outer door locked. She wore old clothes for cleaning—today a pair of baggy, ancient cutoff jeans and a white sleeveless T-shirt—and she preferred not having a potential client come walking in and seeing her looking as though she'd just cleaned the office.

She frowned at the door as the person knocked again. Then, after a few seconds, someone called, "Serena, your car's in the parking lot. Who or what are you hiding from?"

Her heart nearly stopped. Trav! No call, no warning, no nothing. Just dropping in as though she should be glad to see him. Who did he think he was?

The phrase *valued client* flashed through her mind, and she clenched her jaw in resentment.

She approached the door. "The office isn't open on weekends."

He laughed. Laughed at her silly, lame excuse for not opening the door. "I really hate you," she whispered, knowing full well that she was going to have to let him in and cringing when she visualized him seeing her like this. Her hair was tied back from her face with a piece of yarn, and the little makeup she'd used this morning had to be gone. Not to mention her clothes! Well, from now on, she wouldn't wear the oldest, most unbecoming things she owned just because they were comfortable for cleaning.

"Come on, open the door," Trav said. "I've got some papers for you. I swear I'll only take a minute of your time." He had worked very hard at putting Serena in perspective during his absence, and he felt pretty certain that he could see her now without being swamped by confusing emotions. Their telephone conversations had helped him reach that conclusion; neither of them had even hinted at anything remotely personal. Obviously Serena wanted a strictly business relationship, same as him. As different as they were from each other, it was their only sensible course.

But why wouldn't she open her office door? Was she really so rigid that she wouldn't see anyone outside of normal business hours?

"Ridiculous," Trav muttered, and rapped again. Actually, pounded was more like it. "Serena, for pity's sake! This will only take a minute."

Gritting her teeth, she turned the dead-bolt knob and yanked the door open. Her expression wasn't exactly welcoming; she was, after all, embarrassed about her appearance and resentful that he had caught her red faced and in what she considered a none-of-his-business situation. Did he need to know she cleaned her office? Not on a bet, she thought angrily.

"What is it?" she snapped, letting her feelings show.

If Trav noticed her bad humor, he didn't let on. He was staring, almost openmouthed. "You...you look terrific," he finally stammered. It was true. She *didn't* look like a lawyer. In fact the phrase *the girl next door* popped into his mind and wouldn't leave. God, she was gorgeous. Not movie-star glamorous without her usual makeup and stylish clothes, which was the only way he'd seen her so far, but fresh faced and more beautiful than any woman he'd ever known.

His compliment made Serena think about lies and liars. There was very little she despised more than a liar, even when the lie was a cover-up for shock. Yes, he was shocked; she could see it in his eyes.

"Thanks a bunch," she drawled, deliberately sarcastic. Then that phrase *valued client* came to mind, and she changed her tone abruptly and drastically. "What can I do for you?"

Trav was confused again. This woman with the red gold curls, perfect nose and long slender body had the power to demolish every promise he'd made himself, every common-sense argument he'd devised against too much personal involvement and, to top it off, was beginning to change the definition of the word *commitment* for him from "ball and chain" to "happily ever after."

Silently he held out the file folder in his hands. "Uh, I ran across these the other day in a cupboard in the motor home.

Figured you'd need them." He hesitated a second. "Do you want the door locked again?"

Her answer was an absently murmured "Yes. As I said, I'm not open for business on weekends." Serena took the folder and scanned the papers within, only barely aware of Trav throwing the dead bolt. The papers were varied and related to several different lawsuits against Holden's Used Cars, apparently items he hadn't filed in their appropriate folder when he'd received them.

She closed the folder. "I'll put this in my desk for now." She started for the connecting door between the two offices and realized Trav was still standing in the same spot as when he'd come in, and he didn't give her the impression of impending departure. She stopped and turned. "Was there something else?"

His gaze slid down to her toeless sandals and then back up to her hair. Her cheeks took on a crimson hue as she recalled telling him to relock the door. Very easily he could have misinterpreted that request. *Now what?* she thought before deciding that this was one of those situations that demanded a show of strength.

She lifted her chin defiantly. "Must you stare? Maybe you're waiting for an apology for the way I'm dressed. It so happens—"

He took three long strides to where she stood. "Why would I want you apologizing for looking drop-dead gorgeous?" he asked in a voice that was suddenly husky and sensuous.

"That's absurd," she snapped. "I know how I look." His nearness was making her nervous. And there was a look in his eyes that she'd seen before, too. Damn!

He stepped closer and slipped his hand around the curve of her nape, causing a ripple of utter sexuality to travel her spine. In the wink of an eye, her show of strength completely vanished.

"Trav...don't," she whispered. How could he change her from a thinking, intelligent woman to a simpering idiot with just a touch?

No, it wasn't just his touch doing it; the expression in his eyes would undermine any woman's principles.

"Don't what?" His voice was as whispery as hers, only deeper. Much deeper and very suggestive. "Serena..." He urged her forward and moved closer to her at the same time. She knew he was going to kiss her and she also knew she should stop him.

She did nothing except stand there with a racing pulse, staring into his magnetic eyes and waiting for his mouth to reach hers. The first touch of his lips on hers brought a moan of agonized delight from her throat. He dropped all restraints and gathered her into a tight embrace that had them each straining to the other. His mouth opened and so did hers. Their tongues met and danced together. The file folder slipped from Serena's hand to the floor, and she never even noticed it was gone. Trav walked them into her office and closed that door, as well. "Just in case Karen decides to drop in. She has a key to the outer door, doesn't she?"

"Yes," Serena mumbled thickly.

A hunger was building between them that both recognized and neither could prevent or even slow down. Breathing hard, they sank to their knees on the carpet. With his hands stroking her back, Trav buried his face in the sensual curve of her jaw and shoulder, breathing in her scent, forgetting everything he knew about anything, certainly forgetting that he wanted to remain a single, uncommitted man. The only thing in his mind was that he had to have this luscious lady. Right now. Right here. Her feverish response told him that she was feeling the same about him, an exciting, mind-blowing thought that made him hot enough to explode.

They were at the undressing stage, each groping and tugging at the other's clothing. Trav pulled Serena's T-shirt over her head and tossed it on the carpet. She had his shirt unbuttoned and yanked it down his arms. Breathing loudly and erratically, they stopped to kiss again, to nip at each other's lips, to kiss foreheads, cheeks and chins. Their need for each other was unquestionable, and if there were any questions roaming their dazed minds, the answers didn't seem at all crucial.

It was only a few minutes later that they were stark naked and lying on the carpet. That is, Serena was on the carpet; Trav was on top of her. Looking into his eyes, she slid her legs apart, giving him every freedom and an invitation besides to finish what he'd started.

He licked his lips and pressed them to hers. Then he whispered, "I've never, ever known anyone like you."

Before she could formulate a sensible response to a statement she found both challenging and debatable, he had thrust into her. Supporting his weight on his elbows, he held her face in his hands and stared into her eyes while he moved.

Her mouth was partially open—it was the only way she could breathe—and no human heart could beat any harder than hers was doing. Was she falling in love with him? Looking into his captivating eyes while he made love to her gave the idea credence.

But she wasn't ready yet to fall in love again. Tears filled her eyes.

Trav's own eyes narrowed at the sight of the flood in hers. But he didn't ask why she was crying. She wasn't pushing him away, and that was all that mattered right now. She was probably merely emotional about the intensity of their passion anyway; Lord knew he was.

He altered his position by sliding his hands under her hips and laying his head beside hers. His eyes closed as his pleasure expanded. Her legs lifted to clasp around him. Her fingers kneaded and massaged his back. Little whimpers came from her. He was in heaven.

"I could do this forever," he whispered.

"An ambitious project," she whispered back.

"You're special, Serena."

"Am I? In what way?"

"Do you want specifics?"

"Yes."

His voice became lower, more ragged. "You're just wet enough and you're tight. Really tight." He felt her swift intake of air. "You wanted specifics."

"Guess I didn't anticipate..." She released the breath. "It's okay. I asked for it." She took his face between her hands and looked into his eyes. "Did I ask for this, too?"

He couldn't stop moving. "Did either one of us ask for it? Some things just happen, sweetheart."

"And the two of us naked and...and making love on the floor of my office just happened, all on its own?"

"I think it did." The pupils of his eyes had grown darker than normal. "It'll happen again, too, Serena. Again and again. Whenever we're alone. You probably won't want to believe this, but I didn't come here with seduction in mind." He released a long breath and pushed into her as far as he could go. "Can't say I'm sorry about it, though." Recalling some of his vows since the last time he'd seen her and wondering if he'd feel like renewing them later, he smirked a little. "Not right now I'm not."

She frowned. "And just how should I take that?"

He looked at her for a long time, then kissed her lips. Coming up for air, he whispered, "You shouldn't take anything but me right now, which you're doing incredibly well." He buried his face in her throat and groaned, "Oh, baby, you're the best."

Maybe she was and maybe she wasn't, but right at the moment, she was too far gone to care. The ultimate ecstasy was creeping up on her, and she had to have it. It was gathering within her, still not defined or guaranteed. She lost all interest in talking or anything but that torturous need in the pit of her stomach and between her legs, and the only sounds coming out of her mouth were pleas for the final rapture.

Trav felt powerful because he'd brought her to this point. She might be snooty and haughty in her business clothes, but naked and under him, she was all woman. *His* woman.

He took her to the next plateau, the one she needed so badly, slowly and seductively. By the time she cried out her release, tears were streaming down her cheeks, and she was clutching at him with frantic fingers. His own climax was a roaring, rousing success, and he collapsed on the floor beside her, smugly satisfied with his performance and the enormous pleasure they had both attained.

Serena lay with her arm crooked over her eyes. It seemed to take forever to breathe normally again. She knew Trav was laying next to her—she could feel the warmth of his body even without touching him. Neither spoke or moved for a long time, and during that time, Serena's mind returned to reality. She had done it again—made love with a client. Made love with Trav. On the floor of her own office, for God's sake. And she had even wondered about falling in love with him. Oh, yes, she remembered every tiny detail of her own wanton behavior and certainly she remembered Trav's remarks. What was that one about not regretting what they were doing right then? Did that mean he was re gretting it now that it was over?

She sat up. His eyes opened and he smiled. "Hi."

A bit of wisdom struck her then: acting like a deflowered virgin at this point would only make her look like a fool. Trav hadn't forced her this time any more than he had the first. Even though she didn't quite grasp the rules, it would be much better if she played his game rather than got all indignant and righteous.

"Hi." She forced her lips to smile back at him, and it wasn't at all easy to do, either. Actually she was in the biggest, most disturbing quandary of her life. Did she like Trav or did she only like his body?

He took her arm. "Come on down here."

"Um, I really shouldn't...." Her objection came too late. She was lying down again, this time in his arms.

Her head was on his shoulder, and he stroked the hair back from her forehead with a gentle hand. "We need to talk, Serena. Something's happening with us—"

She cut in, speaking hurriedly, nervously. "Yes, but I don't see any good reason to talk about it. I mean, it's nothing serious."

A frown appeared between Trav's eyes. Maybe she was right. Didn't he prefer it that way? Nothing serious. Some great sex and no commitments. Yes, he did prefer it that way. Why in hell was he trying to make her talk about it? Thank God she was a woman with good sense. They could see each other whenever he was in town, play around when they felt like it and live their own lives beyond that.

He stretched contentedly. Actually he already felt like playing around again. Serena was a very potent lady, and holding her naked body was arousing him with surprising speed and intensity, considering how drained and spent he'd felt only a few minutes ago.

Dipping his head, he licked the nipple of her left breast.

Her eyes widened in alarm as a sensual shudder passed through her body. "Trav..."

"Just relax, sweetheart. We don't have to talk about it, but we sure do have to do it." He grinned beguilingly.

Her mind raced, searching for a way around this. "I...I really have to get home."

"More than you have to make love with me?" he said in a husky, teasing tone.

"We already made love." She tried to wriggle away from him, but he threw one of his legs over hers. It was then that she felt how aroused he was again.

Boldly he rubbed his erection against her hip. "Hmm, you feel good."

So did he. Serena shut her eyes as a delicious, weakening sensation began gaining prominence in her system. She knew what it was: desire. Again. So soon. *Much* too soon.

Something within her rebelled. Was she going to permit two missteps to develop into a full-blown affair? My God, her father would be appalled if he ever heard about it. And if it went on for long, everyone would hear about it. It certainly wouldn't help her burgeoning law practice to be known as Trav Holden's mistress.

Careful to give him no warning of her intentions, she rolled away from him and hastily got to her feet. "I really have to go," she said, avoiding looking at him while she pulled on her clothes.

Trav hoisted himself to an elbow and silently watched her scurrying around for a few minutes. He'd been making her want him again, and she had suddenly reversed herself on him. Maybe he would never completely understand Serena, but then she might not ever totally comprehend him, either. Fine. That could be the very best kind of relationship a man and woman could have.

Pushing himself to his feet, he picked up his briefs. "I have a dinner to attend tonight. Maybe you've heard about it."

She was getting into her T-shirt, sliding it down over her head. "Yes, I've heard about it."

"How about going with me?"

Serena smoothed the T-shirt down her torso. "I'm already going, with my cousin Lola and her husband. Besides, you'll be seated in a place of honor. A date couldn't sit with you."

"She could if I insisted."

Serena gave him a startled look. "Well, whatever you do, don't insist. Do you think I want our . . . our—I don't even know what to call it—spread all over town?"

Trav had just pulled on his jeans. Zipping his fly, he leaned against a wall and folded his arms, narrowing his eyes to hit her with a probing look. "You don't know what to call what we've been doing?"

"Not without getting pornographic, I don't," she said sharply. Going to her desk, she fished a hairbrush out of a drawer. "Or clinical," she added while furiously attacking her mop of curls with the brush.

"So making love is either pornographic or clinical to you?"

"No," she said with a resentful nuance to the word. "But I thought we were talking about what *we've* been doing." She suddenly felt limp and sat on the edge of the desk. "Listen to me. You're my client. What's more, you're my most important client. Ethically I shouldn't be sleeping with *any* client, but only a really stupid lawyer jeopardizes his or her professional relationship with an important client by...by..." Exasperated, she rolled her eyes. "You know what I mean."

"I don't think anyone could ever call you stupid, so if it's so ethically incorrect for a lawyer to cross a professional line with a client, how come you keep doing it with me?"

She did her best to appear calm and collected. "I'm not going to do it again. I hope you can understand how I feel about this and..." Her jaw dropped. "What's so funny?"

He was laughing like crazy. Walking over to her, he chucked her under the chin. "You are, sweetheart. I'll finish dressing and get out of your hair, but I'll see you at that dinner tonight." Leaning forward, he planted a kiss on her lips. "I can hardly wait until the next time we're alone, and if you've got one truly honest bone in your body, you'll admit the same thing."

Chapter Thirteen

Serena railed at herself all afternoon. Trav had made no noises regarding anything serious or permanent between them, so he was obviously content with the status quo: an occasional roll around some bed or whatever was handy, in today's case, the floor—and an attorney-client relationship the rest of the time. Yes, he'd suggested they talk, but did they really have anything to discuss, other than her stupidity? How could she be so damned dumb? Did she have some critical flaw when it came to choosing men? Charlie was such a sensible, steady person that this type of flaw—if she had inherited it—could only have come from her mother.

And yet she knew deep down that her mother had been the epitome of gentle and highly moral womankind. Anyone who had died so young hadn't had the chance to pick up imperfections, especially an awful flaw such as Serena felt was her affliction.

This flaw had some very disturbing aspects. First of all, she had never been promiscuous, not in high school, college or law school. She had never just slept around for sexual gratification. The only men she had made love with had meant something to her. She had believed herself in love with them.

But she wasn't in love with Trav Holden!

Or was she?

The subject in general and those questions in particular had her going in circles. She was glad when Lola called around three, and hoped her cousin would take her mind off of Trav and men, period.

Lola rushed right into her reason for the call. "I'm still at the store but I'm leaving for home in a few minutes to get ready for tonight. What I wanted to tell you was that I mentioned selling the store to Duke, and all he said was, 'Do whatever makes you happy, honey.' Now, don't you think he would've had more to say about it? I mean, before I agreed to marry him, he was downright nasty about it. Said *his* wife would never hold down a job, et cetera, et cetera. Then he did this sudden about-face on me and he's been sweet as pie about it ever since. I swear I don't know what to think anymore. Help me out, coz. What do *you* think about it?"

Serena groaned inwardly. She was the last one to be giving another woman advice about men. Especially today.

But she couldn't ignore Lola's plea. Quickly she searched her brain, adding up what she'd seen of Duke and Lola's relationship. It seemed solid, she realized, solid and good. Their love for each other couldn't be questioned, not when one saw them together.

"Let me say that in my opinion you are a very fortunate woman, Lola," she said quietly. "I think Duke wants your happiness above all else. And I think he realized that marvelous fact when you were balking about getting rid of the store before you agreed to the marriage. It was why he did that about-face and why he won't tell you what to do now."

Lola was silent for a long moment. "Lola?"

"That's a lot to take in, but it makes sense. I've got to think about it. We're still picking you up at quarter to six tonight, right?"

"I'll be ready."

"See you then. Bye. Gotta run."

"Bye." Serena put the phone down with a heavy sigh. Why was it so simple to solve Lola's problems and so impossible to do anything about her own?

The sky had clouded over and was threatening rain by five. Serena ignored the good smell of Candace's pot roast coming from the kitchen and finished getting ready for the evening ahead. Because the temperature had dropped with the overcast sky, she chose a summer-knit, plum-colored dress with long sleeves and a high neck. Montana evenings could be chilly even in August, and from the look of the sky, one could hardly doubt that a good downpour was in the making.

Ready at five-thirty, she sat on the back porch and watched the dark thunderheads rolling overhead. Every so often, lightning streaked through the clouds. It was the kind of sky most artists would love to capture on canvas, Serena thought while admiring the fierce beauty enveloping the area.

The screen door opened, and Charlie came out. "Candace said supper'll be ready in about ten minutes. Mind if I sit with you?"

Serena moved over on the porch swing. "Of course I don't mind."

Charlie sat down and studied the sky. "Looks like we're in for a drenching."

"I've been watching the lightning. It's beautiful, isn't it?"

"Sure is." Charlie chuckled. "This kind of lightning is, anyway. When it starts aiming for the ground, it's not quite so pretty." He cleared his throat and turned his head to look at his daughter. "Honey, has something been bothering you lately? Oh, I know you're working hard to get your practice going, but you seem so... I don't know...*distracted* might be the right word."

She should have known Charlie would catch on to her changing moods. None of them—her, Lola or Ron—had ever had much luck in keeping Charlie in the dark about something.

And yet there were some things a woman couldn't discuss with her father.

No, that wasn't the truth of it at all. She couldn't discuss Trav and their inappropriate behavior with anyone. After all, he was a ladies' man, and she was just another notch on his bedpost, hardly a relationship to boast about.

Preparing herself to lie, she took her dad's hand and held it. "Thanks for asking, but my only distraction is my work. I guess I'm worrying about it a lot more than I anticipated."

"Serena, if it's money..."

"It's not. I mean, money's going to be a problem for years yet, but it's my problem. At least I'd like it to be my problem." She smiled. "Is that okay with you?"

"I don't like you being upset and unhappy."

Was she really that transparent? "I know you don't," she murmured softly. Even though it had only been months, she was starting to find it difficult to remember when she hadn't been unhappy and upset. That had to change. She couldn't live out her life unhappy because of one man's deceit.

But deep down, she knew it was possible. And meeting men like Trav—dammit, sleeping with men like Trav—was not going to lighten her mood.

She changed the subject. "Remember when I told you about Tom Powers dropping in and introducing himself?"

"I remember."

"Well, he asked if he could call, and I told him yes. I even gave him my card and I haven't heard a word. I probably should have asked you this before, but is he married?"

"Powers? I don't know about that, Serena, but I do know he's old enough to be your grandfather."

Serena couldn't help laughing. "Dad, he is not. He's older than me, of course, but he's really very attractive." Her smile faded. "And he's a lawyer."

Charlie suddenly looked exultant. "That's it, isn't it? There you were, in Washington, D.C., with lawyers and politicians everywhere you looked. People who spoke your language, people you could relate to. Now, here you are in Rocky Ford, and there's no one to talk to. That's why you're not happy, isn't it? No wonder Tom Powers seems attractive to you."

Serena was embarrassed to find herself choking up. What Charlie had said, after all, did have a ring of truth, even if it was only a part of her misery.

A long stretch of silence ensued, until Charlie asked, "Why don't you like Trav Holden, Serena? Mind you, I'm not saying you should. But he seems like a real nice guy, and I can't help wondering why you and him didn't hit it off."

"Oh, Dad," she said on a disconsolate sigh. "Why don't any two people hit it off? I don't know. Trav and I are just very different." *Not too different to make love on the floor of my office,* she thought wryly.

She was relieved to hear Duke's huge four-wheel-drive pull into the driveway. "They're here," she said, getting to her feet, then bending over to kiss Charlie's cheek. "Good night, Dad. Have a nice evening."

"*You* have a nice evening," he called after her. "Let your hair down, kick up your heels and have some fun."

Serena glanced back at him in perplexity just before she went around the corner of the house, which put him out of sight.

In all of her life, Charlie had never told her to let her hair down, kick up her heels and have fun. What on earth had he meant by such unusual advice? He certainly couldn't have meant it the way it sounded! Not her own father.

Rocky Ford's community center was nothing to get excited about. It was a squat little building that had initially been constructed for a real-estate developer who had gone out of business within eight months of opening his doors. After him, the building had been rented to a half-dozen tenants, each of whom had left his mark in some unattractive way. When Kathleen's group had gotten control of it, their first chore had been to knock out some unnecessary walls and paint the entire interior a nice eggshell white. It was still a squat little building, but it was clean and functional for their particular usage. It did have one very big plus—a large parking lot, which was where Duke parked his vehicle at five minutes to six.

They got out, and Serena noted that Duke and Lola held hands while walking to the front door of the building. Someday, she thought with a feeling of pathos, a man would hold her hand and look at her the way Duke looked at Lola.

Unless, she thought cynically, she continued to be attracted to jerks just because they were sexy.

The muscles of her stomach clenched in self-recrimination, but there was no time for either recriminations or pity. They had reached the door, and Duke held it open. She smiled and murmured, "Thank you," as she moved past him.

"Looks like everyone's here," Lola said as she waved and smiled in several directions. Serena saw about three dozen people, standing around chatting and laughing, all dressed nicely. Some of them she knew, and some she didn't.

It took about thirty seconds for her to spot Trav. He was standing with a group that included Kathleen, the mayor and several business owners.

Lola began filling her in on group protocol. "Liquor, including beer, is taboo at any function of the group. But as you can see in that corner over there, there's plenty to drink." Serena saw a large coffeepot with accoutrements on a table and a refrigerator from which people helped themselves to soft drinks.

There were tables with tablecloths and place settings taking up much of the room. "Dinner will be catered," Lola told Serena. "This building doesn't have a kitchen, which is fine, as I don't think any of the members would want to do the cooking for these affairs. Actually a dinner like this is rare. I haven't been a member long enough to have gained firsthand knowledge, but that's what Kathleen told me."

Serena was only half listening. Her heart was first in her throat and then at the bottom of her stomach. Trav looked like a dream in a summer-weight gray suit that definitely had not come off the rack. His creases were knife sharp. His shirt and tie were coordinated perfectly with the suit, and his shoes, even from a distance, looked like the expensive handmade footwear so many of Washington's bigwigs favored.

What really did she feel for this man, other than a lust over which she obviously had no control? Just looking at him from across the room made her feel overheated and achy in some very telltale areas of her body. It was humiliating to lust after a man who considered her just another easy mark, she told herself angrily.

But why wouldn't he like women when so many of them threw themselves at him? Even Kathleen, who was years older than Trav, was gesturing and smiling with all of the feminine charm she possessed.

Serena turned away, disgusted with womankind in general, herself included. *We're all suckers for a handsome face and a good body, dammit, all of us.* Just then an explosion of lightning and thunder rocked the building as rain began pelting the walls with a fury and the lights went out.

"Serena?" It was Lola.

"I haven't moved. I'm right here," she replied.

Duke took her by the arm. "We're going to stay together. Serena's on my left, Lola, and you're on my right."

Lola laughed. "This is cozy, but now what? If the lights don't come back on, this party is over, my friends."

Kathleen was speaking loudly. "We have a few candles, so bear with us while we get them lighted."

It wasn't pitch-black, but it was close. Serena sensed someone on *her* left, and from the scent of his after-shave, she guessed his identity. Her pulse sped up. He was pressing against her, his side to her side, a safe enough position, but did she trust him to stay put in the dark?

"Are you okay?" he asked in a very low voice.

"I'm not afraid of the dark, Trav."

"Serena, who're you talking to?"

"Trav Holden, Lola."

"Oh, hi, Trav. I'm Lola Sheridan, Serena's cousin. The guy in the middle is my husband, Duke."

"Hello, Duke."

"Hi, Trav. We'll shake hands when there's some light."

Someone opened the door to look out and made an announcement. "It's coming down in buckets, and there isn't a light anywhere to be seen. It looks serious, folks."

Serena felt Trav's hand slowly sliding down her arm. "What're you doing?" she whispered, praying he was the only one who heard.

Somehow he found her ear in the dark and whispered into it, "I know what I'd like to be doing, but in reality, I was reaching for your hand. Do you object?"

"Yes."

His mouth was still at her ear, his breath sending shivers up and down her spine. "How much nerve have you got?"

"What?"

"A man and a woman could get away with an awful lot in this kind of dark, even in a room full of people. And wouldn't it be exciting?"

Her mouth dropped open. "Are you actually suggesting . . . ?"

"Put your hand on my fly, and you'll know precisely what I'm suggesting."

"Are you crazy? Yes, that's exactly what you are. Well, I'm not! Move away from me, Trav. You're pushing me into Duke."

Trav chuckled softly and he didn't move an inch, except for the hand on her arm, which kept sliding up and down her sleeve, brushing unnecessarily against her breast. "This evening is turning out much better than I thought."

"And you're not only crazy, you're a . . . a pervert!"

He laughed again, then groaned. "Hell's bells, good old efficient Kathleen's got a candle lit."

After the first small flame, others appeared, until there were about a dozen candles burning. The room was bathed in a soft yellow glow. Faces appeared.

"Oh, damn," Trav muttered as he put a few inches of space between him and Serena, who breathed much easier.

Then Kathleen located her guest of honor in the dim, flickering light and came over. "I'm terribly sorry about this, Trav. Oh, hello, Serena." She spotted Duke and Lola. "Hi. Isn't this a mess? At least the phone is working. Don is calling the power company right now to find out how long this outage is going to last."

"I suppose it's too late to cancel dinner with the caterer," Lola said.

"Definitely too late."

"Well, we can eat it by candlelight, Kathleen."

"We might have to."

Trav spoke up. "Kathleen, I'd like Serena to sit at my table. Will you please arrange it?"

Kathleen gave him a startled look, then pursed her lips with a display of complete and total disapproval. "I'll see what I can do. All of the place cards are out already, you know."

"I know, but I'm sure a smart lady like yourself can rearrange the seating to accommodate one small change," Trav said smoothly.

Lola nudged Duke in the ribs. Serena wished for invisibility. Trav grinned and Kathleen seethed. She finally agreed, then stiffly walked away.

Lola peered around her husband. "Good show there, Trav, old man. Except you really upset Kathleen."

Duke laughed. Trav laughed. Serena again wished for invisibility, and Lola giggled.

Kathleen's voice rose above all others. "We've spoken with a representative of the power company, and he said there's a transformer out. It was struck by lightning and will take several hours to fix or replace, depending on the damage. At any rate, we're going to be eating by candlelight, so if everyone holding a candle will put it on one table or another, we'll get started. Our food has been delivered, and we don't want it getting cold. I'm sure you can all find your places, so please, let's get started."

Trav took Serena's hand. "Come on. I know exactly where we'll be sitting."

"See you later," Lola said with a teasing lilt in her voice. "Have fun."

As she was being dragged along by Trav, Serena sent a dirty look over shoulder, hoping Lola would feel its impact, but she and Duke had already gone to their table.

When Serena was seated at the head table along with Trav, the mayor and his wife, Kathleen and two other couples, she realized that because of her intrusion, Kathleen was a fifth wheel. Where was her husband? Serena knew Kathleen was married, or she had been, the last Serena had heard. The present situation was abysmal. Obviously Kathleen had intended the table to seat eight people. Now there were nine, and Kathleen was the sore thumb, which she probably hated to the point of murderous impulses.

Serena physically cringed. She would never forgive Trav for this, never! Did he have no tact or sensitivity at all? Turning her face toward him, she hit him with a venomous look.

"Hey," he said quietly. "What's that all about?"

"You have humiliated me beyond words," she said, pasting on a phony smile when she realized Kathleen was watching. "We can't discuss it now," she added under her breath.

"Will you discuss it with me later?"

"Gladly!"

"Fine, then I'll drive you home, and you can lambaste the hell out of me."

"Suits me," she snapped.

It suited Trav, too, but he was too smart to say so. Instead he sat back and smiled convivially at his dinner companions around the table.

The evening was cut short by the raging storm outside and the lack of light inside. People wanted to get home, and so the speeches were very brief, even Kathleen's when she presented Trav with the Citizen of the Year Award, an attractive bronze plaque.

He thanked her and everyone else, then said, "If we weren't under siege here, I'd bore you all to tears with the story of my life." Everyone laughed and Trav grinned. "Maybe the storm is a blessing, huh? Anyway, thanks again. I sure never expected it." He sat down.

Kathleen rose again. "I guess that better be it for tonight, friends. See you all at our regular meeting. Oh, incidentally we have several guests tonight who are considering membership." She smiled charmingly. "To them, I have a special message. Please don't take the storm as a sign against joining."

Laughter broke out again as people began rising and heading for the door. It was still pouring, Serena saw as a couple dashed outside to their car.

"Ready to go?" Trav asked.

Lola walked up. "Ready, Serena?"

"I'm driving her home," Trav said. "She wants to give me hell."

"What?" Lola couldn't help laughing. "Serena, are you riding home with this peculiar man?"

"He is peculiar, isn't he?" Serena said dryly. "I don't know what to make of him and I definitely don't know if I should get in his car with him."

"You promised to give me hell and now you're reneging?" Trav said in a deliberately hurt voice.

"Yep, peculiar," Lola remarked. "Well, coz, it's up to you. Who're you riding with?"

"She's riding with me," Trav said. He turned slightly, and in the shadowy light, only Serena saw what was in his eyes.

Her knees got weak. "I guess I'm riding with him," she said in a voice so husky Lola's left eyebrow shot up.

"Call me tomorrow," she said to her cousin with a pointed look before turning to Trav. "Good night, Trav, and congratulations. That's a very nice plaque and an award to be proud of."

"Thanks. I think you're right. Good night, Lola, and say good-night to Duke for me. We'll all have to get together sometime."

With her gaze moving back and forth between her cousin and Trav Holden, Lola slowly nodded. "You know, I have the feeling we'll be doing that. Be careful out there tonight. Anything could happen on a rainy night like this."

Trav nodded, too, but his was accompanied by a very solemn expression. "You're right, Lola. Anything could happen."

Lola grinned. "And maybe it will, huh?" She walked away.

Chapter Fourteen

I should have told Lola more of what's been happening between Trav and me, Serena thought unhappily as Trav drove from the parking lot onto the street. *She only sees Trav's handsome, charming exterior and has no idea how... how chaotic I feel because of him.*

The windshield wipers were on high and slapping back and forth with frenetic energy. Uneasily she shifted her weight, seeking comfort beyond the physical. She shouldn't be in Trav's car; if she'd gone with Lola and Duke, they would be dropping her off by now.

Her gaze jerked to Trav as comprehension dawned. "This is not the way home. Where are you taking me?"

His profile looked granite hard. "Someplace where you can give me hell." His glance fell on her as he turned his head slightly. "Wasn't that what you wanted to do?"

Her lip curled in a sneer. "You think this is funny, don't you? You think *I'm* funny. For your information, groping in a public place just because the lights are out is not my idea of mature behavior *or* of fun."

"Don't forget the part about humiliating you beyond words."

"Take me seriously, you...you cretin! Why wouldn't I be humiliated over your forcing Kathleen to seat me at the head table? Do you have the slightest idea of the spot in which you put both her and me?"

"Didn't seem like a major problem to me."

"Oh, really. Could that be because you've always had everything your way, Mr. Big-shot Holden?"

He laughed. "Big-shot, huh? If you think that's an insult, you don't know me very well."

"Which I'm the first to admit. Take me home. Turn this damned car around and take me home!"

"How come you got in it? You knew I wasn't planning on taking you home right away. You knew exactly what was in my mind. It was in your mind, too—that's why you came with me. It's still in your mind, only you don't want other people thinking we might be sleeping together and you're trying to rectify something that won't be rectified by my taking you home. Everyone who was at the community center knows about us, baby, every single person. Why are you letting it bother you? They're all doing the same thing. Or they did when they were young enough to do it."

She was glaring at him. "You are the crudest individual I've ever known."

One of his questions remained in the back of his mind: why *had* she gotten into his car? Yes, she felt like telling him off; no one she'd ever known deserved a tongue-lashing more than him. But she couldn't deny there was more to it. She'd gotten in his car because of some extremely complex factors that she might never understand, but was it possible that he was right about her knowing his thoughts back at the center and she'd come with him because she wanted sex with him again?

She didn't like the way her mind was working, but fair was fair. He *did* affect her; he *did* make her think about sex; and last but certainly not least, he seemed to have some sort of magical power over her libido. It was not uplifting knowledge.

Trav's next comment floored her. "And you're the most dishonest individual *I've* ever known."

She all but exploded. "I am not dishonest! I have never stolen one thing in my entire life, and the few lies I tell are only to avoid hurting people's feelings."

"That really got your goat, didn't it? Well, let me tell you the facts as I see them, babe. You lie to yourself all the time. I've never known anyone who had to have life and reality so thickly sugarcoated before she could swallow it the way you do."

"That is the most insulting thing anyone's ever said to me! How dare you! You said I don't know you very well, which I freely admitted. Well, buster, let me tell you this— you don't know *me* at all!"

"I know what makes you moan and whimper." Reaching out, he laid his hand on her thigh.

She grabbed it and tried to throw it off, but now he had hold of her hand. "Let go, damn you," she shouted.

"Come closer." He tugged on her hand in an attempt to pull her across the seat. "Use the seat belt in the middle. I want you next to me."

"Go to hell!" He could hang on to her hand but he couldn't force her to sit next to him. She knew where he was taking her, too. To his motor home at Access Creek. She was full of anger, resentment and other passionate emotions, and her stomach ached and her hand tingled in his. If he got her out of this car and into his motor home, he would win again. She wouldn't be able to say no, and . . . and . . .

Let your hair down, kick up your heels and have fun to-night.

But Charlie hadn't meant for her to have the kind of fun Trav had in mind. No father would advise his daughter in that manner.

She gave her head a shake, hoping to clear it. It felt crowded with unanswerable questions, and they never budged. The back of her neck felt rigid as a board, and she lifted her free hand to rub it.

"You okay?" Trav asked.

"Do you care?" Her voice dripped sarcasm.

"I've been trying to figure that out," he said after a long hesitation that caused Serena to narrow her eyes in speculation.

Her heart skipped a beat. *Did* he care about her? Beyond the obvious, that is? She knew he wanted to take her to bed again. God, a complete moron would know that. But was more developing between them than the most potent chemistry she had ever encountered? Hadn't she been trying to figure out her feelings where he was concerned? It was damned startling to hear that he'd been doing the same. Maybe even unbelievable. Was this just another line?

"It's really coming down," Trav said, unexpectedly veering from the topic. His beautiful, costly motor home parked on the bank of Access Creek had come to mind, and he'd heard that the creek had a history of occasionally flooding low-lying areas during hard rainfalls. No one could say this wasn't a hard rainfall, not when the wipers couldn't begin to keep the windshield clear of the sheets of rain buffeting it. Whether it had rained enough to bring the creek to flood level was anybody's guess at this point, but it wasn't a question Trav could completely ignore, even for this scintillating conversation with Serena.

Her thoughts weren't on the storm. She wanted to hear more about his "caring," even though he'd admitted that he was trying to figure it out, indicating that he probably didn't know any more about it than she did. But was it just a line or the truth? Was he truly troubled over feelings for her he hadn't counted on?

Lord, how should she take that possibility? Did she want him troubled over serious feelings for her? Did she want him *having* serious feelings for her?

There was enough shock value in that whole idea that she didn't feel like fighting anymore. Trav barely noticed her silence. His mind was on the creek and what he might find when they got there. Just from the dark, heavy sky preceding the storm, he figured that he should have anticipated an unusual rainfall and moved the motor home to higher ground.

At long last, he turned onto Access Road; it was only a few more miles to the creek. He glanced at Serena and realized that she had fallen completely silent.

But he wasn't ready to reopen that argument. Later, maybe, once he knew the motor home was safe and secure. Actually he'd enjoyed arguing with Serena. He hadn't been at all angry and still wasn't. That silly argument had only been foreplay to him, and even now—though deeply concerned about his home on wheels—he had only the warmest feelings for Serena. And plans. Oh, yes, he had marvelous plans for the two of them. The motor home would be especially cozy with the rain pelting it. In truth he could hardly wait.

Approaching the creek area, he peered into the watery darkness. To his surprise, the lights he'd left on in the motor home were still on. "The electricity is on out here," he said. "Maybe it was never out."

"I'm sure the area draws its power from more than one transformer," Serena said absently. She was much more concerned with what appeared to be water up ahead. "Is there water on the road?"

"It's the creek." Trav stopped the car just short of the encroaching flood. "I've got to move the motor home. Will you drive the car and follow me out of here?"

"Where will you take it?"

Trav thought a minute. "Actually it doesn't have to go anywhere except to higher ground. I'll move it back from the creek a couple of hundred feet. My property slopes from its hind side to the creek, so the unit will be safe at the far end of the acreage.''

"Oh . . . fine.'' She was looking out the window at the distant lights of the motor home. "You're going to get very wet going from here to there.''

"Wet never killed anyone. See you in a few minutes.'' Opening the door of the car, he dashed out into the rain, pushing the door closed behind him.

"But your suit . . .'' she called too late. His beautiful suit was going to be ruined. Well, the cleaners could probably resurrect it, and certainly his motor home was a hundred times more valuable than the suit.

But just how deep was the water around the motor home? Squinting through the windshield, she tried to see the unit more clearly and to locate Trav to follow his movements.

She couldn't see him at all. Once out of the headlights, he had vanished. Her stomach lurched. What if he had tripped over something and fallen? Maybe his face was in the water right now and he was drowning! Her pulse ran wild with the shock of sudden fear. This was serious business. A flood, for heaven's sake, and he was out in it. Why had she so passively accepted his plan to rescue his motor home?

Every single chapter of her life that included Trav was a major event of one kind or another, she thought frantically. Did he live that way all the time? If so, he must function solely on adrenaline. What woman could keep up with that for long?

Sighing, she sat back and told herself to stop worrying. Trav was a big boy and had survived without her worrying about him for thirty-odd years. But her face was turned in the direction of the motor home, and she watched its wavery lights with an intensity she couldn't dispel.

Then she blinked several times in stunned dread; the lights had gone out!

What did this mean? she thought frantically. Had the power outage finally reached this area? Now she could see nothing of the motor home, and her heart felt as though it had risen to her throat to choke her.

That's it, she thought while groping for the door handle. She was not going to sit in this car, warm and dry, while something horrible was happening to Trav. Would he sit by and do nothing if it were her out there? After all, he'd rescued total strangers!

The second the door was open, Serena felt the rain. Not only was it coming down in buckets, but it was falling with a force that immediately caused it to penetrate her clothes. Even before she got the door closed, her face and hair were wet. And it was noisy, hitting everything so hard it was all she could hear.

She started walking in the direction of the motor home, relying entirely on memory as she could see nothing but falling rain. She was drenched to the skin almost instantly. Her hair was in her eyes, and she pushed it back.

Suddenly the motor home's headlights flashed on. Trav was behind the wheel. Serena was about twenty feet in front of the unit, feeling dazed and very much like a drowned rat. Trav jumped up from the plush driver's seat and ran for the side door.

"Serena!" he shouted as he ran into the rain again.

The headlights had surprised her. She didn't understand motor homes and other recreational vehicles, and she was trying to comprehend why the other lights had gone out when the headlights worked.

Trav ran up to her and grabbed her by the arm. "What in hell are you doing out here? Come on. Get inside before you drown."

She was shivering. The rain was cold and so was she. "That's...what I...thought happened...to you," she stammered.

He began steering her to the door of the motor home. "You thought I'd drowned? I told you to stay in the car. Don't you think I know what I'm doing with this unit? Hell's bells, woman, it's dark out here. What if you'd gone in the wrong direction? You could have ended up in the damned creek!''

"I knew the . . . right direction," she mumbled.

"Yeah, well a lot of people get disoriented and turned around in a storm like this." He couldn't be unkind enough to mention her poor sense of direction the night she'd led him on that merry chase in search of her "shortcut," but he was thinking about it. "Here's the door," he announced, pulling it open. "There are three steps up. Can you make it?" He didn't wait for an answer, just picked her up, threw her over his shoulder and took the steps into the unit.

Next she found herself deposited on a chair. "Stay there," Trav ordered, opening a cabinet for a blanket and tossing it at her. "The water's rising fast, and I've got to get this baby out of here." He hurried back to the driver's seat and started the engine.

Water was running off Serena. She saw the puddles forming on the carpeted floor and grimaced at the mess. The motor home began moving, and she hugged the blanket around herself and shivered. The big unit rolled and bounced along very slowly. Trav was intent on his driving and never glanced back at her. She was too cold and miserable to care if he ever looked at her, and she wondered whom to blame for this fiasco. She hadn't had to come with him, after all, no matter how charmingly he'd trapped her into it. She could be home right now, warm and snug in her own bed.

It seemed like an hour to Serena, but it was more like fifteen minutes before the unit stopped. She heard Trav heave a sigh of relief. The engine went dead, and the only sound was the rain battering the skin of the motor home.

Trav got up and surprised her again by turning on some lights inside the unit. She could see him now, and he was as soggy as her. But it was obvious he had other things on his mind than his personal discomfort.

"The unit's safe here. Listen, I'm going back for the car. While I'm gone, get out of those wet clothes. I'll get you something to put on." He went to the back of the motor home and returned with a robe, which he laid on the sofa. "I shouldn't be long."

He went outside and she was alone. This time she didn't try to watch him through a window. She was totally disgusted with herself. There hadn't been a reason in the world for her to get wet—apparently to the point of looking weak and pitiful—and then get thrown over Trav's shoulder like a sack of potatoes because he thought she couldn't climb a few steps on her own. She could have driven the car to this location and waited for him to get in and take her home.

She put the back of her hand to her forehead in a world-weary gesture. Did she ever do anything right where Trav was concerned?

When Trav came back, Serena was curled up on the sofa in his robe. Her wet clothes were in a plastic garbage bag, which she had found under the kitchen sink. Her wet hair was slicked back from her face, although the wisps around her face were already getting dry enough to curl. She looked positively adorable to Trav.

"Hi," he said, pulling the door closed behind him. "Are you okay?"

"I'm not drowned, even if I should be," she said with acute cynicism.

"You should have stayed in the car." Even while saying it, he was glad that she hadn't. She was out of her own clothes and wearing his robe, definitely a step in the right direction in his estimation. "I've got to get dry, too. I'll only be a few minutes."

"Don't hurry on my account."

She was not in the best of moods, he realized from the tone of her voice. But he had every confidence that he could cheer her up. Grinning to himself, he headed for the back of the unit.

Serena heaved an immense sigh. Was there ever a more stupid woman in the history of the world? How was she going to deal with Trav when she was wearing a robe with nothing under it? She may as well take it off right now, sit here naked and await her fate with a smile on her face. He was going to make a pass, and she was undoubtedly going to love it.

"Oh, damn," she moaned under her breath, laying her head back on the sofa and staring at the dim little lights in the ceiling. How could they be working without electricity? Were they hooked to a battery? This huge vehicle was completely confusing.

Trav returned wearing a robe, too. Great, she thought. Now they were both practically nude.

He stopped at a panel on the wall and pushed a button. A motor somewhere in the unit started, and he glanced at Serena with a smile. "The generator. We'll have better lighting and everything electrically powered will work now. I'm going to make a pot of coffee. I think we both could use something hot to drink."

Coffee? Serena's spirits perked up. A cup of hot coffee would be fantastic, and he didn't seem at all inclined to make a pass at her. Was it possible for this bizarre evening to end on an impersonal note?

A surge of disappointment struck then, surprising and annoying her. Okay, so she enjoyed sex with Trav, but wasn't she trying her level best to avoid an all-out affair with him? She should be grateful that he only intended warming her up with a cup of hot coffee when they both knew how many ways he could raise her temperature that were a lot more pleasurable.

She decided to try a normal conversation with him. "So you can have electricity either with the generator or by plugging in to…in to…" She was almost immediately lost. What was there at Access Creek to plug in to?

Trav nodded, though his gaze was on the coffeepot and what he was doing rather than on her. "I told you there was electricity on my land. Have you ever been to an RV park?"

"No."

"Well, it's really very simple. In a park, they run the utilities underground and everything pokes up every few feet so motor homes and such can hook on to them. It's the same principle with my land. There's a short power pole with a plug. This unit and every other unit has a long attached cord that connects with that plug. *Voilà!* Instant electricity.

"Now, since we're not connected with public power, I'm using the generator. Same result, only I'm also using some diesel from my fuel tanks to run it. Do you see the possible pitfalls?"

"Vaguely. But you had lights between the power pole and the generator."

"Battery operated. That's why they weren't very bright."

"Then these units have all sorts of power sources."

"Yes." Trav switched on the pot. "There. We'll have coffee in about ten minutes." He opened a cabinet and took out a bottle of brandy, which he set on the counter. "Coffee and brandy will chase any chill, believe me."

"It's knowing how much is enough that's important."

Trav turned and looked at her with a tongue-in-cheek expression. "Surely you're not thinking I would ply you with liquor to lure you into bed."

"In the blink of an eye," she said calmly.

He laughed with genuine relish. "You, Serena Fanon, are a doll."

"I think you have me confused with some of your other female friends," she said with a sniff. "I never have been, nor will I ever be, a doll."

"A matter of opinion, my sweet. Strictly a matter of opinion." He seated himself in a chair across from her spot on the sofa. His robe was knee length, and he wasn't completely dedicated to keeping it closed.

Serena looked everywhere but at his long, bare, muscular legs with their sprinkling of dark hair.

"Tell me about your family," she said, having hit on that subject as a safe one.

His expression changed before her very eyes, from amused and relaxed to hard as stone. "No family," he said brusquely.

"None at all?" she asked, taken aback by his answer. "Do you mean you're an orphan?"

"I mean that I have no family." He got up and checked the coffeepot, though it was perfectly obvious that it wasn't done brewing. Aw, hell, he thought. He might as well tell her. What was the big deal anyhow?

Turning, he leaned his hips against the counter. "I never knew my dad because he disappeared before I was born. My parents were never married. When I was just a little guy, my mother played with me and took care of me in a haphazard manner. But then, as I got bigger, she lost interest in me. I never figured out why and I still don't know. But she didn't give a damn about anything I did. I could stay out all night, and she'd never even notice. Men paraded through her life and bedroom. That's what was important to her, the only thing.

"I left home the night I graduated high school. I never went back, and she never tried to contact me. She died when I was twenty-six, and I went to her funeral. I felt nothing. End of story."

Serena was staring, feeling as though her heart were breaking. When he didn't say any more, she said in a near whisper, "That's the saddest thing I've ever heard."

Their eyes met and held for a long time. Then Trav turned away. "I used to think so, too. Let's talk about something else."

Chapter Fifteen

Trav brought her a steaming mug of coffee and brandy. She took it with uplifted eyes challenging his. "You know what I think? I think you don't like women," she said.

He nearly choked on the swallow he'd just taken from his own mug. "Sweetheart, if there's one thing I do like, it's women." The grin he gave her oozed sex appeal. "Haven't I proved that to you several times?"

Her gaze was steady as a rock. "And you're intending to prove it to me again tonight, aren't you? You don't have to answer, I knew from the first. Let me put it another way. You don't respect women. You might like them for sex, but you don't respect them."

"Ah, a little psychoanalysis. This lack of respect for the fairer sex is, of course, due to my mother's lack of affection for me, her only child."

"Make fun of it if you want, but it's still true." She sipped from her mug. "Isn't it?"

He got up and turned off the generator. Instantly the ceiling lights got dimmer. Instead of returning to his chair, he sat next to her on the sofa.

Finally he spoke. "I respect you."

"Because I'm a lawyer or because I'm a woman?"

"I know some male lawyers that I have no respect for. Draw your own conclusion."

"Then you want me to believe your respect is because I'm a woman?"

"I know a lot of women I don't respect." His eyes swung around to her. "What do you suppose it all means?"

She glared at him. "That you're making fun of me."

"Sweetheart, you're no psychiatrist." He took the mug from her hand and reached across her to put it and his own on the counter. Then he snuggled up to her and whispered, "Let's make love. You're driving me crazy in that robe."

"It's hardly sexy."

"It's sexy on you." He nuzzled her ear. "And I know there's nothing under it except silky skin and feminine delights. Kiss me, babe. Open your mouth and kiss me. Go under my robe and touch me. Drive me wild with desire."

"You're incorrigible," she whispered hoarsely.

"I'm excited. I'm bonkers for your body. Is that being incorrigible?" His hand slid between the panels of her robe to her breast. "Oh, damn, you feel good," he groaned. "Touch me, sweetheart. I'll be going down in flames very soon if you don't touch me."

"Explode, incinerate, combust spontaneously or anything else you can think of. See if I care."

"You care. You're as excited as I am." He was rubbing her nipple, and the deceitful little thing was standing up for him! "Let's go to bed and do this right," he whispered just before mating their mouths in a kiss that turned her bones to mush.

"Oh, I just hate you," she whispered raggedly while twining her arms around his neck.

"Yeah, I can tell." Bringing himself to his feet, he picked her up from the sofa. "Now, this might be a little tricky, sweetheart, because we've got some sharp corners to negotiate."

"You *could* let me walk."

His mouth brushed hers. "Yeah, but would you walk to my bed or to the door?"

"Then your carrying me to your bed is coercion?"

"Guilty as charged, Counselor. Watch your head."

They made it to his bedroom without a bump or a scratch, and he stood her on her feet so he could remove her robe. She not only let him do it, but she untied the sash of his and pushed it down his arms to puddle on the floor next to hers.

There was one puny little light burning in the bathroom, but it cast enough glow into the bedroom for them to see each other. Serena couldn't tear her eyes from his. Right from the beginning, she'd been mesmerized by his eyes, sometimes crinkled in amusement, sometimes deadly serious and sometimes completely unreadable. Right now they contained a hot light and the hint of a smile. It was a satisfied, elated expression, she thought. He was again getting exactly what he wanted, and his eyes reflected his feelings.

But then, he might be seeing the same thing in hers. She didn't have to be here, so wasn't she getting what she wanted, too?

His hands moved over her, leaving a wake of sensitized, tingling skin. "You are so beautiful," he said in a husky, low voice.

She blinked. The smile was gone from his eyes. He had become very serious very fast.

But *serious* to Trav only meant he was ready to make love to her, she thought, and realized that she no longer felt resentful of his feelings, whatever they were. Apparently she could have him like this; certainly it was all he'd offered her. Other than their business relationship, of course.

But if she was looking for a husband—which she wasn't, she thought belligerently—then Trav was not the man for her.

So... it was an affair or nothing.

Right at the moment, an affair seemed just fine to her. Certainly it wasn't an option to stop what was beginning to steam up the windows of his bedroom. His hands on her bare skin, and hers on his marvelous body, was really the most delightful pastime. Add to that the cozy sound of the rain outside, some very delectable kisses, the fact that they were both naked and knew precisely how this was going to end up, and there was no way she could suddenly get huffy and walk out of there.

Kissing her with potent desire, Trav took her by the shoulders and quite efficiently steered her down onto the bed. It was easy to accomplish because she wasn't the least bit resistant to anything he did. His lust for this incredible lady dug deeper into his own psyche, and a thought flitted through his mind that maybe, just maybe, he had found the one woman in the world he couldn't live without.

Male friends had slapped him on the back and told him it would happen someday. Bob Conroy, his good friend in Miles City, had said it several times. Trav had always laughed and taken the teasing with good humor, but he'd never really believed it. Just because those guys had fallen hard for one particular woman didn't mean that it would ever happen to him. Let them think what they wanted, was his credo. In fact that doctrine held true for every phase of his life; he really didn't care what other people thought of him or anything he did. He had many friends all over the state, so he felt he must be doing something right.

Right about there, he stopped thinking. Making love with Serena was like ingesting some strange, powerful drug; she brought his physical senses to a fever pitch and made thinking seem intrusive to their pleasure.

He stopped kissing her to look into her eyes. Her lips were parted and her pupils dilated. She was breathing in small gasps, and every nuance of her expression was sexually permissive. Again Trav had that peculiar sensation of emotion burying itself deeper into his subconscious. In fact he felt choked up, as though he was on the verge of tears. Since he couldn't remember the last time he'd shed tears over anything—hell, he must have been just a kid—this aberration couldn't be completely ignored.

But he would think about it later, he decided, dipping his head to taste her lips again. His tongue gently circled them before sliding into her mouth. His erection was right where it should be, nestled between her legs and exciting them both to the point of neither being able to lie still. He kissed her breasts and her smooth, creamy throat. Her hands roamed his body, seemingly taking particular delight in the firm, masculine curve of his buttocks.

"Great buns," she whispered throatily.

His laugh came from deep in his chest. "So glad you think so, my dear."

"Said the big, bad wolf," she murmured, instantly realizing that though said in fun, it was the very best description she'd come up with since meeting Trav. It was a depressing thought and one she quickly put out of her mind. After all, lying under "the big, bad wolf" with her legs open in blatant invitation wasn't the smartest thing a woman could do.

But then, hadn't she already accepted the fact that she wasn't overly smart when it came to men?

Trav's kisses were getting hotter, more demanding, and they successfully dislodged all thoughts of wolfish men and stupid women from Serena's brain. His lips and tongue played hers like a fine instrument, and his hands on her body were equally adept. She felt adored, as though she was something precious, and she reveled in the sensation. Perhaps that was Trav's magic with women; he made them feel special.

He rolled them over, putting her on top. She sat up and looked down at him. "I want to see you," he said raggedly, running his hands over her breasts and belly. "My, you're a beautiful woman."

For the first time, she believed he meant it. Until this second, she'd thought all of his compliments and flattery to be nothing but a line of malarkey.

"My, you're a beautiful man," she said in return.

His eyes crinkled at their outer corners, indicating amusement. "Do you really mean that?"

"Do you?"

"I asked you first."

"Makes no difference who asked first."

Laughing, he pulled her down to lie flat on him. At the same time, he feathered kisses over her face. "What a woman," he whispered thickly, and rolled them over so he was on top again.

She could see in his eyes that the foreplay was over. Her chest felt constricted in anticipation. She wanted him inside her more than she'd ever wanted anything.

Her wish was granted very quickly. Trav watched her face while he moved inside of her.

"You have a mouth that could drive any man crazy," he said hoarsely.

"That's what your eyes do to me," she panted.

"Oh, baby." He burrowed his arms beneath her and held her as tight as he could, considering what else was going on in that bed. She brought her legs up to wrap around him, and no two people could have been more closely joined.

They rocked together, moving as one entity, until the pressure built to the explosive stage. Then they had to move more freely, faster, harder, and Trav let go of her and put his hands, palms down, on the bed to support himself for the final ride.

Serena was in another world. Her release was so strong, so exquisite, that she nearly blacked out. Moaning, she pulled Trav's head down to devour his lips. He was immersed in the hottest kiss of his life when his own release rocked his very foundation. Tearing his mouth free, he shouted, "Serena . . . baby . . . *baby!*"

They were both so weak and sapped, they fell into a lethargy that barely permitted breathing. Somehow Trav got himself off of Serena and curled around her backside before he closed his eyes.

They fell asleep almost instantly to the sound of raindrops pattering against the motor home.

Trav awoke with the delightful sensation of soft, female flesh enclosed in his arms and pressing into his belly and groin. Serena's legs were enticingly tangled with his, though she was too dead to the world to be aware of anything. He smiled a little when he realized how aroused he was becoming again. He'd slept, he'd rested, the rain had slowed down to a mere sprinkle and he wanted this beautiful lady again.

Without a qualm, he slid his hand down her belly. Tenderly he kissed the side of her neck while he unhurriedly worked her legs apart, moving one to rest on his own, which gave him all the space he needed to play and explore.

Very gently he stroked her until she was wet. His own body was already in demand mode, but touching her so intimately made waiting for even a few minutes feel like exquisite torture.

Yet he wanted her hot and at least partially awake. Making sure he remained gentle, he rubbed the bud of her desire until she began making little whimpering noises and started moving her hips to match the rhythm of his hand. Her bottom chafing his arousal was too much to bear, and he adjusted their positions just enough to enter her from behind. Immediately his hand returned to where it had been doing so much good.

Serena wasn't sure if she was dreaming or if this was real, but never had she felt as she did now, as though she were drowning in raw sex. Her eyes remained closed by choice, because if this was a dream, she didn't want to wake up. Low moans came from her throat, and she reached behind herself to caress the man who was giving her such incredible pleasure.

"Is it good?" Trav whispered.

"Yes ... yes ... don't stop."

"Don't worry about that, baby."

It was only minutes before the first delicious spasms had Serena crying out. But one shot of pleasure for her wasn't enough for Trav this time, and he stopped everything until she had taken a long breath and seemed pretty calm.

Then he started the whole process over again, rubbing her, kissing her, stroking her and moving his own body inside of her, gently, ever gently, until she was moaning and wild again. She had heard of multiple orgasms but had never related them to herself. Now she was learning what they were all about, and her feelings for Trav expanded each time she went over the edge.

She didn't know how long it went on; emotionally dazed, she lost count. "Trav..." she pleaded huskily. "I can't...not again."

He turned her over, slid into her and rode her hard, until he came to a roaring climax himself. Then he literally collapsed on her.

"I might never move again," he managed to say, albeit weakly.

She, too, could barely speak. "Move just enough to get off of me," she said thickly. Her eyes were already closed, and her body was aching for sleep.

He rolled to the bed, and neither said another word.

Serena opened her eyes. It took a minute to figure out where she was, then her stomach dropped. It must be terribly late. Charlie ... what would Charlie think?

Turning her head cautiously on the pillow, she looked at Trav, who had apparently moved away from her since their last encounter. "Oh, my Lord," Serena breathed, remembering how long it had lasted and everything Trav had done to her. It was suddenly difficult to breathe at all. She had considered her appetite for good sex merely normal and healthy, but what had happened with Trav tonight made her wonder.

A stabbing pain suddenly shot through her. Was he as considerate and attentive to every woman he liked? Surely she wasn't jealous. Only women in love were jealous—and God knew she wasn't in love with Travis Holden!

Serena swallowed the lump that had mysteriously and uncomfortably appeared in her throat. She wasn't in love with him, was she? In love with a used-car salesman? What about her dream of marrying a man in the fields of law and/or politics? Had returning to Montana destroyed any chance of fulfilling that dream? Was Trav it? Was he all there was for her in Rocky Ford?

Heaven knew he was the sexiest man alive, if that was any consolation. If he ever decided to get married, his wife would never lack sexual attention. The woman might not ever get a solid night's sleep, but she'd never have reason to complain about a sexless marriage.

A big sigh inflated Serena's chest. What time *was* it? She'd left her wet watch on the small table in the living room section of the unit, and she couldn't see a clock in here. Of course, there might be one; it was just too dark to tell. And she knew Trav wasn't wearing his watch, either. Trav wasn't wearing anything.

The thought of him about a foot away in this big bed, naked, hot as a pistol and probably avidly eager to make love again if she woke him up raised her blood pressure by noticeable degrees.

Okay, she thought in disgust. So she was in serious lust with Trav. That didn't mean she loved him, did it?

And it sure as hell didn't mean he loved her!

Throwing back the sheet, she swung her feet to the floor. She had to find out what time it was. It felt very late, and if Charlie was walking the floor worrying about her, she would never forgive herself.

Grabbing a robe off the floor, she put it on and padded barefoot into the front part of the motor home. Picking up her watch, she nearly jumped out of her skin. 4:12 a.m.

She practically ran back to the bedroom. "Trav, wake up! I've got to get home!" He groaned but never moved a muscle. Walking around to his side of the bed, she bent over and shook his arm. "Trav! Wake up. You've got to drive me home. It's 4:00 a.m." My God, she thought. It would be five by the time she got home. What if Charlie was up and she'd have to face him? She gave Trav's arm a furious shake. "Wake up, dammit!"

His eyes opened a crack. "What're you doing? Come back to bed."

"Get up and find me something to put on. I can't go home wearing this robe." Panicked now, she began opening cupboards. "You must have an old pair of jeans and a sweatshirt or something."

Trav sat up and rubbed his eyes with the heels of his hands. "What time is it?"

"I already told you. It's after four." She moved a sliding door and saw a closet. There were jeans and shirts hanging in it, and she yanked a pair of jeans off a hanger. "Dammit, Trav, get moving. It's going to be daylight very soon." She threw off the robe to put on the jeans.

"Hey, baby," Trav said in a seductive tone of voice, "if you come over here, I'll give you a present."

She sent him an impatient look and pulled on the jeans. "No more presents tonight, sport. Please get up and get dressed. You have to drive me home."

"Well, hell," Trav grumbled, but he got out of bed. Instead of immediately looking for some clothes, however, he came up behind Serena, put his arms around her and took her breasts in his hands, one in each. "Very nice," he said while nuzzling her ear. "I'd sure like to play again, sweetheart," he whispered. "Let's go back to bed."

Her heart did a somersault. His hands felt fantastic on her nipples, and his breath in her ear was giving her goose bumps.

"I'd love to," she said huskily. "But I can't, Trav. I really have to get home."

He turned her around and studied her eyes. "You really would love to go back to bed?"

"Yes," she whispered.

"You like me, huh?"

She was leery of admitting feelings of that nature to Trav. Actually she didn't trust how he might use the knowledge.

"I like you just about the same way you like me," she said evenly.

He frowned. "Is there a hidden message there? Am I supposed to understand it?"

"Take it literally. Now, please get dressed."

Trav's frown stayed firmly in place all the time he pulled on enough clothes to drive her home. Did she like him or didn't she?

And why in hell was it so important all of a sudden whether she did or didn't?

"At least it stopped raining," Trav said as he held the passenger door open for her to get in.

Serena set the plastic bag with her wet clothes on the floor near her feet. "Hurry, Trav, please," she implored.

He shut the door and jogged around the front of the car to jump in and start the engine. They were in motion in the next second.

"It'll take about fifteen minutes to get you home," he said. "Not a lot of time, but enough to ask you to see me later today. You could drive to Access Creek. I'll fix us some dinner. I'm really a pretty good cook." He sent her a glance. "What do you say?"

"Dinner and what else?" she asked softly.

"Do you have to ask?"

She inhaled a long, slow breath. She may as well face facts. There was no other man on the horizon, especially one in law or politics, and she couldn't get enough of Trav in bed. Apparently he was enduring the same driving desire with her. Maybe she should be flattered and thrilled. How many women ever found a man who was so perfect for her in bed?

"No," she said quietly. "I don't have to ask."

"Will you come?"

She laughed wryly. "With you, I have no doubt."

He laughed, as well. "Very funny, but I meant will you come to the motor home later today?"

"I knew what you meant. I just couldn't pass up the pun. Yes, I'll drive out this afternoon."

He reached out and squeezed her hand. "Great."

Was it great? Serena wasn't so certain. There was the chance, after all, that she was falling in love.

Which just might be a bigger disaster than falling in love with Edward had been. At least he'd pretended to be in love with her, too.

She cursed under her breath, silently so Trav wouldn't hear. He already thought she was an easy mark in bed; he certainly didn't need to learn that she could swear like a sailor when the situation called for it.

The rain had stopped, and the woman in the little rental house on Rancho Lane awakened to heavy, humid silence. She had enjoyed the storm, even though her lights had gone off with the first earsplitting crack of thunder. Apparently something electrical had been struck by lightning. She hadn't called the power company because she knew the electricity would come back on when they repaired whatever it was that had been damaged.

Now she lay in her bed in the dark and wished the rain hadn't stopped. It had been so pleasant hearing it on the roof. Pleasant and soothing. God knew her nerves needed soothing. She hated being so cowardly, so nervous about something she had every right to do.

She'd been doing a lot of driving lately, and there was no street in Rocky Ford that she didn't know very well. She had also tackled the outlying ranch roads, and one afternoon she had accidentally come upon the Sheridan Ranch. It was a beautiful ranch and the place Lola Fanon had moved to after marrying Duke Sheridan. The rest of the Fanons all lived in Charlie's big house.

It was very interesting to her that Serena was an honest-to-gosh lawyer and had opened her practice in a very attractive building. Surely she would be successful.

Excitement suddenly coursed through her veins. Maybe she could approach Serena as a potential client. She could invent a legal problem and . . .

A shiver racked her body. As happened every time she thought of approaching one of the Fanons, she felt instant fear.

But it was why she was here, in their town, in Rocky Ford, Montana. When was she going to do it, when they were all too old and gray to give a damn?

When Charlie had gotten old and died?

"Oh, my God," she whispered, shocked to realize that very scenario could occur. She had to get herself together and carry out her goal. She had to, before it was too late!

Chapter Sixteen

Serena made it into the house at the crack of dawn on Sunday morning with no one being the wiser. At least, if Charlie and Candace heard her come in, they were too tactful to mention it later on. Serena especially hoped they hadn't seen her in Trav's clothes. Staying out all night was bad enough when you were living under your father's roof, but coming home wearing a man's clothes was really too much.

At any rate, that night was a turning point for her. She stopped acting as though she barely knew Trav Holden and went out with him openly. No matter where they went or what they did, they always ended the date in bed.

And they had started talking to each other, really talking.

"How'd you get started in the used-car business?" Serena murmured drowsily one evening while they were lying in bed after two solid hours of making love. He told her.

"What happened to your mother?" Trav asked her on another evening. She told him.

"Tell me about your brother, Ron," he requested after a Sunday-afternoon bout in his motor home. She spent an hour talking about Ron.

They were getting to know a great deal about each other.

"You have a reputation with women," Serena said one evening, and then held her breath, waiting to see how he would react to that remark.

"Do I?" he said casually. "What kind of reputation?"

"I can't believe you don't know."

He stretched lazily. As usual they were in bed, touching each other when they felt like it, kissing and fooling around until they became aroused again. Nothing in Serena's past had prepared her for this erotic chapter of her life, and she wondered where a couple like her and Trav went from here.

"Well, I suppose I can guess," he said with a laugh. Then he hugged her close. "Do you have a reputation with men, sweetheart?"

"You're my only affair, sport."

"Really? What about the guy in Washington?"

He'd figured that out for himself, Serena thought. Lola was really the only person who knew the painful details about Edward, and Lola wouldn't let a secret out of the bag if you pulled out her fingernails. Candace knew a little of it, and so did Charlie, but they wouldn't talk about it, either, especially to Trav. No, whatever he knew or thought he knew, he had picked up from her, so she may as well admit it. Besides she certainly hadn't committed a crime by falling in love with Edward; she had merely been too trusting.

"Well, yes, there was someone in Washington. But only for a few months," she murmured.

"And it wasn't an affair?"

"No, it wasn't."

"Meaning you never slept with him?"

Serena stirred uneasily. "I didn't say that."

"Then you did sleep with him."

"Trav, I really don't want to talk about that part of my life with you. Do you want to tell me about the women you've slept with?"

He shrugged. "If you want to hear about 'em, sure, why not?"

"There've been dozens, haven't there?" she said in a tiny voice.

"Dozens? I've never added them up. Want me to?"

She pinched him on the arm. "You cad. No, I don't want you to add them up."

"Ouch! Are you always so violent?"

"Stop teasing me. You think you're so damned funny, don't you?"

He wrapped his arms around her. "Nope. What I am is the guy who's hot for your body." He grinned wickedly. "Let's make love."

She gave him a sassy look. "Someday I might say no, sport."

His grin broadened. "It'll never happen, sweetheart, not with me."

"Conceited jerk."

He kissed her.

It wasn't that Serena was unhappy with the affair—God knew one date was barely over before she was impatient for the next—but there was an empty, achy feeling in her midsection that pestered her unmercifully. It was quiet and unobtrusive when she was with Trav, but alone or even with other people, she felt it gnawing away at her vitals. Sometimes it felt like hunger, even though she'd just eaten, and sometimes it felt like a flu symptom when there were no others and she knew she wasn't ill.

Then there were the times she caught herself sitting at her desk with work in front of her and staring out the window instead, with a totally blank mind. Granted, she could see nothing from her desk chair except a few tree branches and a patch of sky, but the lethargy of her brain was disturbing.

Obviously she had a problem, and obviously it had to do with Trav; that much was easy to deduce. Beyond that, nothing made much sense. They talked about almost everything now, even about making love, how great they were together in bed. But falling in love? No, never. It was as though the words *marriage, commitment* and *I love you* had been eliminated from their vocabulary. The thing was, Serena never pressed Trav for that sort of discussion because she had nothing positive or concrete to bring to it. What would she tell him, that she had a hole in her stomach because of him but had absolutely no idea what to do about it? Ridiculous!

She did wonder, though, if Trav weren't experiencing some of the same sort of emotional confusion. He hadn't taken his motor home and visited any of his other car lots since the nineteenth, and from remarks he'd made in the past, she was positive that before this he had rarely stayed in one town for more than a few days. She couldn't doubt that he was lingering in Rocky Ford because of her, but what about his business? How long could he ignore his normal routine before problems started popping up at his other car lots?

She finally mentioned it one night after they had made wild, impassioned love in his bed and were lying together, physically sated.

"How much longer are you planning to stay in Rocky Ford?" she asked.

Her hand was on his chest, and she felt it heave in a sigh. "Not much longer," he finally said. That answer was not delivered in an especially pleased tone of voice, however, and Serena raised up on an elbow to look at him.

"You don't want to go?"

His dark eyes probed hers. "What do you think?"

She lifted one shoulder in a shrug. "I don't know, but you do have a business to run. You can hardly ignore your other lots."

"I'm not ignoring them. I'm in phone contact."

"Yes, but that's not as good as spending time at each one, is it? If it was, I'm sure that's what you would have been doing all along."

"No, it's not as good," he agreed. He twined his fingers into her curls. "Getting tired of having me underfoot, sweetheart?" he asked softly.

"Don't say something so utterly absurd," she said almost sharply. "If I felt that way, would I be in this bed with you every chance I got?"

He looked at her for the longest time, and she looked back. There was something in his eyes that made her pulse beat faster, something unsaid in the very air they were breathing.

But the only thing he eventually said was, "Guess not." He stared at the ceiling, and she lay down again. After a few minutes, he slid his arm under her head and brought it to his shoulder. "I'll probably leave on Friday. I really do have to make the rounds."

Her whole body went rigid. "How long will you be gone?"

"I don't know, a few weeks, a month. It depends." He turned to his side and faced her. "Will you miss me?" Under the sheet and blanket, his hand slowly slid downward, heating her skin as it went and building a fire in the pit of her stomach. She was wet before he ever touched her.

"I'll miss you," she whispered raggedly.

"Show me how much, sweetheart. Show me."

His mouth claimed hers, and she kissed him almost savagely. He was a drug she had to have, more necessary than the air she breathed or the food she ate.

But as intense and overwhelming as this powerful need was, was it love?

The whole town felt different to Serena after Trav left. It was as though he had taken the life and spirit of the place with him. Her work seemed unexciting and humdrum, and she couldn't muster up any enthusiasm for the activities she had once enjoyed.

He was only gone a few days when a thought hit her with the impact of a battering ram: he might not be in love with her, but she sure as hell was knocked dead by him. So he wasn't a lawyer or a politician. Who cared? So his career was considered a little shady by some. Many people accused used-car salesmen of taking advantage of their customers' naivete about engines, transmissions and such. Wasn't that the crux of the lawsuits she was handling for Trav? And did she trust him herself? Not about cars, for Pete's sake, but regarding other women?

"Oh, God," she groaned helplessly. Falling in love with Trav was just begging for heartache.

But it was too late, wasn't it? The deed was done. That hole in her gut was because he didn't love her back. She was his Rocky Ford girlfriend. Wasn't *that* an attractive image?

Trav called often. She never asked him when he'd be back in Rocky Ford and she never failed to shed tears after they hung up. If his call came to the house in the evening, she let herself have a good cry in her bedroom; if it came to the office during the day, she wiped her eyes and forced herself back to work.

It was Thursday afternoon of the second week following Trav's departure that Karen answered the phone in the front office and then called out so Serena would hear her in the back office, "It's for you, Serena. A Mr. Edward Redding."

Serena went stiff in her chair. Why was he calling? She didn't want to talk to him and she'd told him so when he'd called before. What more was there to say? Dammit, why was he doing this to her?

"Serena?" Karen was standing in the doorway. "Did you hear me? There's a call for you on line one."

"I heard," Serena mumbled. Karen was looking at her peculiarly. "Karen, we're out of coffee. Would you take my

car and run to the store and get some? Here's some money."
She fumbled in her purse for a ten-dollar bill.

"Glad to. But . . . are you all right?"

Serena forced a smile. "Yes, I'm fine. Go get the coffee,
please. I'm dying for a cup." She wasn't but she didn't want
Karen overhearing this conversation. Karen was a great
secretary, and Serena even considered her a friend. But she
did like to gossip, and a call from an old boyfriend was no
one else's business.

Nodding, Karen left. When Serena heard the door to the
hall close behind her, she reached for the phone. "This is
Serena."

"Hello, darling. How are you?"

The sound of his voice angered Serena all over again.
"Why did you call again? I asked you not to. And how did
you get this number?"

"Darling, it's not at all difficult to call information and
get the phone number of an attorney in a two-attorney
town." Edward's little chuckle conveyed pride in his own
wit.

"I'm not going to talk to you, Edward. Goodbye." She
started to hang up, but Edward's voice had taken on a
frantic edge.

"Serena, wait! I'm in Montana—in Billings—and I'm on
my way to Rocky Ford to see you."

Slowly she returned the phone to her ear. "You're what?"

"I should be there in time for dinner. You will see me,
won't you? Darling, I have incredible news and I love you
so much. I know you don't hate me, Serena. How could you
when we were so much in love? Tell me how to find your
office, darling. I'd rather meet your family after we talk.
Wait at your office for me, and then we'll have dinner together. I can hardly wait to see you. You're all I've thought
about since you left Washington."

Serena's troubled gaze moved to the window. What if it
was Trav saying those things to her?

But it wasn't Trav, and she had to tell Edward to stop trying. Apparently doing so on the phone wasn't effective; she was going to have to speak very plainly right to his face.

"Very well," she said coldly. "My office is in the Ridgeport Building at 1331 Franklin Street. I'll wait until six."

"Thank you, my love. I'll be there around five-thirty."

Getting any real work done for the rest of the afternoon was impossible for Serena. For one thing, she kept wishing Trav would call. He'd been calling every day this week and hadn't done so yet today. She had no intention of going out to dinner with Edward; she could tell him everything he needed to hear right in this office. But the idea of Trav calling when Edward was here was extremely discomfiting, and she had the strongest premonition of that happening.

Five o'clock finally rolled around, and Karen left for the day. Serena literally fell back in her chair with relief, as she had also been worried about Edward getting here sooner than he'd estimated and walking in while Karen was still at her desk.

Being alone made her feel much better. She left the hallway door unlocked so Edward could come in, and then took her time straightening her desk just for something to do until he arrived. Actually she wasn't at all nervous about seeing Edward again. She didn't even hate him anymore. She simply wanted no more contact with him, and that was what she must make him understand and accept. To think that he'd come all the way to Montana in another attempt at reconciliation was almost unbelievable. Obviously he still didn't grasp how badly she'd been hurt and how much she despised lies and deceit. Maybe he even thought of himself as the injured party. Given his monumental ego, she wouldn't put it past him.

About five-twenty she called home. "Hi, Candace. I'm tied up at the office, so don't hold dinner for me. I'll eat whatever's there when I get home."

"If you're not going to be too long, I could keep a plate warm for you, Serena," Candace offered.

"Not necessary. I really don't know how long I'll be. Please don't worry about it. You and Dad enjoy your dinner, and I'll see you both later."

After goodbyes, Serena put down the phone. At that precise moment, she heard from the other room, "Serena?"

Her voice became cold as ice. "In here, Edward."

He came to her office door, looking boyishly abashed. "Is it safe to come in? I mean, you don't have a frying pan or a rolling pin in here, do you?"

Her expression did not warm up over his stab at humor. "Come in and let's get this over with."

He looked the same—crisply clean, handsome and sure of himself. His blond hair gleamed like spun gold, and his tan slacks and shirt fit as all his clothes did—perfectly. Unquestionably he was a special-looking man. Wasn't that what had attracted her to him in the first place? And in many ways, he really was special. He was well-educated, intelligent and witty when he wanted to be. He'd made her laugh many times during what she finally realized were clandestine meetings and not the romantic dates she had thought.

But then her laughter had turned to tears, because he'd crushed her feelings for him under the lethal weight of lies and treachery. She could look at him now, admit his good looks and feel nothing. It was a satisfying sensation, because now she could also admit that one small part of herself had been concerned all afternoon that seeing Edward again would undermine her decision to *never* see him again.

"Sit down if you'd like," she said coolly.

His expression remained boyish, changing only a little with the addition of a conciliatory grin. It was the very expression that had initially won her heart in Washington, that I'm-so-cute-how-could-any-woman-resist-me? expression. All it did for her today was reinforce her resolve.

"Are you really going to stay behind that desk?" he asked in a teasing tone. "Don't I get even one little kiss?"

"You get nothing from me, Edward, except for some conversation. Do you want to hear what I have to say standing or sitting? That's really your only decision in this meeting."

Leaning against the doorframe, he folded his arms. "My, my, haven't we become hard?"

"My, my, I wonder why."

"And cynical. Darling, you were never cynical. Is that what this dreary little town is doing to you?"

"No, it's what Washington did to me. Wait a minute. Let's get specific here, Edward. Why beat around the bush and blame Washington or anything else? If I'm cynical now, it's strictly because of you."

"How many ways can a man apologize?" Edward approached the desk, laid his hands on it and leaned over toward her. "Do you want me on my knees, darling?"

"I *want* you back in Washington, where you belong!"

"What if I told you I'm a free man?"

She blinked in surprise. "You . . . you're divorced?"

"I told you I had good news." Smiling, he walked around the desk and bent over her chair, putting his face mere inches from hers. "My own true love, I'm asking you to marry me."

"Well, isn't this just the most precious sight?" Trav drawled from the doorway. The sickish roiling of his stomach didn't show on his face; he merely looked hard as nails and amused, both at the same time.

Serena nearly fainted. "Trav!" Pushing her chair back from the desk, she got it tangled up with Edward. "Get away!" she told him irately.

Edward seemed dazed, mentally disoriented, as though the idea of Serena even knowing another man was an impossible concept. "Serena, who is that man?"

"No one important," Trav said before Serena could answer, again speaking in that laid-back drawl. He studied

Edward until he had memorized the man's slick features, then he looked at Serena, who had finally made it out of her chair but looked so flustered she didn't know what to do next.

"Just tell me one thing," Trav said to her. "Is this the guy from Washington?"

Serena almost choked. This was a nightmare. "Trav," she said weakly, "why didn't you call?"

His left eyebrow shot up. "Oh? You need a warning when I'm coming to town now?" His expression got even harder. "You didn't answer my question. Is this the joker from Washington, D.C.?"

"Joker!" Edward said indignantly. "I'll have you know—"

"Can it," Trav growled at him. "I'm talking to Serena, not you." His eyes bored into her. "Are you going to answer me?"

"Yes," she whispered. "He's from Washington."

"Thanks. That's all I needed to hear." He touched his forehead in a mocking salute. "See you around, babe."

"No," she said in a choked voice when he walked out. "No, Trav, don't go."

But he was already gone. The next office was still reverberating from the loud slam of the hallway door, and it felt as if the sound were clawing at her very soul. Her knees buckled and she sank back into her chair.

"Well, I hope he doesn't think he scared me," Edward said with a puffed-up, belligerent expression on his face.

Serena turned her head to look at him. "Macho doesn't suit you or impress me, Edward, so turn it off." She sounded tired and beaten, with very little strength to her voice.

"Oh, my poor darling," Edward said sympathetically. "Let's go somewhere nice and have a drink and a good dinner." He smiled cajolingly. "And we can talk and make plans."

She shook her head in disbelief. "Do you honestly think I'd go anywhere with you, let alone make plans? My future does not include you, you...complete jerk!" She pushed herself to her feet. "Go now, Edward. Leave and never come back. That may sound melodramatic, but it's exactly how I feel. I never want to set eyes on you again."

"But...but I got a divorce so I could marry you," he stammered.

"If I really believed that, I might harbor some guilt, but you know what, Edward? First of all, I think it's another lie, and second, if it does happen to be the truth, it was the biggest favor you could ever do for your wife. I'll bet she's not one bit unhappy about it. One thing more—when I finally learned you were married, I never once hinted that you should divorce your wife or desert your children. So I don't feel any guilt about it. Actually, Edward, I feel nothing for you, your life or mistakes except for a great deal of disgust."

He backed up as though struck. But it was apparent that he wasn't going to take this without a fight. Serena wondered when his lips curled angrily just how far he would go in defense of his callous, selfish behavior in Washington.

"You're cold, Serena. Cold and hard. In Washington you were sweet and—"

"Stupid! Leave, Edward. Leave now before I call the police to put you out of my office and then file a lawsuit in Washington, D.C., against you for sexual harassment. Incidentally I have an excellent case for that charge and I doubt if the publicity would do your career any good."

"I can't believe you would do that."

"Believe it, Edward. Do believe it."

He stared at her for a long moment, then turned on his heel and walked out.

Her legs were suddenly too weak to hold her up, and she sank to her chair. Edward wouldn't bother her again, but maybe Trav wouldn't, either.

Moaning, she laid her arms on the desk and put her head on them. How strange and unpredictable life was. Who could ever have foreseen Edward coming to Montana? And Trav deciding to return to Rocky Ford, then dropping in at the office without a call—probably to surprise her, which he certainly had—at the very same moment that Edward was proposing marriage was a scenario from hell.

The worst part of her anguish was a certainty that Trav not only wouldn't listen to an explanation, but he wouldn't want one. She simply didn't matter enough for him to fight for her. Sex was an inexpensive, readily available commodity, and what else did they have? She was, as she'd thought about before, only his Rocky Ford girlfriend. His current bed partner.

That was when the tears started. Devastating self-pity had her sobbing her heart out. Then the pity turned to condemnation, and she once again cursed her gullibility with men. She was an easy sexual mark and lacked the sense God gave a goose. Why wouldn't men like Edward and Trav take advantage of her? She'd been there for the taking, hadn't she?

Eventually she realized it was getting dark outside. Sighing soulfully, she got up, went into the bathroom and looked at herself in the mirror. Her eyes were red and swollen, and most of her makeup was gone. She looked terrible.

But she looked no worse than she felt. Bathing her eyes with cold water, she decided to forego more makeup. After locking up the office, she drove home.

Her feet dragged as she walked to the house and went in. Everything was quiet except for the television set in the living room. She peered in and saw Charlie alone.

"Where's Candace?"

He turned with a smile. "Hi, honey. Candy was tired and went to bed early." He got a good look at his daughter's forlorn face and rose from his chair with a frown. "What's wrong?"

The dam burst. "Oh, Dad, I've botched things so miserably," she wailed.

Charlie put his arms around her for a long, comforting hug, then led her to the sofa, where they sat down. Holding her hands, he looked at her with love and concern. "Now, tell your old dad what you've botched and why you feel so badly about it."

Chapter Seventeen

Twenty minutes later, Charlie knew everything. Almost everything, that is. Serena had omitted the most-personal aspects of her and Trav's relationship from her story, but she was sure from the knowing look in her dad's eyes that she hadn't had to go into detail for him to fill in the gaps.

"And you're in love with him," Charlie said quietly.

Her head bobbed in a shaky nod.

"Figured something like that was happening with the two of you."

Serena's voice was lifeless. "That's where you're wrong, Dad. It was only happening to me."

Charlie shook his head. "Nope, you're the one who's wrong. That boy loves you, too."

Serena's eyes suddenly blazed with anger. "Then why didn't he say so?"

"Did *you* say so?"

The anger deflated as suddenly as it had appeared. "Neither of us wanted to fall in love. I think for Trav it worked out perfectly. I wasn't so fortunate.''

Charlie looked puzzled. ''You didn't *want* to fall in love? I don't understand that attitude, honey. Don't you want a home of your own? A husband? Children?''

Serena's voice became very small. ''I . . . wanted to marry a man in my career field, Dad.''

''Is Edward a lawyer or a politician?'' Obviously Charlie was still very perplexed.

Serena slumped back against the sofa cushion. ''No.''

''But he was in the swing of things in Washington.''

''Very much. I guess he was,'' she added listlessly. ''He never discussed his actual work. He just kept dropping hints about his enormous responsibility and the confidentiality of it all.''

''He's probably no more than a damned clerk,'' Charlie said with a derisive snort. ''Told you all of that garbage just so he could keep you in the dark about his real life.''

''You're probably right.''

''Well, when you saw him today, was there any of the old spark left?''

''God, no,'' Serena said with a shudder. Her eyes were suddenly brimming with tears. ''What I felt for him—what I *thought* I felt for him—wasn't one-tenth of what I feel for Trav.''

''But Trav's not in law or politics. Could you live with that?''

''I have asked myself that so many times I've lost count. But all the time, I was falling in love anyway.'' Her eyes were swimming again. ''And he doesn't love me, Dad,'' she said sadly. ''You should have seen him today. He didn't even care that Edward was in my office and proposing marriage. The only thing he said was . . . well, I told you.''

''Yes, he asked if Edward was the guy from Washington. Hasn't it occurred to you that he's been jealous of 'the guy from Washington'?''

"Jealous? Trav?" The idea was astonishing, and she dismissed it immediately. "Believe me, he's not the jealous type. I'm sure it's been the other way around all of his life. Women by the droves, suffering, jealous, depressed and unhappy."

Charlie almost laughed and maintained a straight face only through monumental effort. The picture Serena had so dramatically painted of Trav and countless suffering, jealous women was the funniest thing he'd heard all day.

But it was deadly serious to her, so he cleared his throat and patted her hand. "Let's talk about solutions."

Now it was her turn to look perplexed. "Solutions to what?"

"To your little dilemma."

"Are you talking about Trav? Dad, there is no solution to our situation. No woman can make a man fall in love with her."

"That's true, but every woman can find out for sure what a man *does* feel for her. I don't think you really know. From what you've told me, I think the two of you were so careful to avoid the subject of commitment that you don't really know how each other feels about much of anything. Serena, the one thing you can't do is give up without at least a conversation with Trav. Good grief, girl, he might be going through the same trauma that you are right now. What a shame it would be if you suffered with unrequited love for the rest of your days and so did he. 'Course, I've heard of folks running into each other again after thirty-forty years and finally getting together. Seems to me, though, that thirty to forty years could be put to better use than silent suffering."

In a way, Serena couldn't help wondering if Charlie was taking this as seriously as he should. There wasn't a sign of a smile on his face, but wasn't there something just a little bit off-key in his voice?

Nevertheless, she had bared her soul, and he had given her some hope. It was more than she'd arrived home with. "What do you think I should do?" she asked.

"Find 'im. Talk to 'im."

"And if he refuses to talk to me?"

"He won't."

"You don't know him, Dad. He's perfectly capable of refusing."

"Don't sound so depressed, honey. At least give it a try. Do you know where he is now?"

"Probably at Access Creek."

"Then get yourself together and go out there and see him. Trav is an intelligent man, and you're an intelligent woman. You can't permit a permanent breach over something so ludicrous. You at least have to try to right the apple cart, Serena."

Serena drew a long, suddenly nervous breath. Did she have the grit to find Trav and insist on a conversation? What if he yelled at her? He had the ammunition to cut her to ribbons, should he choose. No one else in the world knew the things Trav knew about her, primarily how she became a tigress in bed.

But only with him. Did he know that?

Maybe he should. She kissed her Dad's cheek. "Thanks. I'll clean up and drive out there." Her lips quivered in a feeble smile. "The worst he can do is throw me off his land, right?"

Charlie smiled. "Don't think about the worst, honey. Think positive."

Think positive had been Charlie's advice on many occasions in the Fanon family, Serena thought while she drove out to Access Creek. It was his own credo, obviously. Many men might have crumpled under the strain of being widowed young with two small children. Not Charlie. He'd packed up his little family and moved them to Montana to start over. And he'd given them a good life. Then he'd taken in his niece, Lola, when her own parents were killed in an auto accident, and had made her a member of the family. They were all lucky to have Charlie.

But Serena's ultimate decision to see Trav and attempt a discussion was her own. She had considered her dad's advice while taking a shower and changing clothes, and it was good advice. But it was only good because it coincided with what she knew had to be done. Trav had to be told that she'd known nothing of Edward's visit until today, and that she certainly hadn't anticipated a marriage proposal.

The night was very dark and so was Access Road. Serena's stomach churned as she drove. Facing Trav was a daunting prospect and all she could think about. There was the possibility that he hadn't gone to his property on the creek. It had been her first thought, but with that motor home for an address he could be anywhere.

She approached his piece of land with her heart in her throat and felt an enormous surge of relief when she saw the dark bulk of the motor home. If Trav was here, he was either sitting in the dark or in bed, as there were no lights burning.

But there was no car parked next to the unit, so it looked to her as though he wasn't home. "Damn," she mumbled. Using the headlights of her car to get to the door of the motor home without tripping over something, she knocked. "Trav?" she called.

There was no response from inside the unit, and she finally tried the doorknob. It turned; the unit wasn't locked. Gingerly she mounted the steps and went in. "Trav?" Was he sulking in his bedroom? Ignoring her and hoping she'd go away?

Well, she wasn't going to go away, and he could like it or lump it. Feeling around, she located a light switch and then made her way to the back of the unit. The bedroom and bathroom were empty.

Okay, she thought. Maybe he's at the car lot. Turning off the motor home's lights, she left it as she'd found it, dark and unlocked, and returned to her car.

During the drive to the car lot, she tried to compose herself by thinking of the best parts of their relationship. Their talks, for instance. Maybe they'd avoided certain subjects, but still, their talks were warm and pleasant memories.

Yet she was kidding herself, she thought unhappily, if she tried to simplify what really was a complex, lustful, tempestuous love affair. Or to pretty it up with wishful thinking.

She almost headed for home. What made her even hope that Trav would listen to her? He had an image in his mind of Edward leaning over her and proposing marriage. One did not easily eradicate images of that sort. She knew that from firsthand experience, because she had a few images of her own—remnants from Washington—that were as sharp and defined now as they'd ever been.

But she could not compare herself discovering Edward's treacherous secret to Trav walking into her office today. The two events were nothing alike, and she was not guilty of anything—as Edward had been in Washington—even though it might have appeared to Trav today that she was the most deceitful of women.

The car lot was closed, which she'd known would be the case, although it was almost as bright as day from its many pole lights. There were chains across the driveways, however, so she parked on the street, stepped over a chain and walked to the office. Its lighted windows were deceiving. No one answered the door, and after peering into every window she could reach, she gave up on Trav being there.

Returning to her car, she sat there thinking. Was she going to forget about talking to Trav tonight? His motor home could be gone in the morning. Wherever he was, he could return, get in that damned house on wheels and vanish from Rocky Ford. After that, who would tell her where he was if he issued instructions to his employees to keep mum?

On the other hand, she had his legal files.

Her shoulders slumped in utter dejection. He could get his files through another attorney. If he didn't want to ever see her again, there was nothing she could do to stop him.

"Except for some determination," she said under her breath as she started her car. She was *not* giving up! She'd done nothing wrong, and he was going to hear the truth if she had to wait in her car next to his motor home all night!

Everything was the same at Access Creek when she got there. Turning off the ignition, she settled down to wait.

She realized she must have dozed when she awoke with a start. Nothing had changed. The motor home was still dark, and no cars had come along. Serena checked the time. She'd only slept about a half hour.

But her muscles felt cramped, and she got out of the car to stretch her legs. Her stomach growled, and she recalled that she'd had nothing to eat since lunch. Eyeing the motor home, she pondered going in and getting something from Trav's refrigerator. Even angry, he wasn't the type of man to begrudge her a sandwich.

It took several minutes of walking around her car, enduring hunger pangs and worrying about trespassing before making up her mind. She would hurry, just grab something and come back outside to eat it.

Once she was inside the unit with the lights on, however, her crime didn't feel so terrible, and she didn't hurry at all. She'd spent enough time in here to feel at ease. And he'd left the door unlocked, which could be construed as an invitation for her to wait inside.

But that idea didn't hold much water, not if he believed she was still with Edward.

Sighing, Serena opened the refrigerator. She took out cheese, ham and milk, got the bread from a cabinet, made a sandwich and poured herself a glass of milk, then sat at the dinette to eat.

It wasn't that late, only around ten, and Trav might not show up for hours. Lord only knew where he was and what he was doing. She wouldn't let herself think that he might be seeking consolation from another woman, but he was somewhere and might not come home until the wee hours. Could she really wait in her car that long? And was there any point to that much physical discomfort for her?

She would wait in here. She was hardly contaminating the place, after all, and if he hadn't wanted guests, he should have locked the door.

After wiping down the dinette table and making sure everything was as clean and neat as she'd found it, Serena sat on the sofa. She was too antsy to read, and Trav didn't have anything she thought interesting, anyway. Sports and hunting magazines had never appealed to her, and that was all he had, other than some thick spy novels, which weren't her cup of tea, either.

Just sitting there in the silence made her sleepy. Her head was nodding when she decided to heck with it and stretched out on the couch.

But then, as she lay there, her pulse began beating faster with another idea. Did she have the courage to do it? Putting her courage or lack thereof aside, what was so great about Trav walking in and finding her asleep on his sofa? Her other idea was much better because he would immediately get the picture. Maybe they never would have that fight she'd been sure was imminent since driving out here.

Oh, my, yes, it made much better sense. She should have thought of it right away.

Getting up, she walked to the back of the motor home. A shower first, then bed. This time she *would* hurry, as she didn't want Trav walking in with her in his shower; the whole thing would be much more effective with her in bed.

Feeling almost light-headed from the brilliance of her plan, she turned on the shower and began tearing off her clothes.

Later, just as she was snuggling down in Trav's bed, a thought struck her. *This isn't like you, Serena Fanon.*

But what was? she thought cynically. Did she even know herself anymore? Maybe she never had. Maybe there was no place for girlish dreams in the real world, and hadn't she lived on hopes and dreams for many years? Probably every damned one of them had been and still was immature and improbable.

If nothing else came out of today, at least she had finally, at long last, grown up. Reaching for the light switch, she pushed it to Off.

The darkness was soothing, and she closed her eyes.

It was a few minutes after midnight when Trav pulled up behind Serena's car. He'd known something was out of kilter when he'd spotted the lights burning in the front section of the motor home, but it wasn't until he'd gotten closer that he'd seen Serena's car.

Drawing a long breath, he turned off the engine and sat there in the silence. She was inside, obviously waiting for him.

But why? Where was her Washington lover?

He'd fought self-pity all night, and he sure as hell wasn't going to give in to it now. Even with that vow, his eyes burned. He cursed violently rather than let even one tear escape. He hadn't cried since childhood, and he'd be damned if Serena Fanon was going to make him blubber like a baby.

Pushing open his door, he got out and gave it a slam, not caring a whit how much noise it made. He hadn't spotted her peeking out a window, so she was either deliberately keeping out of sight or had fallen asleep on the sofa.

He grabbed the knob of the motor-home door and yanked it open. The sofa was the first thing he saw, and Serena wasn't on it. Stepping up into the unit, he frowned. Serena must be in the back, in the bathroom. Maybe she'd gone there to collect herself when she'd heard his car.

Okay, fine. He'd collect himself, too, he thought with cynical amusement. This confrontation was hardly going to qualify for the good-time-of-the-year award, after all. Going to the refrigerator, he took out a beer, opened it and swigged down a good third of the bottle in one gulp.

He had finished the bottle—with much less haste than the first swallow—before he realized that he hadn't heard even one small sound from the back. Not a peep. If Serena was hiding in the bathroom, she was just barely breathing to be so quiet. She hadn't brought her car here and gone somewhere else, had she?

Trav shook his head at such an inane idea. He'd been thinking crazy, off-the-wall thoughts since leaving Serena's office, things about being in love with her. The very first woman he'd ever fallen in love with, and she was carrying a great big torch for that jerk from Washington. Smart, real smart.

But he'd already figured out that he wasn't very smart when it came to Serena. Right from the first, he'd treated her like any other woman, and she wasn't any other woman. Why in hell had it taken him so long to know that?

He'd come to that conclusion about 4:00 a.m. last night after rolling and tossing for hours, missing her so much he ached, thinking of her beautiful face and body, thinking of her, her intelligence, her smile. Thinking of every tiny thing that had ever occurred between them and ultimately admitting that she was not just another woman; she was the woman he wanted to spend the rest of his life with.

What a revelation that had been. He'd gotten out of bed, fired up the motor home and started driving to Rocky Ford. He had to talk to Serena, find out if she was feeling anything even close to what was causing him the agony of insomnia. Since he'd been clear across the state—and Montana was an enormous state—it had taken him until this afternoon to get here. Walking in her office and seeing that . . . that . . .

Trav clenched his jaw. In his tormented mind, he'd already called the man every name in the book, and maybe it wasn't even the guy's fault. Maybe Serena had been in contact with him all along. Maybe she'd invited him to Rocky Ford. Maybe she'd been dying to hear that marriage proposal.

But if all that were true, what was she doing in his motor home tonight?

Trav had been sitting in the dinette, and he slid across the seat and got to his feet. If Serena wasn't in the bathroom, she was in the bedroom, and what was she doing in there?

It was time to find out. Although his mouth had gone dry, Trav began quietly moving to the back of the motor home.

Chapter Eighteen

The darkness in the back of the unit surprised Trav, and it shouldn't have because driving up he'd noticed lights in the front and none in the back.

But why would Serena be sitting in the dark?

After snapping on the overhead hall light, he could see into both the bathroom and bedroom. The bathroom was empty, but the bedroom certainly wasn't. Serena was in his bed, one arm thrown over her head, one foot peeking out of the covers. She looked sound asleep.

Folding his arms across his chest, he leaned against the doorframe and looked in at her. If she was feigning sleep, she was doing a damned good job of it. Actually she looked knocked out, breathing through her mouth, even snoring a little.

But why come here to sleep? Just then she moved slightly, the sheet and blanket slipped and he caught a glimpse of a bare shoulder. His heart took a wild leap in his chest. Was she really naked under those covers?

His heart continued to beat hard, thundering in his own ears. Would she be here at all if that joker from Washington was still around? Today he'd given her no chance to explain anything. Not that he was all that sure there was anything to explain. After all, hadn't he seen what was going on with his own two eyes?

Or was it possible that his brain had misinterpreted what he'd seen?

He suddenly felt sweaty. What if he'd rushed to the wrong conclusion? What if he'd misjudged Serena and that scenario in her office?

Not only did he feel sweaty, but he smelled of cigarette smoke and beer. Considering that he'd spent hours in Danny's Saloon, where at least half of the patrons chain-smoked, how else would he smell?

A shower. He had to have a shower before waking Serena. No way was he going to climb into bed with her when he smelled like a tavern.

And climbing into bed with her was exactly what he was going to do. She wouldn't be there if she didn't want him with her.

Feeling as though a ten-ton burden had just vanished, he quietly reached into the shower stall and turned on the water. He tried to keep everything quiet, but even the spray sounded loud to him. Wincing over the noise, he stepped into the stall.

In the bedroom, Serena opened her eyes. Instantly she knew Trav had come home. He was in the shower right now. Her blood began racing like a white-water river. She hadn't expected to fall asleep, but either today had exhausted her or the many restless nights she had undergone while Trav was away had finally caught up with her.

But the big question was, should she let him know she was awake or should she pretend to still be sleeping? He had to know she was here, in his bed. What was he planning to do after his shower? There was some comfort in the fact that he hadn't shouted her awake and kicked her fanny out into the night. But second-guessing what he'd do once he knew she was awake was a little risky to her mental health. Certainly it was darned effective at undermining her courage.

No, she wouldn't think about it, she decided adamantly. Whatever happened happened. Why worry about it beforehand? Either he'd come out of that shower friendly or growling like a grizzly bear.

It really might be best if he thought she was still sleeping, she decided nervously. Lying there and listening to his progress in the bathroom, she tried to remember what her position had been when she'd first awakened. Of course, that was silly. People moved around in their sleep. As long as she was still and her eyes were closed, he would accept any position.

"Hmm," she murmured as an idea to better her case took shape in her mind. Quickly she drew one leg from under the covers, exposing it clear to her hip, and then pushed the blankets down until her bosom was just barely concealed. From this pose, he would know that she was naked as a jaybird in his bed, and if he didn't get the message from that, maybe he never would.

The shower went off. Serena took several calming breaths, preparing herself for an easy, rhythmic breathing pattern that one only attained in a sound sleep.

As Trav came out of the bathroom stark naked, Serena gulped and closed her eyes.

He stopped at the bedroom doorway and gaped. How in hell had she gotten into that erotic position? Had the shower disturbed her just enough to make her squirm around and lose some of the covers?

But wasn't it interesting how sexily the blankets had been rearranged?

She was awake, the little fake! Oh, she'd been sleeping before, no question about it. But she was awake now and pretending she wasn't.

He knew something then and he almost yelped for joy. She loved him. No woman would do all of this for a man she didn't love. She was probably bursting with things to tell him and had come out here this evening with the intention of forcing him to listen. And where had he been? Nursing his wounds in Danny's Saloon.

Hell, he should have been here. Look how much time they'd wasted.

Still, it was damned gutsy of her to suppose he wanted her in his bed after today. Maybe she needed to be shown who was boss in this twosome.

Grinning inwardly, though maintaining a straight face, Trav snapped off the hall light and felt his way to his side of the bed in the dark. He lay down, turned his back to Serena and pulled up the covers to his waist.

Her eyes popped open. Was he actually going to act as if she weren't here?

Then she sniffed the air—beer! Was he too drunk to *know* she was here?

That took the wind out of her sails. It hadn't occurred to her that he might come home drunk, for pity's sake. Why would it? As many times as they'd had a drink or two together, Trav had never overindulged. In fact anytime they were out and he had to drive them home, he never went past one glass of dinner wine.

Suddenly she felt terrible. She wanted to bawl. What he'd seen in her office today had ripped apart his standards, and he'd probably spent the whole night in a tavern drinking himself into a stupor. Someone else must have driven him home. It might even have been a woman.

That thought started her tears, and she let them flow down her temples to course into her hair and the pillow. She'd done all of this for nothing. Damn saloons, liquor and loose women the world over! Trav was too drunk to talk about anything serious, and she couldn't stay here for the rest of the night, hoping for a chat in the morning.

She was just on the verge of sliding out of bed when Trav flopped over and threw an arm and a leg over her.

"Hey," he said with a thick slur. "What's this? Who's in my bed?" He snuggled closer. "Never mind, baby doll. It doesn't matter who you are. Give us a kiss."

Shocked and wounded for eternity, Serena wrestled herself free and all but jumped off the bed. "You...you cretin," she shrieked. "Any woman will do for you, won't she? Don't you have any morals at all? Any scruples? I wish I knew what in hell made me think I was in love with the likes of you! A woman would have to be fifty percent blind and fifty percent brain-dead to love you!"

Trav sat up and switched on the ceiling lights. "Got'cha," he said evenly.

Her eyes widened. "What do you mean, you got me?"

His gaze was moving over the flushed skin of her nude body. "Damn, you're beautiful." Delicately he cleared his throat. "Did I hear you say you were in love with me?"

"You don't sound drunk now," she retorted.

"Maybe because I'm not."

"But you did a few minutes ago." She caught on. "You deceitful snake! You were pretending."

"Guess we're both guilty of that crime."

Without asking, Serena went to the closet for one of his robes, which she put on and tied tightly around the waist.

"What's your game?" she asked derisively.

"What's yours?"

"Dammit, can't you answer a simple question?"

"Can't you?"

"You're purposely being argumentative. I...I came here tonight to explain about Edward...."

"So his name is Edward."

"Edward Redding. I've told you that before."

"Nope, you haven't. He was proposing to you. Did you say yes?"

"Would I be here if I had?"

"Might be. Maybe Eddie's not as good in bed as I am. Some women are capable of marrying one man for certain reasons and keeping another on the side for sex."

"I'm sure you'd know all about that," she said with scathing sarcasm. "It's what I've been battling ever since I met you. You'll never settle for just one woman, will you?"

Trav leaned against the headboard. "I might. Depends on the woman." After a hesitation he added, "Until I met you, I didn't think there was any such woman."

She blinked at him, then swallowed. "Uh, what should I say to that?"

"Before we get into that, tell me why Edward came to Montana. Did you invite him?"

"Never!" she gasped. "I told him before leaving Washington that we were through. He called me once—actually it was the same day you asked me out for the first time—and I told him not to call again."

"Why were you through? What did he do to hurt you so much?"

Serena perched on a corner of the bed. "All the time he was dating me in Washington, he was married with two children. When I found out—quite by accident—I told him our relationship was over. I do not date married men and break up families. He insulted my intelligence, my integrity and my own self-respect. I could never forgive him, never."

"Yeah, but what about your feelings for him? I mean, before you found out, did you think you were in love with him?"

Her eyes rose to meet his. She wasn't going to lie about this or gloss it over. "Yes," she said. "I was in love with him."

Trav snorted. "Love just doesn't disappear because your sense of morality receives a major clout."

"Oh? And you're an expert on the subject?"

He fell silent. They stared at each other for a long time. He finally spoke. "You're right. I'm no expert on love. You're my first experience with the emotion. Serena, I love you." He suddenly raked his hair with all ten fingers. "Damn, I didn't want it to happen." His eyes narrowed on her abruptly. "You didn't, either, did you?"

She stole a breath. "No, I didn't want to fall in love with you, either."

"Because I'm not good enough for you."

"*What?*"

"Do you think I never caught on to your superior attitude? Do you think it didn't hurt?"

She was guilty as sin and utterly ashamed of her snobbishness of the past. "Trav...I...I did have some foolish ideas for a while, but please believe me—"

"Why wasn't I good enough for you? Because I wasn't educated? Because I have no family? Tell me why, Serena. I have to know."

"It's so silly, Trav, and I don't feel that way now. Not at all. Why make me tell you something that will only cause hurt feelings?"

"They're my feelings. If I want 'em hurt, it should be my decision."

"That's absurd," she scoffed.

"And maybe I'm not as sober as I wanted you to believe." Moving fast, he got to his knees and took her by the shoulders. She gasped in his face, but he held on. "Tell me the truth. Why did you feel I wasn't good enough for you."

She was trapped and knew it. But if they had any future at all, wasn't honesty best? Even over something like this?

"All right," she conceded. "You're not going to like it, but here goes. Ever since I decided on the law for a career, I also dreamed of marrying a lawyer. Or a man in politics. As it turned out, neither Edward nor you fulfilled that dream. Obviously my dreams do not coincide with the reality or direction of my life."

"I should have smashed that bastard's face this afternoon in your office," Trav said angrily.

"For what reason? Because he was trespassing on what you considered your property, or because I loved him first?"

A muscle in Trav's jaw jerked. "Did you love him the way you love me?"

"You're going to break my heart, aren't you?" she whispered sadly. "You'll love me only until the next pretty woman comes along. How does a woman live with that knowledge, Trav?"

"How does a man live with the knowledge that the woman he loves doesn't believe a word he says? And that she's ashamed of the way he makes a living?"

"I'm not ashamed."

"You were. I sensed it, you know. Long before this, I sensed it."

"Why didn't you say something? We talked. You could have said something."

"So could you." Trav let go of her and sat back on his heels. "We're both damned good at evasion, aren't we? So...where do we go from here?"

"Where do you want to go?"

Trav's lip curled. "I've got an idea. Instead of answering a question with another question, let's say how we really feel, okay? I won't pretend I'm a saint, Serena, or that I ever was. I've always liked women, and there've been a lot of them. But I'll tell you this, babe. I'm not a liar or a cheat, and if I commit myself and my future to one woman, that's the end of the old life for me. I would never break your heart, but do you have the guts to put me to the test?"

"I have a...certain amount of courage," she said huskily.

"Yes, you do. But do you have the courage to marry me?"

His question took her breath. "Are...are you proposing?"

"Dammit, Serena, don't you dare answer one more of my questions with another question. Do you have the courage to marry me?"

"I...have the love," she whispered. "I don't know about the courage. You scare me, Trav. I can't help it."

"And you scare me," he muttered darkly. "How do you think a man feels when the woman he loves is ten times more educated than he is and probably a hell of a lot smarter?"

"I'm not one bit smarter. More educated, yes, but no smarter. Look at what you've accomplished with used cars." She scooted a little closer to search his eyes for the truth. "Are you really scared of me?"

"Scared witless. But I love you. I honestly never believed it would happen to me." He shook his head. "I still can hardly believe it did. I knew it at 4:00 a.m. last night, and I couldn't get to Rocky Ford fast enough to see you." He raised a hand to touch her face. "What're we going to do about us?"

She placed her hand over his and held it to her cheek. "Do you believe Edward means nothing to me?"

It took a minute, but he finally answered. "I believe it. Can you believe I'll never look at another woman for as long as I live?"

She had to smile. "You'll always look, Trav. The burning question is, will you touch? That's what I have to come to grips with. Can you look without touching?"

His hand slid down to her throat and then inside her robe. "All I know is that I can't look at you without touching." He rolled her nipple between his thumb and forefinger and felt its instantaneous response. "Take this robe off," he growled, going for the sash.

She let him untie it and push it from her shoulders. Then she also let him push her down to the bed. On her back, she stroked his marvelous hair and handsome face.

He lowered his head until she could feel his breath on her lips. "Tell me you trust me," he whispered raggedly. "I will never give you a reason not to trust me, but you have to believe, Serena. You have to believe."

It was suddenly so clear: trust him or lose him. He wouldn't always be in Rocky Ford. In fact he would be gone much of the time. But he would always come back. It was as though some incredibly potent power had just planted that thought in her mind, because it felt like a permanent part of herself. Trav would always come home to her.

Besides, wasn't this problem of trust hers and not his? Wasn't it something she had to work through on her own? He'd already worked through his jealousy of Edward; dare she be petty enough to do any less?

"I have to be honest, darling," she whispered with tears in her eyes. "I love you and want to trust you with all of my heart. I'm going to try with every fiber of my being. I despise nags, shrews and people who drive their spouses crazy with unfounded jealousy. If you can live with my promises, I can live with yours."

"Then you'll marry me?"

"Yes."

He grabbed her into a smothering hug and then kissed her with all of the love and passion in his soul.

When they came up for air, he whispered, "Neither of us is going to be sorry, Serena. We're going to have a good marriage, and if we have children we're going to love them and tell them we love them every day of their life."

Serena's eyes began spilling tears again. "Yes, my love," she said on a sob of raw emotion, "that's exactly what we'll do." No one had told him he was loved as a child, and maybe love was what he'd been searching for all of his life.

A lovely peace settled upon her. She would never stop telling him she loved him. Not ever.

She began in the very next heartbeat.

Serena would have been content with a simple wedding, but Trav insisted on an affair to remember. His guest list was pages long. Add all of the Fanon friends to Trav's, and this wedding was going to be huge.

But Lola, Candace and Charlie volunteered to help with the myriad details of planning a big wedding, and the day finally arrived with everything in order. Serena wore a gorgeous champagne-colored gown with a slender silhouette that flared around her ankles and a stunning hat of the same color. It was not a traditional dress, but then, she didn't consider herself a traditional bride.

Nor was Trav a traditional groom. Serena felt they were a unique couple, madly in love but planning almost separate lives. What else could they do? Even though Trav was going to have a lovely home built for them on his property at Access Creek, his business was spread over the entire state. Her career was in Rocky Ford, and if she was at all successful, she would have precious little time to travel with Trav.

And yet she had never been happier. The church ceremony was lovely and emotional, then everyone went to the community center for the reception. The chilly, damp weather would not permit an outdoor reception such as Lola and Duke had had, but the community center had been decorated beautifully, and there was music and lots of good food and drinks for the multitude of guests.

Whether it was correct protocol or not, the reception line started with Charlie. Next to him was Candace, then Lola, Duke, Serena and Trav. As the guests arrived, they went down the line shaking hands and talking to the family. There were so many people there Charlie didn't know—Trav's guests, obviously—that he just smiled and welcomed them all without trying to find out who they were.

A young woman put her hand in his. Looking into her lovely gray green eyes, Charlie's smile faltered. She looked familiar, as though he should know her. Her hair was a rich, dark auburn, smartly arranged in an elaborate pattern of knots and rolls. Brushed straight, without the fancy hairstyle it must be very long, Charlie thought.

"Do I know you, young lady?" he asked.

She smiled and spoke in a naturally husky voice. "No, sir, you don't."

"Friend of Trav's, huh?"

She merely smiled again, extracted her hand from his and moved away to repeat the process with Candace.

Charlie wanted to watch her—there was something about her that nudged his memory and made him a bit uncomfortable—but immediately a couple had taken her place in front of him.

The woman moved down the line, looking into each set of eyes as she shook hands and murmured compliments on the wedding. She all but held her breath when she reached Serena.

"Your gown is lovely," she said quietly.

Serena smiled. "Thank you. I don't believe we've met." She glanced at Trav, who was conversing with two guests. This beautiful young woman in a stunning salmon-colored knit suit must be one of his guests, but she didn't want to interrupt him for an introduction.

She took care of it herself. "I'm Serena Holden, and you're...?"

"Andrea." She smiled at the bride. "Your wedding was very special."

"Thank you." She wanted to ask Andrea's last name and wondered why she hadn't given it. But the line was on the move again. Andrea quickly shook hands with Trav, murmured "Congratulations" and moved away to disappear in the crowd.

Serena frowned. It seemed forever before there was a lull and she could actually speak to Trav. She wanted to ask about Andrea in the worst way, but questions about a beautiful woman on their wedding day seemed like jealousy, so she pushed the mystery woman to the back of her mind.

After a few minutes, Tom Powers came down the line. He took Serena's hand and kissed her cheek. "All the happiness in the world, Serena," he said softly.

"Thank you, Tom."

"I wanted to tell you something. I'm closing my office in Rocky Ford." He grinned. "You're stealing all of my clients, young woman."

"Oh, I'm sorry."

"Nonsense, that's the name of the game." He turned to Trav. "Congratulations. You're a very lucky man."

Trav put his arm around his wife's shoulders. "No one knows that better than me, but thanks."

Serena introduced them, then became busy with another guest. Later, searching the crowd, she realized that Andrea was no longer present. Who was she? Glancing at Trav, Serena frowned slightly. If she was an old flame of Trav's, she would have said more than a quick, impersonal "Congratulations," wouldn't she?

No, Trav didn't know her, either. But if she wasn't Trav's friend and she wasn't her friend, why had she been here?

Every so often throughout the festivities, Andrea popped into Serena's mind. When she got the chance, she asked Lola about her. "Beautiful woman, about five foot four inches tall, 120 pounds, dark auburn hair. She said her name is Andrea. Do you remember talking to her in the reception line?"

"Sorry, Serena, but I really don't. There were so many strangers."

"I know."

"Was there something about her that bothered you?"

Serena thought a moment. "Yes, to be honest, but I can't put my finger on it. I was hoping you had noticed her."

Lola smiled then. "Forget her for a minute. I've got something to tell you. I put the store on the market. It's for sale... and I'm pregnant!"

Serena hugged her cousin. "Oh, Lola, I'm so happy for you. Who else have you told?"

"Charlie and Candace. And Duke, of course," she added with a laugh. "Everyone's thrilled for us."

"They should be." Serena's eyes took on a dreamy cast as she looked through a throng of people to where Trav was talking to a circle of friends. "Isn't he the most handsome man you've ever seen?"

Lola laughed and squeezed her cousin's hand. "Yes, coz, he's the most handsome man I've ever seen."

Serena started, then laughed. "Next to Duke, I meant to say."

"I know what you meant." She spotted Candace across the room. "It's her turn, you know. She can't live like she's been doing for the rest of her life."

"She's still in love with Ron, Lola."

"This might sound crass, but I'd bet the right man could make her forget her first love. What do you think?"

"It's possible," Serena said slowly, then added, "I hope so. Ron would never have wanted her to grieve ad infinitum."

"She grieves alone, too, doesn't she? I mean, she's always sweet and uncomplaining, and yet you just know that she cries when she's alone. She's really a very special woman, Serena."

"Very." Serena smiled conspiratorially. "Maybe we can find someone for her. On the qt, of course. She would never agree to even meeting a man with romance in mind."

"I know. We'll be very tactful and subtle about it, agreed?"

"Agreed."

Trav walked up and put his arm around his wife. His eyes showed his adoration, and Lola sighed happily for the two of them.

"It's time for us to leave, sweetheart."

"Getting anxious to start that honeymoon?" Lola teased.

"Damned right," Trav retorted with a big grin. He looked into his wife's eyes again. "Ready to go?"

She looked at him with all the love in her heart and soul. "Yes, my darling. I'm ready to go."

Epilogue

Andrea sat in her car long after leaving the community center. Her heart was hammering in her chest. She had actually held Charlie's hand and looked into his eyes. And Lola's, Candace's, Serena's.

Tears began dribbling down her cheeks. Finding a tissue in her purse, she wiped them away.

But nothing in her life had affected her as strongly as today had, and the emotion remained rooted in her system.

Finally she started the car and drove to her little rental house. She took off her salmon knit suit and hung it in the closet, then put on jeans and a sweater and made herself a cup of tea.

The day had been both disturbing and satisfying.

Was that the combination of feelings she would endure over the final step in her plan?

The time to do it was getting closer; she could feel it in her bones. Looking into Charlie's eyes today had bolstered her courage.

Yes, the grand finale was getting closer. The Fanon family was in for a major shock. Were they strong enough to survive it?

That really was the sixty-four-thousand-dollar question, wasn't it?

*   *   *   *   *

Watch for MONTANA LOVERS, the next book in Jackie Merritt's delightful MADE IN MONTANA miniseries, coming in November 1996, only from Silhouette Special Edition.

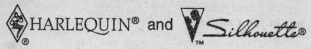

HARLEQUIN® and **Silhouette®**

are proud to present...

HERE COME THE GROOMS™

Four marriage-minded stories written by top Harlequin and Silhouette authors!

Next month, you'll find:

Married?!	by Annette Broadrick
Designs on Love	by Gina Wilkins
It Happened One Night	by Marie Ferrarella
Lazarus Rising	by Anne Stuart

ADDED BONUS! In every edition of *Here Come the Grooms* you'll find $5.00 worth of coupons good for Harlequin and Silhouette products.

On sale at your favorite Harlequin and Silhouette retail outlet.

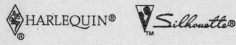

HARLEQUIN®   **Silhouette®**

HCTG996

MILLION DOLLAR SWEEPSTAKES
AND EXTRA BONUS PRIZE DRAWING

No purchase necessary. To enter the sweepstakes, follow the directions published and complete and mail your Official Entry Form. If your Official Entry Form is missing, or you wish to obtain an additional one (limit: one Official Entry Form per request, one request per outer mailing envelope) send a separate, stamped, self-addressed #10 envelope (4 1/8" x 9 1/2") via first class mail to: Million Dollar Sweepstakes and Extra Bonus Prize Drawing Entry Form, P.O. Box 1867, Buffalo, NY 14269-1867. Request must be received no later than January 15, 1998. For eligibility into the sweepstakes, entries must be received no later than March 31, 1998. No liability is assumed for printing errors, lost, late, non-delivered or misdirected entries. Odds of winning are determined by the number of eligible entries distributed and received.

Sweepstakes open to residents of the U.S. (except Puerto Rico), Canada and Europe who are 18 years of age or older. All applicable laws and regulations apply. Sweepstakes offer void wherever prohibited by law. Values of all prizes are in U.S. currency. This sweepstakes is presented by Torstar Corp., its subsidiaries and affiliates, in conjunction with book, merchandise and/or product offerings. For a copy of the Official Rules governing this sweepstakes, send a self-addressed, stamped envelope (WA residents need not affix return postage) to: MILLION DOLLAR SWEEPSTAKES AND EXTRA BONUS PRIZE DRAWING Rules, P.O. Box 4470, Blair, NE 68009-4470, USA.

SWP-ME96

As seen on TV!
Free Gift Offer

With a Free Gift proof-of-purchase from any Silhouette® book, you can receive a beautiful cubic zirconia pendant.

This gorgeous marquise-shaped stone is a genuine cubic zirconia—accented by an 18" gold tone necklace.

(Approximate retail value $19.95)

Send for yours today...

compliments of ▼ *Silhouette*®
™

To receive your free gift, a cubic zirconia pendant, send us one original proof-of-purchase, photocopies not accepted, from the back of any Silhouette Romance™, Silhouette Desire®, Silhouette Special Edition®, Silhouette Intimate Moments® or Silhouette Yours Truly™ title available in August, September or October at your favorite retail outlet, together with the Free Gift Certificate, plus a check or money order for $1.65 U.S./$2.15 CAN. (do not send cash) to cover postage and handling, payable to Silhouette Free Gift Offer. We will send you the specified gift. Allow 6 to 8 weeks for delivery. Offer good until October 31, 1996 or while quantities last. Offer valid in the U.S. and Canada only.

Free Gift Certificate

Name: _____

Address: _____

City: _____ State/Province: _____ Zip/Postal Code: _____

Mail this certificate, one proof-of-purchase and a check or money order for postage and handling to: SILHOUETTE FREE GIFT OFFER 1996. In the U.S.: 3010 Walden Avenue, P.O. Box 9077, Buffalo NY 14269-9077. In Canada: P.O. Box 613, Fort Erie, Ontario L2Z 5X3.

FREE GIFT OFFER   084-KMD
ONE PROOF-OF-PURCHASE

To collect your fabulous FREE GIFT, a cubic zirconia pendant, you must include this original proof-of-purchase for each gift with the properly completed Free Gift Certificate.

084-KMD

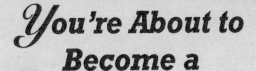

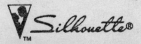